Getting Lucky

Getting Lucky

Kamryn Donavan

URBAN BOOKS
http://www.urbanbooks.net

This is a work of fiction. Any references or similarities to actual events, real people, living or dead, or real locales are intended to give the novel a sense of reality. Any similarity in other names, characters, places, and incidents is entirely coincidental.

URBAN SOUL is published by

Urban Books
10 Brennan Place
Deer Park, NY 11729

ISBN-13: 978-1-59983-025-4
ISBN-10: 1-59983-025-6

First Printing: September 2007

10 9 8 7 6 5 4 3 2 1

Printed in the United States of America

Introductions

Unit 109

His name is Vernon. No, no . . . it's Victor. Or did he tell me his name was Vincent?

For all Peaches could remember, the strange man sleeping in her bed at least had a name that started with a *V.*

Peaches had never been good at remembering a guy's name, which is probably because she never stayed with one long enough to learn his name. A guy could introduce himself, but she would never be interested in any of that small talk. All she wanted to know was how much money he had in his pocket. From there, she would make up her own name for him. Like the man in her bed, his name was Mr. 1000. That is how much he had spent on her the entire evening. At least a hundred in tips and private lap dances . . . the rest is what he paid her to take him home.

Peaches called out to him, hoping the sound of her voice would jostle him from his sleep.

She stood at the foot of her bed, naked and fresh from the shower, ready to get this strip-club trick out of her bed so she could go on with her day.

This was not her normal routine. She had brought plenty of guys home from the club before, and then after sex, she would quickly send them on their way. Mr. 1000 was different, though. He was the first one she had actually allowed to sleep over—mostly because he was the first one to spend so much money on her in one night. The sex had something to do with it too. Mr. 1000 had worked her over so good that she almost felt obligated to reward him with a few hours of sleep next to her, but now his time was up.

This time Peaches used her foot as a wake-up call. "Hey! Wake up, man! I'm not running a damn motel here."

That was enough to rustle him from his slumber. The man rolled over and smiled at Peaches, still rubbing sleep from his eyes. "Hey there, baby girl."

Peaches did not have a smile to return. "This ain't Motel Six. If you wanna sleep, you need to take ya ass home."

"You kicking me out already, baby girl?" The man chuckled as he threw back the covers to show her how he was arousing himself. "You sure you don't wanna take another ride before you send me packing?"

Peaches marveled at how such an ugly man could be blessed with such a large one, but she quickly figured that was God's way of balancing things out. Since his ugly face could not reel in the ladies, his big dick and overflowing wallet sure would. As tempting as it was to take another ride on Mr. 1000, she had to remind herself that he was for business, not pleasure.

"Do you have some more money?" she asked, keeping a straight face to let him know that she was serious.

The man laughed then jumped out of bed to reach for his clothes. "You sure are something else, baby girl," he said with a hint of laughter in his voice.

Knowing that he was watching, Peaches pranced over to the closet to slip into her robe, making sure to put an extra jiggle in her step.

"Damn, baby girl, having that much ass should be against the law!"

Peaches laughed to herself, wishing she had a dime for every time she had heard that line. When it came to her, God had certainly made the scales unbalanced, blessing her with good looks and a body that could make a grown man cry.

"So are you working tonight?" the man asked, attempting to kill the awkward silence between them.

"Of course I am. I'm there every night making that paper."

The man went into his wallet, then handed Peaches forty dollars. "This is just a li'l something extra for you," he whispered in her ear as if someone else were in the room listening.

A smile spread across her face as she slipped the money in her pocket. She said thank you, trying her best to sound appreciative, but such a measly gesture was not what brought such a look of pleasure. She just found it hilarious that he was giving her money, not knowing that she had already lifted sixty bucks from his wallet while he had been asleep.

"So will I see you there tonight? I'll save a private dance just for you."

"Will that be a private dance on the house?"

Peaches scoffed at him. "Sweetie, I'm a working girl. The only thing I give away free is advice."

The man put his arm around her waist and pulled her closer. Peaches wanted to push him away, but she decided that would not have been a good business move. In order to make the big money, she at least needed to pretend as if these nasty men actually appealed to her. Instead, she played it off by giving him a quick peck on the cheek, then walked away as if she had to grab something out of one of her dresser drawers.

"My sexy baby girl," the man said, chuckling as he went back to putting on his clothes. "So did you enjoy last night?"

Peaches felt relieved, finally able to express an honest emotion with him. The sex had been more than she could have ever imagined, and she did not mind letting him know.

From the apartment next door, there was a big thud heard against the wall. The man turned to Peaches and opened his mouth to say something when another bump was heard, followed by muffled yelling.

"I guess someone's not too happy over there," he said.

Peaches walked over to the wall and started pounding on it with her fist. "That's just my stupid-ass neighbor and her retarded boyfriend. She's always getting mad at him, throwing shit around and cursing him out."

The man shook his head. "Ya know, you should think about getting out of these apartments, baby girl. You are young and I'm sure you make some good money. Have you ever thought about buying a house? That way, you wouldn't have to worry about sharing a wall with noisy neighbors."

Peaches had been told that by several of her strip-club tricks, but buying a house and being Ms. Responsible was not on her agenda. She wanted money. She wanted fancy clothes, flashy jewelry, and an expensive foreign car.

The man continued to go on and on about the benefits of owning a home, and Peaches obliged him with an occasional "Oh really?" as if she were interested in what he had to say. Before long, she had eased her way towards the front door with him in tow. He had definitely overstayed his welcome.

"Baby girl, you were the bomb last night," he said as he held the front door open.

"Of course I was," she joked with him. "You weren't too bad yourself."

As they spoke, there was more banging heard from the apartment next door. Peaches walked over to the living room wall and pounded on it with her fist, yelling for her neighbors to keep the noise down. When she walked back over to the door, the man gave her a kiss on the cheek.

"I'll be talking to you later, baby girl," he said before finally walking away.

As he made his way down the walkway, Peaches called after him. "Hey, man, what is your first name? I'm really bad when it comes to remembering names."

The man turned and gave her a look of disappointment, as if he was hoping to shame her into feeling bad about having slept with a man whose name she could not remember. Peaches had no shame, though.

You're a trick, she wanted to tell him. *Would you rather I just called you that?*

"My name is William," the man finally answered before continuing on to his car.

Peaches waited until he was gone before laughing aloud. She figured Victor was close enough to William in the alphabet.

No wonder I got the names mixed up.

Just as she was about to go back into her apartment, her next-door neighbor came rushing outside after her boyfriend. Both of them were yelling loud enough for the entire complex to hear.

Even though this sort of thing happened at least once or twice a week, Peaches never got tired of watching them. If the neighbors were going to run outside and yell out all their personal business, they obviously wanted an audience. Peaches felt it was her duty to give them exactly what they wanted. However, she was not like the rest of the complex, hiding in their windows to see what was going on. She always made sure to be out there on the front porch watching every second of the action. She just loved drama, especially when it was happening to someone other than herself.

Unit 110

Jewel grabbed the first thing she could think of.

In the blink of an eye, her oldest son's remote control car went sailing across the living room, coming to a crash against the wall, narrowly missing Romello's head by an inch or two.

Romello ducked out of the way, then looked at his girlfriend as if she had lost her mind. "You are a crazy nut!" he hissed at her.

Jewel bent down to pick another toy to be hurled at him, but when she looked up her intended target was already out the front door.

"Just where in the hell do you think you're going?" she screamed, hot on her boyfriend's heels.

"Just go back in the house!" Romello yelled back at her.

"How the hell are you just gonna walk out the house?"

Romello laughed. "What? Do you expect me to stand around while you throw missiles at my damn head? I'm telling you, Jewel, you are a nut!"

"Don't you dare walk away from me while I'm trying to talk to you, Romello!"

Romello ignored her threat and continued walking. "You're not talking, you're screaming! I don't wanna hear it!"

"Well, where are you going?" Jewel asked, still yelling at the top of her lungs. When she got mad, there was just no keeping her quiet.

"I'm going to my damn car. Is that okay with you?"

Jewel broke into a sprint to get to his car before he did. She threw her thick frame in front of the driver's-side door to keep him from opening it.

"You're not leaving here," Jewel huffed, trying to catch her breath. "Your ass is gonna stay right here until you tell me what I want to know."

Romello threw his hands up in frustration. "Damn it, Jewel, I just came out here to get my damn cigarettes. Why do you have to turn everything into a theater production? You are such a damn drama queen." Without much force, he moved her from in front of the door, then went inside the car to get his cigarettes.

Jewel stood there glaring at him, still trying to catch her breath. All that yelling and fast walking had her winded. Chasing after Romello was usually the only exercise she had, outside of having sex.

"Well, are you gonna answer my question or not?" she asked, finally bringing her voice to a more tolerable, calmer volume.

Romello lit a cigarette and inhaled deeply. He looked at his girlfriend hard and long before answering. "Look, Jewel, I had a long, tiring night, last night. Right now, all I want to do is go back in the house and get some damn sleep. Do you think you can let me do that without giving me any more grief?"

Jewel folded her arms across her chest. "Well, just where in the hell were you last night? I don't know how many times I tried your cell phone. I left at least twenty messages! Were you that damn busy that you couldn't answer the phone or return one of my calls? Now you have the nerve to come waltzing in this morning as if it was no big deal. You'd be lucky if grief is the only thing I give you."

Romello closed his eyes, trying not to let his anger get the best of him. "You know that when I stay out all night I'm out there trying to hustle. I can't always answer your damn calls or call just to check in. I'm out there taking care of business, trying to get bills paid." He started walking back toward the apartment, frustrated that they had to have this discussion once again.

"I'm tired of going through this every damn morning," he mumbled under his breath. "I'm out there trying to make money to pay these damn bills. Somebody's gotta do it . . . you won't get your fat ass up and get a damn job!"

Jewel cringed. It always hurt her when Romello called her fat. That was just something else on the laundry list of things that would always bring on an argument. He didn't like that she was no longer the hot size four that she was when they'd first met—that was nine years and three kids ago. He just could not accept her size eight body now. As Romello often told her, she was not "perfect" anymore.

"Fuck you!" Jewel yelled back in retaliation. "I'm not fat, and I don't need to be out there working. I stay home and raise your damn kids!" She started chasing after him again. "There you go walking away from me again, Romello! Don't you think I'm gonna let this die. I want an answer from you. I want to know where you've been all night, and don't give me that 'I'm a hustler' crap!"

Romello opened his mouth for a smart remark, but was distracted by the sight of Peaches standing on her front porch with her robe halfway open. He stopped walking, hoping the light morning breeze would be strong enough to give him a better look.

It did not take long for Jewel to realize what had caught her boyfriend's attention so quickly. She stopped in her tracks and turned her anger towards her neighbor.

"What, you think we're putting on some kind of show for you?" she yelled at Peaches. With every bone in her body, she could not stand that girl. To everyone, she would say it was because she did not like what Peaches did for a living; truth be told, she was jealous of her.

Even as a straight woman, Jewel had to admit that Peaches was gorgeous. She had perfect caramel skin, and a body that Jewel knew she never would have been able to rival, even if she had still been a size four. What got under her skin even more was that she knew Romello had it bad for Peaches. On more than one occasion, she had caught him giving her a lingering eye. A few times, she had even heard him flirting with her. It killed Jewel that Peaches was the object of Romello's desire, while she was the one who had had his children.

Peaches laughed at her. "Well, I thought you wanted people to watch. I mean, isn't that why you come running out here yelling like a lunatic all the time?"

Peaches waved flirtatiously at Romello. Jewel was ready to go into a rage when she saw him raise his hand to wave back. She gave her boyfriend a shove, trying to get him to start walking back towards the house again. Romello did not budge.

Jewel turned back to Peaches. "Go put some damn clothes on, girl! Don't you have any decency?" She knew the angrier she got, the more it amused Peaches, but she just could not help herself.

Peaches stepped off the porch and held her robe wide open, laughing even harder. "When ya got it, ya flaunt it," she taunted. "Don't be jealous, honey. With a few sit-ups and some Jenny Craig, you might look half this good."

Jewel gasped as she turned to Romello, whose eyes were as big as saucers. "You bitch!" she yelled, referring to both him and her.

She shoved Romello again, but he still would not move. He had been dying to see Peaches naked ever since he had moved in two years ago—there was no way he was gonna go in the house now, no matter how many times Jewel tried to get him to move.

Damn! he kept saying in his head.

Peaches closed her robe again. "Well, you two have a nice day," she said cheerfully before stepping back onto the porch. As she opened the front door to go inside, she turned to look back at Jewel over her shoulder. "And can you please keep all that noise down? A girl's gotta get her beauty sleep, ya know." Peaches disappeared into her apartment.

"Well, maybe you could sleep if you didn't have all those men running in and out of your bedroom!" Jewel paused to wait for a response before directing her frustrations back to Romello. "You dirty sonofabitch. I hope you got a good look. If you wanna fuck her so bad, why don't you move the hell out and just go be with her?"

Of course, Jewel had not meant that at all. Romello was the sole provider. If Romello left, she knew she would not be able to make it on her own. In addition, despite all their arguing, Jewel loved him to death. After nine years, she could not imagine her life without him. Besides, Romello knew that if he ever tried to leave her for another woman, it would be the last thing he ever did.

Romello just looked at his girlfriend with a fiendish grin on his face, then looked around the complex to see if there was anyone else who had witnessed what had just happened. He caught a glimpse of his neighbor in Unit 214 standing in the window. The grin on his face grew broader.

She's another hot one, he thought to himself. *Too bad she's married.*

Without another word, he turned and started walking back towards the apartment as fast as he could so none of the other neighbors could listen to Jewel start in on him about Peaches.

Unit 214

"You really shouldn't be so nosy, Alisha." Craig finished the last of his breakfast before getting up from the table. "No one likes a nosy neighbor."

Alisha turned away from the window. "I am just watching to make sure they don't hurt each other. You know how wild Jewel can be. She has put bruises on Romello a couple of times, although I can't say he didn't deserve it."

Craig laughed. "Who are you kidding, Alisha? You're one of the nosiest people I know."

Alisha rolled her eyes at him then went back to looking out the window.

Her husband was right. She was one of the nosiest people on the face of the earth, although she preferred to call herself "inquisitive," not nosy.

"Would you look at that?" Alisha gasped. "That girl just flashed them!"

"What girl?"

"Peaches! She's that stripper who lives in unit two-oh-nine!"

Craig casually strolled over to the window, shrugged his shoulders, then took a seat at the table again. "No big deal," he mumbled.

Alisha turned to her husband in disbelief. "Yeah right," she said, snickering. "You know damn well that if I wasn't standing here, you would have your face pressed against the window trying to get a look at that girl. Don't sit here and pretend like you aren't interested in seeing her."

Craig shrugged his shoulders. "Who's pretending? Is it that hard to believe that I'm not excited about seeing some naked two-bit stripper?"

"She's a pretty girl."

"She may be *pretty*, but my wife is *beautiful*." Craig got up and put his arms around her waist. "You are the only woman I get excited about seeing naked."

Sometimes it seemed like Craig was laying it on too thick, but she enjoyed his compliments all the same. He definitely knew how to stroke her ego, which was one of the things she loved about him so much. However, Alisha did not really need anyone to boost her self-confidence. She already knew she was a good-looking woman—there was not a man's head that did not turn anytime she walked into a room; it was just nice to have Craig tell her every day that he thought she was beautiful.

"Well, you still have some time before you go to work. Interested in seeing your wife get naked now?"

Alisha did not wait for an answer, as she took a small step back so Craig could watch her undress.

Craig really did not have that much time. He had promised his boss that he would be in early to get a jump on some paperwork. He was just about to open his mouth and tell her, but nature took over once he saw her slip out of her bra. He quickly thought of using traffic as an excuse, then sat back down at the table to watch his wife's striptease.

"Your turn," Alisha giggled playfully as she stepped out of her last piece of clothing. She seductively made her way over to Craig and had him stand up.

"You are so bad," he whispered to her. "I am supposed to be at work early."

Even after three years of being together, Alisha still gave him the feeling of being a nervous young boy during his first time. He fumbled with one hand, trying to undo his pants, while using his other hand to caress her soft cinnamon-brown skin.

"Well, maybe I can get you to call in sick," she whispered as she began kissing his neck. All of a sudden, she whipped her head towards the window. "Did you hear that?"

Craig breathed a sigh of relief after finally getting his pants down. "Hear what?" he asked. "I didn't hear anything."

"I heard something outside the window."

Craig lifted Alisha up, wrapping her long legs around his waist. "I didn't hear a thing," he said. "Don't go getting all paranoid on me now."

Alisha smiled, focusing her attention back to her husband. Craig backed her against the wall as she moaned in anticipation of feeling that first thrust inside her. However, the moment was paused with the sound of a loud banging on the front door.

"Alisha? Craig? You in there?" a woman's voice called from outside. They both recognized the voice as Ladona's.

Craig groaned in frustration, but refused to miss a stroke. "If we don't answer she'll go away," he panted.

Alisha nodded in agreement, as they both continued kissing.

Ladona knocked again. "Hello! Is anybody home?"

"Don't stop. Just ignore her," Alisha insisted.

The more she knocked, the harder it was for Craig to concentrate. He gave Alisha a look as if to apologize, then eased her back to her feet. "I swear your friend has the worst damn timing," he grumbled.

Alisha grabbed Craig's arm to keep him from walking away. "Let's just go to the bedroom. The knocking won't be so distracting."

They both looked at each other, listening to Ladona pound away at the front door. No matter where they went in the apartment, the knocking would definitely be a distraction. Craig finally shook his head.

"The woman is persistent," he said, chuckling. He took off his T-shirt and gave it to Alisha to put on. "Get rid of her quick," he said, gathering their clothes off the floor, then dashing to the bedroom.

Alisha silently cursed Ladona in her mind. Her friend certainly did have the worst of timing. This had not been the first time Ladona had managed to spoil one of Alisha and Craig's impromptu encounters in the kitchen. Craig always joked that it was Ladona's mission to rain on their sex life, but Alisha just dismissed it as Ladona being incredibly needy for attention.

Alisha took a second to collect herself. She slipped on Craig's T-shirt, then walked to the door, determined to make Ladona's visit a very short one.

Ladona continued to knock.

"I'm coming!" Alisha yelled at the door in frustration. She hoped her friend had a damn good reason for stopping by. She always did, though.

Unit 220

Ladona gritted her teeth as she continued peering through the narrow slat of the blinds. Even though her mind kept telling her she had no business standing outside Craig and Alisha's apartment spying on them through the window, she just could not get her body to cooperate. Her feet did not want to move. Her eyes wanted to continue to see.

"That whore," she grumbled under her breath, wishing it could be her.

Even though Alisha was her friend—maybe even her best friend, since she didn't have many—Ladona was still upset seeing her sharing an intimate moment with Craig.

Ladona finally came to her senses and started to walk away from the window, but not before accidentally knocking the window with her keys. She quickly moved from in front of the window. After a few seconds, she found herself looking through the same narrow slat in the blinds. This time Craig was half dressed, with Alisha draping herself all over him.

Oh no, I can't let this shit happen, Ladona said to herself as she marched for their front door and started banging as hard as she could. She was once again determined to foil their time of intimacy. Even though he was Alisha's husband, Ladona had it set in her mind that one day she could swing the odds in her favor.

Ladona faked a smile as soon as Alisha came to the door. *Craig's only with her because she's pretty,* was the first thought that popped in Ladona's head.

"Why are you knocking like you're the damn police?" Alisha snapped at her. "Is the building on fire or something?"

Ladona gave a fake laugh. "I'm sorry, girl. I just wanted to make sure you heard me, that's all. Is Craig here?" She looked past Alisha, hoping to catch a glimpse of Craig somewhere in the room. She was disappointed to see he was nowhere in sight.

That's funny, Ladona told herself. *If they would just limit their intimate moments to the bedroom, I wouldn't have to peep through their kitchen window!*

"He's in the room getting dressed," Alisha replied.

"Uh-oh! I didn't disturb you two from getting busy, did I?"

Alisha shook her head to say no, but the expression on her face said otherwise. "So what's going on? What's got you knocking this early in the morning?"

Ladona thought fast to come up with an excuse. "Well—uh—I just wanted to see if I could catch a ride with Craig downtown. I've got some errands to run, and I figured I'd do a little shopping." After saying it, she felt like patting herself on the back for sounding so convincing.

"What's wrong with your car?"

"Oh. Well, you know how that thing is. Today it doesn't wanna run."

Alisha nodded her head. "I keep telling you to go get another car."

Ladona laughed. "I know, I know, girl. I just can't

afford anything new right now. I'm gonna hold on to that thing until the wheels fall off. So do you think your husband would mind?"

"I don't think he'll mind. Why don't you come back in an hour or so? He should be ready to go by then."

Alisha tried to close the door, but Ladona held out her hand to stop her. "Are you sure he won't mind? Well, maybe you should ask him now while I'm here. I would hate to come back in an hour just to have him tell me he can't give me a ride."

"He'll do it." Alisha tried closing the door again, but Ladona still would not move her hand.

I can't let her go back in there to him, Ladona kept telling herself.

"Is there something else you want?" Alisha asked.

This time she could not come up with anything fast enough. Defeated, Ladona stepped away from the door. "Naw, girl. You go on and get you some rest. I'll come back in an hour."

Without saying good-bye, Alisha quickly closed the door, not knowing that Ladona continued to stand there, staring at the door. She went back to the window to see if anyone would come out of the room, but no one did.

"She may have him now, but at least I'll have him to myself on the ride downtown," she mumbled under her breath.

Ladona had it bad for Craig. There was not a night she did not lay in bed wishing she could have him next to her, touching her the way she touched herself. There was not a moment in the day when she was not trying to come up with some way to get him alone. She always thought that if she had him alone, she'd finally be able to build up the nerve to tell him she was in love with him. In turn, she imagined Craig would reveal that he was secretly in love with her too.

Ladona knew she was fooling herself, though. She knew Craig was in love with Alisha. She could hear it in the way he talked about her. She could see that twinkle in his eyes at the mere mention of that woman's name. As much as she hated to admit it, Alisha and Craig were like the perfect couple; however, Ladona had convinced herself that she was a better fit for him; she was prepared to knock on his door every morning begging for a ride downtown if that is what it took.

"This shit ain't over," she grumbled as she started back to her apartment.

She smiled at the thought of inviting Alisha over and putting poison in her coffee. Of course, she was not that desperate . . .

Yet.

Let the Games Begin . . .

Chapter 1

No one was happier than Ladona to see that summer had finally come around.

Even though she could not stand the heat and the way humidity wreaked havoc on her hair, she was happy to have three months away from the halls of screaming adolescents and school board administrators who did not know their asses from a hole in the wall.

"Have a nice summer, Miss Littleton!" one of the students called to Ladona as she made her way through the school parking lot carrying an armload of items she had collected over the school year.

Without even turning around, Ladona knew it had been Joey.

Yeah, you little fucker, have a nice time in summer school, she said, chuckling under her breath. Joey had made her school year a nightmare. If anything, she was just happy to be away from him.

The entire ride home, Ladona thought of all the fun things she had wanted to do with her time off. At the beginning of every summer vacation, she promised herself that she would do something exciting so that she could be one of those teachers in September bragging about such a fun vacation. Every summer vacation ended up being the same, though. The most excitement she would experience was maybe going to the movies or managing to go out on a date or two with some guy who would end up not calling her again.

This summer is going to be different, she told herself. Unlike all the other summers, this time she meant it. She could feel it in her bones.

As she parked her car in her assigned stall, she noticed her friend Alisha standing out on the balcony waving to her.

Ladona rolled her eyes.

She hated that some women were lucky enough to not have to work for a living because they were pretty enough to get good-looking husbands with good-paying jobs. Ladona resented the fact that she was not one of those women, and she resented Alisha for having someone like Craig.

She sat in her car for a moment, hoping Alisha would go back in her apartment so she would not have to talk to her. She was disappointed when she saw Alisha quickly approaching in her rearview mirror.

"Hey, Ladona!" Alisha called out.

Ladona let out a long sigh and quickly prepared herself for the act she was about to put on.

"Hey, Alisha," she called back to Alisha as she got out of her car.

"How was your last day of school?" Alisha inquired.

"I'm just glad it's over," Ladona replied. "Would you believe the principal had the nerve to approach me about teaching one of the summer school classes?"

"What did you tell him?"

Ladona looked at her friend as if she had lost her mind for asking something so foolish. "I told him there was no way in hell. I mean sure, the extra money would be nice, but I like my sanity too much. I don't wanna see a child for the next three months."

The two of them laughed as they started back toward the apartments.

"There was a moving van here this morning," Alisha announced.

"Oh really? Someone's moving into one-twenty-one?"

Alisha nodded her head and started grinning from ear to ear. "A man . . . and I didn't see him with a woman."

Ladona shrugged her shoulders. "You act like that should make a difference to me."

Alisha nudged Ladona with her elbow. "Come on, girl. He might be single."

Ladona rolled her eyes, annoyed that her friend was always trying to hook her up with someone, even though she knew she should have been more grateful. Had it not been for Alisha, she would not have had those two dates she'd had over the last year.

Ladona considered herself unlucky in the man department. For reasons she could not understand, guys just did not seem to be very interested in her. Lately, the only guys she had been able to attract were either married, jobless, or just plain ugly. A couple of those guys had actually been all three! Alisha had managed to fix her up with some real winners, though—single guys with good jobs and good looks. It always ended up being the same thing, though. After the first date, the guy would promise to give her a call, only never to be heard from again.

She had come to the assumption that maybe she was not good-looking enough for them. She figured that they wanted a trophy girl like Alisha, something Ladona knew she definitely was not. Not that she considered herself ugly, but Ladona knew she was a plain Jane—no makeup, no flashy clothes and no fresh-from-the-salon hairdo.

What you saw was what you got with Ladona, which was usually a baggy pair of jeans and a wrinkled T-shirt.

"Don't even think about trying to fix me up," Ladona said, chuckling.

"But the guy is gorgeous, in that thuggish sort of way," Alisha insisted.

"Well, if he's gorgeous that means he definitely wouldn't be interested in somebody like me."

"Now what makes you say something like that?"

Ladona shrugged her shoulders. "Gorgeous guys go for gorgeous women. I'm not exactly one of the beautiful ones."

"Don't say that. You don't know."

Ladona listened quietly as her friend went on and on about their new neighbor with muscles and his cornrows.

"Oh, so D'Angelo is moving into Macon Street?" she finally interjected. "That's nice."

Alisha laughed. "He sure is as fine as D'Angelo is . . . *or was.*"

"Well, it sounds to me like you're more excited about him than anything else. You're not thinking about stepping out on Craig, are you?" Ladona smiled to herself, hoping that was the case.

Alisha playfully hit her arm. "Don't be silly, girl. The guy is fine, but ain't nobody finer than my Craig."

You got that right, Ladona wanted to agree.

The two of them stopped in front of Ladona's apartment. "Well, like I said, he probably wouldn't be interested in me anyway. If he doesn't fall for you, he will probably be chasing after Peaches."

"I really wish you would stop putting yourself down all the time like that. You are not ugly, girl. There is no reason why he would not be interested in you. You've gotta start being more . . ."

"More confident. Yeah, yeah, I know."

"Well, go ahead and put your stuff away. Stop on by later. Craig's gonna be at the office late, so we can hang out for a little while."

"Sure." Ladona had no intention of going by there until she was sure Craig would be home. She loved seeing him dressed in his business suits.

She watched as Alisha walked back to her apartment. Just as Ladona was about to open her own door, she caught a glimpse of Peaches stepping out onto her front porch.

"Hey!" Ladona called out to her and waved.

Peaches looked up in her direction and gave a hasty wave. "What's up, Miss Schoolteacher?"

"Where are you on your way to, girl?" Ladona asked. *Dressed like that,* she wanted to add.

Only Peaches would have the guts to prance around outside looking like she had just stepped out of a Victoria's Secret catalogue. Ladona shook her head and smiled to herself, thinking that if she had a body like that she would probably be wearing the same things.

I wonder how the school board would feel about an outfit like that, she joked to herself.

Peaches nodded her head toward the parking lot and the shiny red Mercedes that was just pulling in. "I'm going to be a good neighbor," she answered with a devilish grin on her face.

"Who's that?" Ladona asked.

"Probably the finest brotha to ever step foot in this complex."

Ladona watched as Peaches continued on her beeline to the parking lot before finally going into her apartment. She was not sure what Peaches was up to, but she knew it had something to do with throwing herself at some man. The last thing she wanted to see was another one of the *beautiful ones* getting whatever she wanted.

After poking her face in and out of the window all

morning, Peaches was excited his car was finally here. It was not customary for her to play the role of welcoming committee, but when it came to a good-looking black man in an expensive car, she was willing to play just about any role.

The man got out of his car, pausing to watch Peaches as she approached. Up close, the man was even finer than she had imagined.

Roughneck, Peaches thought to herself, bringing a smile to her face. He was definitely the kind of guy she was attracted to—tall, dark, and handsome, with muscles, braids, and an expensive foreign car.

"I'm Peaches," she said as she walked over to him.

The man looked her over from head to toe, then smiled. "Peaches," he said softly, as if giving her name some thought. "I'm Jermaine, but people just call me Lucky."

When he smiled back at her, Peaches thought she was going to melt. He had dimples so deep she wanted to swim in them.

"I'm the one who's feeling *lucky,*" she mumbled under her breath, still loud enough for him to hear.

Lucky started laughing. "It's good meeting you."

"I saw you pulling in, so I thought I'd be a good neighbor and come over to say hello." Peaches looked at his hands and noticed he did not have on a wedding band.

"Well, that was nice of you," Lucky replied.

Peaches ran her hand along the trunk. "I am loving this car, Lucky," she said, putting extra emphasis on his name.

Peaches looked him over from head to toe again, this time noticing his clothes. Even though he was only in a tank top and shorts, she could tell they were expensive. After years of working at the strip club, she had learned how to distinguish knockoffs from genuine labels. The men in genuine labels were usually stingy with the tips.

Peaches assumed that was because they had already spent so much money on their wardrobes.

Lucky smiled proudly. "This is my baby. Only had her a week. I love the way she rides."

Peaches smiled at him flirtatiously. "Guys say that same thing about me too." She paused to wait for his reaction, hoping to get him a little flustered.

Lucky just nodded his head. "I'm sure they do," he replied without batting an eye. He then added, "My baby bought this for me."

The smile disappeared from Peaches's face. "You're married? I didn't see a ring on your finger."

"I'm not married, just seeing someone."

Peaches smiled again. "Well, now I really *do* feel lucky."

As long as there was no ring, a man was fair ground, in her book. Even when it came to bringing a man home from the club, she was adamant about not sleeping with another woman's husband. A stripper with morals, she liked to think of herself.

The conversation continued as the two of them walked towards his apartment.

"So where's your girl? Why isn't she here helping you move in?"

"Works a lot," Lucky replied.

"Well, somebody's gotta pay for those nice-ass wheels. What kind of work do you do?"

"I don't work," Lucky said.

To Peaches, he sounded as if he was proud of that fact. She quickly made up in her mind that Lucky was a kept man, someone she definitely could not date. With no job, there was not a damn thing he could do for her, except give her one hell of a night in bed. At this point, that was all she was shooting for.

"Nice car, nice clothes. I assume she's taking care of the rent too."

Lucky did not have to answer; his smile said it all.

"You sound a little disappointed," he told her.

Peaches shrugged her shoulders. "Not at all," she replied. "Women are kept. Men can do it too, I suppose. So what kind of work does she do to be affording all these nice things for you?"

Lucky shook his head and laughed. "You sure do ask a lot of personal questions."

"Maybe I'm trying to get to know you personally."

Lucky just nodded his head. "Well, I don't like talking about her."

"Sorry," Peaches said defensively.

Standing at the front door, Peaches stood there smiling, waiting for Lucky to invite her inside.

"Well, it was nice of you to come over and introduce yourself," Lucky said, giving her another look from head to toe.

"You aren't gonna invite me in?" Peaches asked.

Lucky tried to explain that he had a lot of unpacking to do, but Peaches was not trying to hear any of that.

"If you need help . . ." she started out saying, trying not to sound too desperate.

Lucky smiled politely. "I wouldn't dream of asking you to help out. You don't seem like the type of woman who'd do any hard labor."

Peaches laughed. "You're right. This body is too precious for all that. But I have no problem hanging a picture here and there."

A picture was all she wanted to get her hands on. She was dying to see what his sugar mama looked like. Peaches figured she had to be a pretty woman to snag someone as fine as Lucky, but she could not understand why a pretty woman would feel the need to buy a man, regardless of how fine he was.

She must be uglier than hell, Peaches finally concluded.

Lucky went on to give an excuse about not having any furniture. "I'd rather invite you in when I have furniture to sit on."

"Who needs furniture?" Peaches grinned, then mumbled, "There's the floor, the kitchen counter, the shower."

Lucky shook his head as he started laughing. "You are something else," he said. "But like I said, I will definitely have you over when the furniture comes. Do you drink?"

"Crown Royal is my poison."

"I'll make a note of that."

That was enough to satisfy Peaches. "Well, that sounds like a date," she replied. "Now, your sugar mama—I mean girlfriend—isn't gonna mind me being over here having a drink, will she?"

"Why would she mind?"

"'Cuz when it comes to me, women always mind." She gave him a small peck on the cheek. "I'll let you get to your unpacking."

Peaches started walking back to her apartment, glancing over her shoulder to see if he was still on the porch checking her out. To her surprise, he had already slipped into the apartment.

"This one's gonna be tougher to crack than I thought," she mumbled to herself. Still, she held her head high, marching back to her own apartment.

As she walked past, she saw Jewel step out onto her porch. "You are something else, girl," Jewel said. "I should've known you'd have your hot ass over there trying to holla at that man."

Peaches stopped and shrugged her shoulders. "Why do you care?"

"I *don't* care. I just think it is trifling. Do you have to try and sleep with every man in this complex?"

"I haven't had *your* man."

Jewel put her hands on her hips and opened her mouth to say something else when Romello came walking out the front door.

"Don't you two ever stop with the back-and-forth?" he asked.

"Talk to your girlfriend," Peaches said as she continued walking. "She's the one who can't seem to stay outta my business."

Romello turned to Jewel and exhaled. "Leave that girl alone, Jewel."

"It figures you would be on her side, anyway. You should just take your stuff and go move in with the girl. I swear, both of you make me sick."

"I'm not on her side. I'm just sick of hearing you going at it with her. Whatever she does and whomever she does it with is that woman's business. All this damn huffing and puffing you be doing makes *you* look bad, not her."

Jewel rolled her eyes at him, then walked back into the house. "Do you think you said that loud enough for her to hear? If you're lucky, it might've scored you some brownie points with her."

Romello walked back in the apartment after her. "Ain't nobody trying to score no damn brownie points, woman," he lied, hoping that Peaches heard what he said. "I'm just being straight up with you, Jewel. It makes you look crazy."

Before he had a chance to react, Jewel swung and hit him on the arm. "You wanna see crazy?"

Romello leaned closer and gave her a kiss on the cheek to show her he was not going to be bothered by one of her fits. "I'm gone," he said, heading for the door.

Jewel reached out and grabbed his shoulder to stop him. "Where the hell are you running off to?"

Before Romello had a chance to answer, the two older

kids started yelling at each other in their room. Jewel looked at him, as if waiting for him to do something about it. Romello just stared back at her with a blank expression.

"Well, aren't you gonna go in there and see what's wrong with your sons?" she asked him.

"I'm on my way to work." He gave Jewel another kiss on the cheek.

"You're going to work? You didn't say you were going out tonight!" she yelled at him as he walked out the front door.

Romello prayed she would not follow him outside and cause a scene, but when he turned around, she was there on the porch. He picked up the pace to his car.

"You come back here, you sonofabitch! These are your kids too! It'd be nice if you took care of them once in a while."

Romello glanced over his shoulder again to see Jewel picking up one of the boy's baseballs from the porch and firing it in his direction. He managed to duck out of the way.

"You're a damn psycho!" he screamed at her. As he continued walking, he noticed a few neighbors peeking through their windows.

Romello broke into a sprint towards his car. It felt like he could not get away from Jewel's madness fast enough. He loved her, but every day it was getting harder and harder to deal with all her fits of anger and jealousy.

Part of him was ready to go. There was not a night he did not think about pulling out of that complex and never coming back. Nine years was a long time, though. That's how long he'd been with Jewel; and after all that time and three beautiful kids, there was the other part of him that felt obligated to stay around, which is why he'd always come back home.

Jewel's obsession with Peaches was another thing that

drove him crazy. She was constantly accusing him of cheating with her. To Romello, that was funny, considering the fact that Peaches was not the one he was cheating with.

Jewel didn't know anything about Maria or Latosha. She certainly had no idea about Serita or even that little Asian girl from out of town who let him hit it only an hour after meeting. Jewel would have had a fit had she known. She may have had her suspicions that he was out there doing dirt, but there was no concrete evidence. Romello was extra careful about that.

Regardless of how many women he had crept with over the years, he was certain there would never be another woman to treat him as well as Jewel did. Unfortunately for her, there were just too many beautiful women walking around to make Romello be faithful. Too many beautiful women like Peaches. He figured that as long as he could keep it all from Jewel and did not bring home any drama or diseases, then he would be okay.

Once Romello got to his car, he turned back towards the apartment and let out a sigh of relief, seeing that Jewel was no longer standing on the porch. He opened the car door and started to get in, but then caught a glimpse of Peaches through her kitchen window. All the stress caused by Jewel seemed to wash away, replaced with dirty thoughts of his fantasy woman.

Romello considered himself an above-average-looking guy. With his thick, short wavy hair, his naturally tanned, muscular physique, and a silver tongue that could charm the pants off a mannequin, Romello was usually a hit with the ladies. However, Peaches had not been so easy to impress. Even after two years of sweet talk and his strongest of games, she just would not give him any play. If it had not been for the fact that Peaches brought home a man damn near every night, he would have thought she was a lesbian.

He was not one to give up that easily, though, especially when it came to his sexual conquests. Peaches was hands down the finest girl he'd ever laid eyes on, and he wanted nothing more than to be able to brag to his friends that he got the chance to "tear it up." *Sooner or later,* he would always tell himself.

Romello glanced at his watch.

He really did not have to go to work. That was just an excuse he often gave to Jewel so he could get out and meet up with one of his booty calls. Usually, he would be able to sweet talk money out of the girls, with an empty promise of making her his exclusive lady. With no real job, that is how he managed to keep the bills paid around the apartment.

Jewel had mentioned they were running low on groceries, and Romello wanted a little change in his pocket, so tonight he was meeting up with Latosha, knowing that today was her payday. A little loving for a little cash—Romello did not see himself any differently than he did Peaches, which is why he didn't really trip off the things that she did. To him, they were both just trying to do what they had to do to get by. He just wished that one day they could do what they had to do *together.*

As Romello rounded his car around the next block, he decided to pull over to a spot along the curb.

"Latosha can wait a little while," he said aloud as he checked out his reflection in the rearview mirror. The thought of being with Peaches was just too strong to put out of his head. He wanted to be with her badly, and was certain tonight would be a lucky night for him.

The thought of being with her was enough to make him risk sneaking back into the apartment complex without being seen by Jewel. He prayed the kids had her so tied up that she would not notice him.

Chapter 2

Romello's heart raced as he crouched low on the front porch, tapping on the door just loud enough for Peaches to hear. He knew that if he knocked any louder, Jewel would peek out of the window, as she always did, wanting to see what new visitor Peaches had at her door.

When there was no answer, Romello decided to sneak around to the side of the apartment to tap on her bedroom window. He thanked God Peaches had an end apartment with a side window he could go to. He also prayed that he would not look in and find her in there entertaining male company.

"Peaches," Romello called into the open window.

Peaches turned from the closet and looked at him. "Negro, what in the hell are you doing creeping at my window?" she snapped at him.

"Come open the front door."

Peaches walked out of the bedroom. As soon as Romello heard the front door open, he made a dash around the building, then darted into her living room.

"Thank you," he said to her as he tried catching his breath.

"What the hell are you doing here?" Peaches said, closing the door again.

Romello motioned for her to lower her voice. "You know my girl has those bionic ears."

Peaches waved him off. "This is my damn apartment. I ain't whispering for nobody. What the hell are you doing here?"

"Sorry to stop by unannounced," he said.

Peaches laughed. "You ain't Tom Cruise. You act like you're on some secret mission, creeping around my bedroom window. Shouldn't your ass be at home with your family?"

Romello relaxed a little. "I'm where I'm supposed to be," he said, trying to sound manly. "I just thought I should come over and apologize to you for my girl's behavior. She be trippin' sometimes. I know that shit be getting on your nerves."

Peaches finally closed the front door. "Whatever your crazy girlfriend says don't bother me one bit. Jealousy is a bitch."

Romello nodded in agreement, as he laughed it off. "Yeah, well—"

"I know damn well you didn't come over here just for that. What really brings you over here?" Peaches took a seat on the couch.

Romello stood at the door and looked around, admiring all her nice things. This was the first time he had actually stepped foot in her apartment.

"I'm really digging that TV. What is it, a fifty-two-inch?"

Peaches laughed again. "You came here to check out my damn TV?" she asked.

Romello laughed, trying to play off his nervousness. "I didn't come over here for that shit. I was thinking that maybe we could chill for a little while. Ya know, be neighborly."

"Neighborly?" Peaches chuckled under her breath.

Romello strolled over and sat down next to her. "I like this couch too," he said, admiring the leather.

"If you want, I can give you an inventory of everything I have and where I bought it from."

Romello laughed. "You are such a smart-ass, girl," he said to her.

The two of them sat in silence as Romello's mind raced with thoughts of what to say next. More than anything, he wanted to reach across that couch and give her a kiss, but he was sure that would land him on the front porch before he could blink an eye.

If this were any other girl, Romello would know exactly what to do and say next, but Peaches was the only girl who made him feel this nervous.

It's only sex you're after, Romello kept reminding himself, but he couldn't help feeling like he had to come at her in just the right way.

"I wasn't disturbing you, was I?" he finally thought to ask.

He was relieved when she shook her head. "Just looking for something to wear to the club tonight," she replied.

Romello tried not to stare, but he could see right through her lace top. "What's wrong with what you have on?" he asked, quickly turning his head away.

"This ain't something I'd wear to the club." Peaches laughed at him.

Building up the nerve, Romello moved closer and put his arm around her shoulder. Inside, he celebrated a small victory when he saw that Peaches did not try to move away. Instead, she just sat there smiling at him, waiting for him to say something else.

"Ya know, you have the prettiest lips," he finally said. "Are they as soft as they look?"

Peaches continued not to say a word, sitting there with the same smile on her face.

Romello laid more sweet talk on her as he moved in even closer to whisper in her ear. "I bet you're a good kisser." Once again, he was surprised when Peaches did not haul off and smack him.

She stared at him with amusement. "So you're here to find out whether or not I'm a good kisser?"

Romello shrugged his shoulders and gave her a bashful grin. "That and other things," he replied.

Filled with confidence that maybe tonight could finally be his night, he softly touched her breast as he began kissing her on the neck. The fact that Peaches did not seem to be resisting turned him on even more. She just sat there motionless, letting him caress her. When he looked up, he saw her staring at him, still with a smile on her face.

"Are you okay?" he asked.

When she nodded her head, Romello took that as a sign that he was cleared for takeoff. He took a chance and leaned in to kiss her on the lips. When Peaches kissed him back, he felt as if he would explode in his pants.

Peaches finally spoke out. "So *this* is what you came here for," she said, chuckling.

"You act like you didn't know." Romello kissed her on her neck. "You know I've been wanting you for a long time. I've had the feeling you wanted me too."

Romello did not notice her roll her eyes as she got up to straddle his lap. "Is that so?" she whispered in his ear. "Well, how about I do this for you?"

Damn, Romello thought in his head as he watched Peaches pull her lace top off over her head. He was so excited that he did not know what to do next. He was not sure if he should touch her or just sit back and admire her bare breasts staring him in the face.

"Damn, girl," he finally uttered.

Peaches started to laugh as she stood up in front of him. "Better yet, why don't I just take the pants off too?"

Romello nodded his head and watched as Peaches did just that, sliding the matching lace bottoms down to her ankles. He wanted to pinch himself to make sure this was not a dream. There had been many nights he had fantasized about this moment, and he was thankful things were about to change.

Fuck Latosha. Fuck getting grocery money tonight, he told himself.

"Damn girl," was all he could utter from his lips again. He sat there a few moments longer, taking in the sight of what he had waited so long to see up close and personal.

"Girl, you are fine as hell," he said, chuckling under his breath as he knelt down on the floor in front of her, ready to taste her with his tongue.

He put his hands on her hips and tried to pull her closer, but Peaches took a step back. "Well, this is just a sample of what you could get for eight hundred," she said coldly, "but to be neighborly, I'd only charge you six."

Romello stared up at her in disbelief, hoping she had not said what he thought he had just heard. Peaches stood there staring down at him with this evil smile on her face.

"Are you serious?" he asked.

"I don't do charity. This pussy ain't free, especially for a man who already has a woman. Either pay out or get out."

Romello was too embarrassed to be mad. He felt he should have known this was too good to be true. Regardless, this only made him want her even more; however, he wasn't willing to pay. He figured he would eventually be able to wear her down.

"Well, I guess I should be leaving," he said, as he rose to his feet.

"That's too bad. I was hoping you would come up with the money. You look like you might be able to hang."

Romello had started walking for the door. As he listened to her talk, for a brief moment he thought about actually going to get some money, but then quickly dismissed that idea.

Hell naw, I do not pay for pussy! Pussy pays for me.

Peaches followed him to the front door. He turned around and took one last look at her standing there in all her naked glory. "Peaches, you are cold-blooded," he said shaking his head at her.

Peaches leaned in and gave him a kiss on the cheek. "I know," she whispered in his ear. "You have a nice night, Romello."

He raced back to his car. Sitting behind the wheel, he laughed at himself for what had just gone down. If she had intended to make him angry, it did not work. The only thing she had done was leave him with a raging stiff one and even more determination to get to her next time.

I hope your ass is ready for me, Latosha, he said as he raced off to his next destination.

Chapter 3

Alisha was starting to feel the maternal bones in her body start to rattle. They were letting her know that maybe now was the time to start having some babies. She just wished they would rattle a little louder so Craig could hear them too.

During the first year of marriage, she let Craig convince her that it was too soon to be having a baby. He said he thought it would be better if they "enjoyed each other" for the first year. During the second year of marriage, Craig used money as an excuse. He did not think he had a good enough income to be able to raise a child properly. Alisha had even offered to go to work, but Craig would not entertain the thought. He insisted on being able to take care of Alisha; he did not want her out there slaving at some nine to five.

This year she refused to take no for an answer. She was bored around the house and was certain that having a baby would cure all of that. The first time she had tried explaining that to Craig, he gave her a credit card and insisted she do some shopping to take her mind off things. Well, after a few outfits with handbags and shoes to match, she realized shopping would not fill the void.

Craig then told her to join a community group and start meeting more people. That was not the answer for her, either. There was no way around it. Alisha wanted a baby, and she had all but gone so far as to replace her birth control pills with Tic Tacs, something she was planning to do when all else had failed.

"Ya know you can always borrow one if you want to," Alisha heard Jewel say, as the two of them sat out on Jewel's front porch.

Alisha turned to her, not sure what she had meant. "Borrow what?" she asked.

Jewel started laughing. "I see you staring at the kids real hard. I was just saying you are more than welcome to borrow one anytime you feel like playing mommy. Hell! Don't stop at one, you can borrow all three!"

Alisha joined in the laughter. "Girl, I'm sorry. I didn't realize I'd spaced out on you like that."

"So when are you and Craig gonna put a bun in the oven? You two would have the cutest little baby."

Alisha sighed as she nodded her head in agreement. "That's the same thing I keep telling him, but he keeps saying he doesn't wanna have one right now."

Jewel yelled out to one of her kids to be careful, then turned back to Alisha. "What's his hang-up?"

Alisha shrugged her shoulders. "That man can come up with every excuse in the book. Did you have all these problems when you and Romello started having kids?"

Jewel looked at her as if she was crazy. "Girl, I was only sixteen when I got pregnant with RJ. Romello and I didn't have time to really discuss anything."

"Sixteen? Had you planned it?"

"Hell no, but it's not like we'd done anything to prevent it either." Jewel smiled as she looked off, remembering how much fun things were with Romello when they were younger. "So what are you planning to do?"

"I really don't know. I mean, I've given some thought to skipping a few pills, but I think that's gonna be my plan Z. All I have to do now is come up with plans A through Y."

Jewel looked at Alisha and smiled. She wanted to tell her friend that Craig was right not to want kids now. As much as Jewel loved her children, there were still moments when she wished she could just be childless and have time to herself, the way Alisha and Ladona and Peaches did.

If she did not have kids, she would still have her cute little figure, and not be walking around feeling like such a fat blob. If she still had her figure, Romello would not have his eye on Peaches.

"Now *you're* the one spacing out," Alisha teased.

Jewel smiled. "Just thinking about the kids," she sighed.

Peaches came walking out of her apartment.

"Oh no," Jewel mumbled under her breath.

Alisha raised her hand to wave. "Good morning, Peaches!"

Peaches waved back, then started walking across the lawn towards them.

"Now you've done it," Jewel groaned. "That slut is on her way over here."

Alisha smacked her on the arm. "Be nice, girl. I don't know why you insist on always talking shit about her."

Jewel thought about what Romello told her about making herself look bad. "It just pisses me off the way Romello drools over her," she told Alisha.

"You act like that's her fault, though."

However, in Jewel's opinion, it was Peaches's fault. If she did not walk around the complex half-naked all the time, Romello would not look at her with that look—the same look he used to give her when she was a size four.

To Jewel, it was as if Peaches was inviting him and all

the other men to look and lust after her. Because of that, Jewel felt her only course of action was to talk bad about her, even though it never seemed to do any good. Most of the time Peaches would just laugh her off or ignore her. That would make Jewel want to say things even more.

"Good morning," Peaches said, looking at Alisha. She turned her attention to Jewel and said flatly, "Good morning to you too."

Jewel rolled her eyes and mumbled under her breath what sounded like a hello. Keeping in mind what Romello said about making herself look bad, she decided she would try to tolerate Peaches.

"Is it hot enough out here or what?" Peaches gasped, taking a seat on the porch next to Alisha. "It's not even ten o'clock yet and you can see the heat waves coming off the asphalt. Why are you two out here baking in the heat?"

"I'm hoping the heat will wear those little rug rats down so I can have a peaceful afternoon under the air conditioner," Jewel said, chuckling. "Besides, Romello has his ass in there sleeping. I don't want him listening in on my gossip."

"That's why I don't want kids," Peaches sighed. "That's just too much damn noise from such little mouths."

"Oh, kids are a wonderful thing," Alisha chimed in. "I want at least three or four."

Peaches scoffed at her. "Girl, that is three or four too many. You should be thankful you do not have any crumb snatchers running around, interfering with your sex life, draining money from your pockets. You and Craig are living the life right now." She turned to Jewel for an amen.

Jewel just shrugged her shoulders, not wanting to comment on that one. Even though that was what she had wanted to convey to Alisha, she figured she would let Peaches be the voice of negativity.

Alisha shook her head. "You make it sound like kids are spawns of Satan intent on ruining their parents' lives."

"That's a close enough description," Peaches said, chuckling.

Alisha playfully tapped Peaches on her leg. "You are so silly, girl. So I hear you went over and met the new neighbor."

Peaches shot Jewel a look. "You just couldn't wait to blab that, huh?" she asked her.

Jewel shot her a nasty look in return. "I didn't say anything about you going over there," she replied.

"Ladona told me," Alisha said. "So what's the dirt?"

Peaches turned to Alisha again and started giggling. "His name is Lucky," she sighed. "I thought the brotha was gorgeous from a distance, but up close—all I have to say is he is f-i-n-e, fine." She leaned in closer and started telling the little bit she knew about their new neighbor. Happy to be the center of attention, she had both girls hanging on her every word.

"So she pays for the car, the apartment, and everything else?" Jewel repeated after Peaches was done talking.

Peaches nodded her head. "The girl is straight taking care of his ass. I mean the dick must be incredible for her to be doing all that."

"And you say he won't even talk about her?" Alisha asked.

"In so many words, he told me to mind my own business," Peaches replied. "I bet you that girl is ugly, though."

That struck Jewel as funny. "Why do you say that?"

"Oh, come on. Do you think a pretty girl would pay for dick like that? Of course not! I know I sure wouldn't. I bet neither one of you would, either."

Jewel smiled to herself, happy that Peaches grouped her in as one of the "pretty" ones who would not have to pay.

"That's a silly thing to say," Alisha said. "There are some pretty girls who would probably pay, just like there are ugly girls who wouldn't have to pay. Looks aren't everything, ya know."

Peaches laughed at what she said. "Who told you that lie? Looks *are* everything. They can get you everything. Just look at what Lucky has."

Alisha shook her head in protest. "He's got himself a stupid girl, not necessarily an ugly girl. I don't believe that looks are everything."

"Not that I be checking out your man or anything—" Peaches started saying before a snicker from Jewel interrupted her.

"As I was saying," Peaches continued as she shot Jewel a dirty look, "it's not that I be running around here checking out your man, Alisha, but he's a very good-looking guy. Now do you think he would have chosen you had you been some ugly, fat beast? Would you have chosen him if he had looked like a swamp creature? I think not!"

"She's right, Alisha."

"Well, look at somebody like Dennis Rodman. He is not exactly the Mona Lisa. Women flock to him like wolves to a lamb, though." Alisha looked around for someone to agree, but Peaches and Jewel just shook their heads.

"Rodman has money. If you want something in this life and you don't look good then you damn sure better have money." Peaches started laughing. "Honestly, do you think all those women would give him the time of day if he was one of those niggas hanging out near the liquor store?"

"I'd step over his bum ass and keep on walking," Jewel interjected.

"I can't believe you two have such a cynical outlook on things. There's more to a person than what they look like on the outside or how much money is in their bank accounts."

Peaches and Jewel looked at each other, then started laughing. "Alisha, you're a sweetheart, but you can be so naive sometimes," Jewel told her.

"And here comes a prime example of how a lack of beauty gets you nothing," Peaches said as she looked out into the parking lot and saw Ladona driving in.

"Peaches!" Alisha gasped. "You are so mean! Ladona is such a cool person."

"Being cool and being good-looking have nothing to do with each other," Peaches replied. "The girl needs a serious makeover."

"I hope you aren't planning to do it," Jewel grumbled. "You'd have her going from spinster to hooker in no time."

"I hear that jealousy coming out, Jewel," Peaches started teasing.

"Stop it, you two," Alisha warned.

As Ladona got out of her car, she noticed the three girls sitting on the porch chatting away. She was not in the mood for socializing, but she was sure they were gossiping about the new guy. She figured she would put up with them long enough to get the scoop on the sexy new neighbor.

"Damn! Aren't you all hot out here under this sun?" Ladona asked, taking a seat next to Jewel on the porch. "You all couldn't have this little powwow underneath somebody's air conditioner?"

"Good morning to you too," Jewel said sarcastically. "Peaches was just telling us about the new guy. His name is Lucky."

"Did you end up sleeping with him?" Ladona asked.

Anyone else would have thought it was a rude question, but Peaches just shrugged it off. "I'm good, but not that good," she replied. "I at least had to find out what's going on with him first."

"So he must be single," Ladona said.

Alisha shook her head. "He's got a sugar mama."

The four girls looked up when they heard a car pulling into the parking lot.

"Speak of the devil," Ladona said.

They all sat in silence as they watched Lucky's Mercedes pull into his assigned parking spot.

"I've been begging Craig for one of those since we got married," Alisha sighed. "I had to settle for that Jetta instead."

"Don't complain," Jewel told her. "At least your man got you a damn car."

"Now that is what I call a body," Ladona said breathlessly, watching Lucky get out of his car. She still did not think he could hold a candle to Craig, though.

"Call him over so we can meet him," Alisha said excitedly.

Everyone started laughing. "Calm down, girl. You're married, remember?" Peaches said to her before standing up and waving him over.

"Hey Lucky! Come over and meet some of your neighbors!" She turned to the girls. "How do I look?"

Jewel snickered. "Well, are those shorts or are they panties? You're giving me a damn yeast infection just looking at you!"

Everyone started to laugh, including Peaches. "Jewel, don't you ever get tired of being jealous?"

Feeling like a lamb about to walk into a den of lions, Lucky started toward the group of girls. He did not feel like being bothered, but he figured it would not have been polite for him to have just waved them off and kept on walking.

"Good morning, ladies," he greeted all of them.

Peaches rushed over to his side and draped herself around his arm. "Lucky, I want you to meet some of your neighbors. This is Alisha, this is Ladona, and *that* one on the end is Jewel."

"Nice meeting you ladies."

Chapter 4

"Craig, I want to have a baby," Alisha announced to her husband before he even had a chance to walk through the front door.

Craig looked perplexed as he set his briefcase down on the table. "No greeting? No 'How was your day at work, honey?'"

Alisha did not get up from the couch to greet him as she normally did. Craig came over and tried to give her a kiss on the cheek, but Alisha turned her head away from him.

"I'm serious about this, Craig. I want to have a baby."

"You must've spent the day down there with Jewel and her kids," Craig exhaled as he started walking toward the bedroom. "Alisha, do we really have to go over this again?"

Alisha got up and followed him. "Yes, we have to go over it again! We're gonna keep going over it until you give me a perfectly good reason why we can't have a baby!"

"My job is too demanding; I wouldn't be able to be here and help you raise a child like I'd want to. Besides, we don't have enough money. Think about diapers, formula, and then there's child care. What about clothes? What about college?"

"You act like we're living on welfare. We have plenty of money!"

Craig neatly hung his suit in the closet, then turned to look at his wife. "Honey, I'm the one who handles all the finances. Don't you think I'd know whether or not we have enough money?"

"That's still not good enough, Craig. Does anyone ever really have enough money to raise a child? Besides, money is not everything. What about love?"

"Love won't put clothes on a baby's back or food in his belly."

Alisha sat down on the edge of the bed as she rolled her eyes at her husband. "You sound so damn ridiculous."

"I'm just telling the truth, though."

Craig walked out of the room to go to the kitchen; Alisha was close on his heels.

"Well, when will we have enough money? I don't want to wait until I'm in my thirties to have a kid. I want one now while we're still young and full of energy."

Craig looked into the foil-covered pan sitting on top of the stove, then looked over his shoulder at Alisha and grinned. "So you think by fixing me my favorite food that I'm gonna agree to have a baby?" he said, chuckling.

That had been part of her plan, but Alisha shook her head to deny it. She sat at the table and watched as Craig started fixing himself a heaping plate of lasagna.

"I don't see what's wrong with waiting until we're in our thirties, anyway," Craig continued. "Thirty isn't as old as you make it sound, honey. What I don't get is why you are in such a rush to have a damn baby. If we have one then that will pretty much be the end of us being able to do anything alone. There would be no trips to Hawaii, no cruises to the Virgin Islands. I mean, just look at my sister and her husband. They never go out as a couple since Joshua was born."

Alisha snickered underneath her breath. "Your sister and brother-in-law never went out and did anything even before they had their baby. They're the biggest couch potatoes I know."

Craig sat down at the table across from her. "Baby, I want to have a baby just like you, but not right now."

"But why, Craig?"

Alisha waited patiently for an answer as Craig took a bite of his food. "Because now's just not the right time," he finally answered. "By the way, the lasagna is excellent. What did you do, add a different kind of cheese this time?"

Alisha rolled her eyes at him. "I'm sitting here talking about having kids while you're worried about my recipe for lasagna?" she said with disgust. "So just what in the world would you do if I told you I was pregnant right now?"

Craig dropped his fork on the plate and looked at her in alarm. "You're pregnant?"

"What if I am?" Alisha asked again.

Craig did not say a word as he got up from the table and started walking towards the living room. Alisha grabbed him by the arm.

"Where are you going?" she demanded to know.

"I can't believe this shit. I told you I didn't want to have kids right now."

Alisha stood up, still holding onto his arm to keep him from walking away. "I'm not really pregnant, Craig. All I did was ask 'what if,' but is this how you would act if I really were pregnant?

Craig let out a sigh of relief. "I told you I'm not ready. I don't know how many times I have to tell you that."

This time, Alisha walked away. Craig reached out to stop her, but she managed to wrestle her arm from his grip. "You can't give me one legitimate reason why. You just keep giving me the same bullshit over and over again."

"It's because I'm afraid!" Craig called after her.

Alisha stopped and turned around to face him. "Afraid of what?"

"I'm afraid of being a father. I'm afraid of not knowing what to do. Okay?"

Alisha searched in her husband's eyes for any hint of deception. She thought that maybe this was just another lame excuse like all the others, but he looked sincere enough; to her, he did look a little scared. She let out a sigh of relief, feeling that she had finally gotten to the real reason.

"Well, don't you think everyone is scared to be a parent? It's not like babies come with instructions, even though they should." She walked over and put her arms around his waist.

"Just be patient with me, Alisha," Craig whispered as he held her in his arms. "I know you want a baby, and I want to give you everything you want, but on this one thing I need you to be patient with me."

Alisha did not respond but in her mind, she was willing to wait until he was ready.

There were some nights Jewel could not stand that the apartment walls were so thin. Tonight was one of those nights.

Things would not have been so bad if she did not have to share bedroom walls with Peaches. She and Romello were forced to listen to the moans of ecstasy on a regular basis, with some nights being louder than others. Tonight was a loud night, with a man crying out "Oh Jesus!"

"What do you think she's doing over there?" Jewel asked Romello as she lay in bed staring up at the ceiling.

"I don't know," Romello snapped at her.

This was one of the few nights Romello did not want to go out. Jewel had thought that maybe tonight would be her night to be moaning through the walls, but after dinner, Romello went straight to the bed and did not seem to have any interest in doing anything.

"Romello, it's been nearly two weeks since we've done anything," she whispered.

"It hasn't been that long, has it?" Romello asked.

"The night the kids stayed at my mother's—that was two weeks ago." She paused to see if he would have anything to say, but Romello gave no response. "So why has it been two weeks?"

"I don't know, Jewel," Romello replied, sounding a bit annoyed. "I've been busy, you've been tired. Shit happens like that, I guess."

"Well, I'm not tired now. Are you tired?"

"Yes."

Jewel sat up. "Well, when are you *not* gonna be tired?"

"After I get some damn sleep, woman. Take your butt to bed."

"It's a little hard getting to sleep when Peaches is over there screwing some man so hard that he's calling on the Lord."

The room was too dark for Jewel to notice the look of anger on Romello's face. He certainly did not like hearing Peaches with another man.

"Well, put cotton in your ears or something."

Jewel leaned over and started kissing Romello on his ear. That was something that always got him in the mood, but tonight she was fighting a losing battle. Romello had Peaches on his mind, and he was not going to let Jewel ruin it.

"Jewel, go to sleep," he said, swatting at her with his hand.

"Come on, Romello. I know you like this," she said, continuing to kiss his ear.

"Not tonight," he said in a stern voice. "I'm trying to get to sleep."

Jewel sat up again and pushed his shoulder. "You make me sick," she hissed at him. "If you aren't having sex with me, then who are you having sex with?"

"Why do I have to be having sex with someone else? Can't a brotha just be tired?"

"Tired from what? You haven't done a damn thing all day except lay on the couch and watch TV."

"Well, I'm tired. Okay?"

Jewel sat there staring at Romello in disbelief as she thought about a time when it seemed like he just could not keep his hands off her. She remembered there was not a day that didn't pass without the two of them having sex at least two or three times, but that all seemed to have changed over the last few years.

It's a wonder I even managed to get pregnant, Jewel would often joke to herself.

However, in reality, she did not find anything about this situation funny. Romello's lack of interest in her was starting to become a major problem, and it seemed no matter what lengths she went to, three or four nights of pleasure each month was about all she could get out of him. Even then, he still did not seem to be too interested.

"It's my weight, isn't it?" Jewel asked in a meek voice.

Romello did not want to answer and admit to her the truth, but he knew if he did not say anything, Jewel would never let the subject go. A part of him figured he should go ahead and have sex with her just to shut her up, but the truth was that he really was tired. Trying to please three other women aside from Jewel was definitely taking a toll on his body.

"It's not your weight," he finally answered.

"Well, when I was thinner it was like you couldn't keep your hands off of me," Jewel whined at him.

When you were thinner, I didn't have as many girls on the side as I do now, Romello thought in his head. In that instant, Romello had to admit to himself that as Jewel had gained more weight, the more girls he'd started messing around with on the side.

Romello heard Jewel start to sniffle. "Well, last week I wore that lingerie to bed. You didn't even pay any attention to me."

"I was probably too tired to notice," Romello lied. He had definitely remembered that lingerie she had worn to bed—it looked a size too small. "Look, Jewel, don't go on and on about this weight stuff. I have been running out damn near every night this week, and you know I hardly get a decent sleep during the day with the boys running around here as if they're crazy. Tonight I would just like to catch up on some rest. Is that really too much to ask?"

Jewel kicked him in the thigh. "Get the hell out of my bed!" she barked at him.

Romello rolled over and looked at her. "Are you kidding?" he asked.

She kicked him again. "If you're so damn tired, take your damn pillow and go sleep on the couch. I don't want you in my bed."

Not wanting to go through an argument, Romello grabbed his pillow and a blanket, then headed out of the room. As he got to the door, he felt a pillow smack him on the back of the head. When he turned around, Jewel was ready to fire another pillow at him.

"You've got anger issues, woman," he said.

"And you won't be back in here until you're ready to have sex with me," she yelled as she threw the other pillow.

Romello ducked out of the way, then went to the living room to make himself comfortable on the couch, satisfied that he would now be able to get to sleep without listening to his fantasy girl doing things to a man that damn well should have been him.

Chapter 5

"So you're not coming home?"

Jewel asked the question but did not wait for Romello to respond. She slammed the phone down, hanging up in his ear. When the phone rang again, she just walked back to her bedroom and took a seat on the bed, unsure whether to scream or cry.

Before leaving the house that morning, Romello had promised he'd be back before midnight, but at 9:30 when his cell phone number showed up on the caller ID, Jewel knew he was gonna break that promise.

Just as the first tear started to roll down her face, RJ walked into the room and asked for a Popsicle.

Jewel shook her head. "It's too late for Popsicles. You and your brother should be in the bed."

"But Mama," RJ whined at her. As he took a step closer, he noticed the tears falling from her face. "Mama, is everything okay?"

She quickly dried her face with her arm and tried to laugh it off. "Mama's fine, baby," she said unconvincingly.

At eight years old, RJ had become such the little man, always worrying about protecting his mother. Even though Jewel thought she was doing a good job of hiding her problems with Romello, she had forgotten that the apartment walls were very thin and that when she got angry she got loud.

"Daddy's gonna be out again?" RJ asked.

"He's gotta work," Jewel said.

RJ looked at her as if he wanted to say more, but he just walked over and put his hand on her back. "Don't cry, Mama," he said softly.

The two of them looked at each other in surprise as there was knocking on the front door. Part of Jewel hoped it was Romello having decided to come home after all, but she knew he would have used his key.

"I'll get it," RJ said, walking towards the bedroom door.

"I've told you about going to answer the door. You take your butt in the room and get in the bed."

The knock at the door got a little louder and more urgent.

"I'm coming! I'm coming!" Jewel called out as she hurried to get to the front door. On her way, she tripped over a toy in the middle of the floor. "Damn it, RJ, I told you to get your toys up from the damn floor!" she yelled to her eight-year-old.

Jewel continued her race to the front door with a limp. Through the screen, she could see the figure of a man. As she got closer, she realized it was Lucky.

"Good evening," she greeted him as she opened the front door.

"Sounded like you were having a little trouble getting to the door," Lucky said, chuckling. "You okay?"

Jewel smiled. "I keep telling those damn kids to pick up their toys when they're done playing. I'm gonna end up breaking my neck one of these days."

"Well, here are some other things they left behind." Lucky held up a bat and two baseballs. "They left these in the yard in front of my apartment. I didn't want them sitting there overnight for one of the other kids around here to come along and take 'em."

"I have told them over and over—RJ! Cesar! Get in here right now!" Jewel turned back to Lucky. "I am so sorry. I probably wouldn't have had all these problems if God had just given me all girls."

"Hey, it's no big deal. I'm just looking out for the kids. Promise me you won't be too hard on them, though. Boys will be boys."

The eight- and seven-year-olds came running to the front door at their mother's call. Jewel turned to look at them.

"Did you two forget some of your toys outside?" she asked them.

The boys looked from their mother to Lucky, who was holding up their bat and balls. Without saying anything, they grabbed their toys from him, then disappeared back into their room.

"Hey! Don't you all know how to say thank you?" Jewel called after them. "And you two better be in there getting ready for bed!"

Faint "thank you's" were heard from the bedroom as Jewel turned back to Lucky once again. "Like I said, I really am sorry about that."

Lucky shrugged it off. "No problem."

"Would you like to come in?" Jewel asked as she held the door open for him.

"Oh no. It's late and you've probably got to get the kids ready for bed."

Jewel shook her head. "My baby girl is in there sleeping already, and the boys know how to get themselves situated. Come on in. I'd love the company."

Lucky gave her a look of hesitation. "You sure it's okay?

What about your boyfriend? He won't trip seeing some strange man in his apartment?"

Just the mention of Romello brought a look of sadness to her face. "He'd have to actually come home to trip about it," she said, trying to make light of it.

"Uh-oh, sounds like there's trouble at home."

After Lucky stepped into the apartment, Jewel poked her head out the door and looked in the direction of Peaches's apartment. She would have loved for Peaches to be out there seeing Lucky walk into her apartment.

"Oh, there's no trouble," Jewel sighed. "It's just that he works a lot. He's usually gone most of the night."

Lucky nodded his head as if he understood where she was coming from. "My baby works a lot too," he said. "It's almost like work is a whole other life."

Jewel felt a little more at ease as she snickered. "I know exactly what you mean."

The two of them sat down. "So how do you like Macon Street so far?"

Lucky shrugged his shoulders. "People have been nice, especially the ladies."

"I just bet they have. I know Peaches has been the friendliest."

"Miss Peaches," Lucky said with a bit of amusement in his voice. "She's definitely something else."

When he smiled, Jewel could not help but admire how attractive he was, with his neatly groomed cornrows and finely chiseled facial features. Lucky reminded her of a male model. To her, he was the right size, the right height, and he definitely had the right look.

"So will your girlfriend be moving in with you?" Jewel asked.

Lucky shook his head. "Not anytime soon," he replied. "Things are working out living separate, so if it ain't broke don't fix it. Besides, my baby's got other obligations right now. Living together just ain't gonna work."

Jewel wanted to know more about those "other obligations" but she thought it would be too nosy of her to ask. "That's so sweet that you always refer to her as your baby. What's her little pet name for you?"

"Lucky," he replied flatly.

Jewel started laughing. "Well, your baby must love the hell outta you. That sure is a nice car she got you."

Lucky finally looked up and started to laugh. "I see your friend Peaches didn't leave anything out, huh?"

Jewel emphatically shook her head. "Oh no, Peaches and I are nowhere near being friends."

Lucky looked puzzled. "But you two were out there together the other day."

"We were just tolerating each other. Truth be told, I cannot stand that girl. In case you didn't know, she's a stripper and she has men running in and out her apartment damn near every night."

"So she's a popular girl, huh?"

"You call it popular, I call it trampy."

"Mama, when is Daddy coming home?" Cesar asked as he walked into the living room.

RJ came running up behind him. "Mama, I keep telling him Daddy's not coming home tonight, but he won't listen to me."

Jewel looked at her sons, wishing the earth would open up and swallow her to spare her from all the embarrassment she was feeling at that moment. "You two get your butts in bed. When you wake up your daddy will be here," she snapped at the boys.

"But, Mama," Cesar started to argue with her, but Jewel shot him a look to let him know he was one word away from feeling the back of her hand.

RJ grabbed his younger brother by the shoulders.

"Come on, stupid. I told you not to come in here bugging Mama while she's got company." The two of them went back into the room.

Jewel turned back to Lucky, too embarrassed to look him in the eye. "I swear those kids," she laughed it off.

"I'm a good listener if you wanna talk about it," Lucky said, sounding genuinely concerned.

"There's really nothing to talk about," she said, still not able to look. Even though she said it, she found herself starting to pour out her story to this complete stranger.

She hardly knew Lucky, but she felt comfortable telling him about most of her issues with Romello, and why she hated Peaches so much. For the next half hour she went on and on about her weight issues and how tired she was of always being left alone. Lucky sat in silence, giving an occasional nod to let her know he understood. When she was finally done, he reached over and put his hand over hers.

"If it means anything, I don't think you're fat at all. You've got meat on your bones. Guys like girls with some meat. And as far as the whole Peaches situation—it's not her fault." Lucky put his arm around her and rested her head on his shoulder as she started to cry.

"You don't even know me and here I am telling you my sob story." Jewel sniffled. "You must think I'm an idiot."

"You just needed someone to talk to. I told you I'm a good listener."

Jewel felt secure with his arm around her. Taking in the scent of his cologne and feeling the warmth of his arms around her, Jewel felt safe and secure—something she had not felt in such a long time. There was also something else she was feeling that made her quickly pull away. It was the tingling feeling of excitement any sex-starved woman would get after being in the arms of such an attractive man. Jewel looked at Lucky and tried to smile as if there was nothing wrong, but the look on her face gave her away.

"It's getting late," Lucky said. "I should go."

"Okay," Jewel said quickly.

She got up from the couch and walked Lucky to the door. "Thanks for letting me bend your ear a little."

Lucky looked at her with a seductive stare. She was not sure if he was doing that on purpose, but it did not matter. All she wanted to do was melt.

"He's a fool," Lucky said in a low voice.

"Who's a fool?" Jewel asked.

"Your boyfriend." Lucky gave her a kiss on the cheek, then turned and walked out of the apartment.

Jewel stood in the doorway and watched him walk back to his apartment.

Even his walk is sexy, she found herself thinking as she went to bed that evening with a smile.

Chapter 6

For Craig, the day began just like any other morning. He was awakened by a kiss on the cheek from his beautiful wife. He showered, then went to the kitchen to pour himself his usual cup of coffee. When he went to the window to make sure all was well outside, he caught a glimpse of what had become an all-too-familiar sight since the summer had begun.

"Alisha, I see your friend Ladona down there messing with her car again," he said as he turned away from the window. "I guess she's gonna want a ride somewhere this morning."

Alisha came over to peek out of the window. She then turned to him and smiled. "Well, I'm sure she's gonna get that old thing fixed one of these days," she said as if she were apologizing for her friend. "Besides, it's not like you have to go out of your way, right?"

That was right. Craig did not have to go out of his way to drop Ladona off for what was starting to seem like every morning; and while it was nice to have someone to talk to while being stuck in bumper-to-bumper traffic, there was something about Ladona that made him a little uncomfortable. Something he just could not put his finger on.

She seemed like a nice enough girl, and Alisha seemed to enjoy hanging out with her, but there was a look in her eyes that made Craig think something just was not right. For that reason alone, he was not too thrilled about being trapped in a car with her almost every morning.

"Well, I don't understand why she just won't get a new car," Craig said as he took a seat at the table to finish his coffee.

"Well, Craig, it's not like teachers make all that much money. Ladona is determined to keep that car 'til the wheels fall off."

"Well, maybe she should find a better mechanic."

Alisha went into the kitchen to start making breakfast. "You sound like you don't wanna be bothered." She turned and looked over her shoulder. "What do you want to eat this morning?"

Craig shook his head. "No time to eat. I've gotta get into work early," he said, looking at his watch. "In fact, I need to be getting out of here now."

He walked over to Alisha and gave her a kiss on the back of her neck. "Have a good day at work, sweetie," she said to him.

"Let me go down there and play taxi once again."

Alisha gave him a scolding look. "Be nice."

"I'm always nice," he said before ducking out the front door.

Out the corner of her eye, Ladona saw Craig walking across the parking lot in her direction. She pretended to be messing with something near the engine, then slammed the hood down, yelling out a stream of profanities as if something was wrong. Of course, nothing was actually wrong with her car. With a rebuilt engine and a brand-new transmission, her car drove just as well as it did when she had pulled it off the lot ten years ago.

"Are you still having problems with this thing?" Craig

asked as he walked up to the car. "Where do you need a ride to this morning?"

Ladona smiled, knowing that she had come up with one hell of an excuse this morning. "Well, I'm supposed to be meeting a coworker for lunch downtown, but I was going to do a little window shopping before then."

"Well, if you want, I can take a look under the hood for you right quick."

Craig took a step towards the front of the car, but Ladona put her hand out to stop him. "Don't bother," she said. "I'll just have to have my mechanic take a look at it sometime this week."

"You need to fire your damn mechanic. It seems like no matter what he fixes, there is always something going wrong. Maybe you should let my mechanic take a look at it for you."

Ladona nodded her head. "Yeah. I'll have to be sure to get that number from you," she lied.

"Well, let's hit the road. I wanna try to get to work early today."

"Craig, you are such a lifesaver. I swear I'll pay you back for all this."

"Don't worry about it. It's no big deal. I just hate to see a lovely lady in distress."

Lovely lady, Ladona repeated in her head.

Ladona waved at Lucky as she and Craig started towards his SUV.

"Who's that?" Craig asked.

"That's the new guy who moved in a few weeks ago. His name is Lucky. I'm surprised Alisha didn't mention him to you."

Craig paused to watch Lucky as he crossed the parking lot to his car. He turned to Ladona and shook his head. "Some pretty-boy thug, huh?"

"Lucky's a nice guy," she said.

Craig gave him one last look before climbing into his truck. "He looks like trouble," he mumbled under his breath.

Ladona smiled to herself as she caught a hint of what sounded like jealousy. However, she did not see why Craig had any reason to be jealous. Lucky may have been good-looking, but to her, Craig had him beat by a landslide in the looks department—especially when he had on his suit. Seeing Craig dressed up every morning, freshly shaven and smelling of expensive cologne, was the reason she looked forward to waking up.

"Is something wrong?" Ladona heard Craig ask, jarring her from her thoughts.

Ladona blushed, quickly looking away. "Oh no," she replied. "I was just thinking about something."

Craig laughed nervously. "For a minute there, I thought something was wrong." *I swear this girl makes me nervous.*

The first half of the drive downtown was filled with an awkward silence. Ladona spent most of the time beating herself up for having Craig catch her staring at him like a lovesick puppy. She was sure after today he would never want to give her another ride. She figured he would tell Alisha all about it, then the both of them would never want to speak to her again.

Ladona racked her brain, trying to think of a way to do damage control on the situation. She wanted to come up with something funny and interesting, hoping that a good conversation would make him forget about her psychotic stare.

"So what's the deal with the new guy?" Craig asked. "What'd you say his name was? Lucky?"

Ladona quietly breathed a sigh of relief, thankful that Craig had finally broken the silence. "I really don't know all that much about him. He's got a girl who pretty much pays for everything he has."

Craig nodded his head as if giving her words deep thought. "He's not one of those gangbangers, is he? The complex is a decent place. We don't need a whole lot of wild shit going on."

"He looks the part, but I doubt he plays the part," Ladona replied. She found it curious that Alisha had not mentioned him to Craig. "You know Peaches is ape shit about him."

"What man isn't she ape shit about?" Craig turned to Ladona and grinned. "What about you? I saw you smiling pretty hard when he waved at you."

Ladona rolled her eyes. "Your wife seems to think Lucky and I would be perfect for each other. I guess the fact that he already has a woman doesn't mean much to her."

"You know how Alisha is, though. She's always trying to fix someone up."

Ladona's stomach turned at the sound of admiration in Craig's voice as he talked about his wife. That little twinkle he had in his eye and that little smile on the corners of his mouth—it all made her want to gag.

"I wish she'd stop, though. I think I'm probably one of those people who will never be married."

"What?" Craig gasped. "Why would you say that? You aren't even thirty yet. You've got plenty of time to find yourself a man, settle down and have some babies."

I have found one, but I just have to figure out how to get him to notice me, Ladona thought to herself as she gave Craig a smile.

Peaches did not particularly like entertaining her male guests in the middle of the afternoon, but when Clarence called saying he'd give her an extra hundred, she couldn't refuse. How else would she be able to make nine hundred dollars for just an hour's worth of work?

Another reason she decided to make an exception for Clarence was that out of all the tricks she had, Clarence was the best. He was not the best sex she had ever had—Clarence could not have sex at all, or at least not penetration. However, when it came to oral, he was hands down, no questions asked, toe-curling good. For one whole hour that is all he would do—lick until she was climbing the walls.

Clarence had some kind of dysfunction with his organ, but Peaches could never remember the name of it. It's not as if the name mattered to her, anyway. As long as it was not something that she could contract, she did not need to know the name. The only thing that mattered to her was that Clarence could not get a stiff one to save his life, but made up for it by burying his head between her legs for a good hour, sometimes more. This was something she definitely did not have a problem with.

I love the taste. I love the smell, Clarence would always tell her when it was over.

And I love the money, so hand that shit over, Peaches would always be thinking in her mind.

Clarence turned and gave Peaches a hug. "An afternoon well spent," he whispered in her ear.

"No more of this daytime crap, though. I like it better at night, Clarence."

"Whatever you say, my sexy peach. You know it's always about you."

"So when am I gonna hear from you again?" she asked, thinking about the trip she wanted to take to Jamaica at the end of the summer.

"I'll give you a ring when my pension check comes in next month," he replied. Clarence started to walk out the door, then suddenly turned to face Peaches again. "You know, you should consider giving an old man a discount or something since I'm one of your best repeat customers."

"Now, Clarence, you know I ain't one for rebates and

discounts and any of that other shit," Peaches said sweetly. "For the best meal in town, you know you're gonna have to pay full price."

Clarence started laughing. "You got that right. It certainly is the best."

Peaches stepped out onto the porch to watch as Clarence made his way to his car. Just as she turned to go back inside, she caught a glimpse of Lucky sitting on Jewel's front porch. The two of them smiled at her and waved.

"Make that money, girl!" Jewel said as she burst into a fit of laughter.

Peaches could care less about what smart remarks Jewel had to say about her. What brought that look of horror to her face was the fact that Lucky had just witnessed her working.

Playing it cool, Peaches waved back at them. "Hello to you too!" she said in a pleasant voice before quickly going back into the house to go jump in the shower.

Peaches wanted to get over to Jewel's and find out what was going on. Not only did it bother her that Lucky had seen a trick leaving the apartment, it was disturbing to know that he would be visiting Jewel, of all people.

As she showered, she was sure Jewel was over there poisoning his head with all types of stories and lies.

She's a slut. She's a whore. She's trying to sleep with my boyfriend. Those were just a few of the nicer things she was sure Jewel was saying about her.

By the time Peaches got dressed and out her front door, Lucky was already gone. Only Jewel was sitting there, feeding a bottle to her eight-month-old daughter. Peaches walked over to her anyway.

"Sorry you missed him," Jewel teased her.

"Since when did you and Lucky become such good friends?" Peaches asked, wanting to slap that smirk off her face.

Jewel shrugged her shoulders. "You didn't know? Lucky and I talk all the time. Over the past couple of weeks we've become pretty good friends."

"Pretty good friends my ass."

"Peaches, I would almost say you're a little jealous!" Jewel started laughing.

"Me, jealous? Never!"

"Well, one thing's for sure. At least Lucky got a chance to see the type of girl you really are."

"And just what type of girl is that, if I may ask?"

Jewel smiled fiendishly. "Poor little Peaches. Looks like you won't be getting lucky with Lucky after all, will you?"

Peaches folded her arms across her chest. "Honey, if you think this little incident has derailed my train, you are sadly mistaken. By the way, I would appreciate it if you stayed out of my business from now on. I do not need you going around telling anybody anything about me. Got it?"

Jewel just laughed, proud of herself for finally having ruffled Peaches's feathers. "What makes you think I said anything to him about how much of a tramp you are? The man saw it with his own eyes, remember?"

"No, what he saw was a man leaving my house. What he saw was my cousin Clarence."

Jewel laughed even harder. "Maybe that is what he *saw*, but what he *heard* was you begging Cousin Clarence to 'eat it up.' You had him in there eating a little peach cobbler, maybe? Next time you should think about closing your living room window."

Peaches smiled. "He sure was, and it was the best damn peach cobbler he's ever had. Don't fuck with me, Jewel, or next time I'll be serving it up to Romello."

That smug expression dropped from Jewel's face. Before she could open her mouth to say something in return, Peaches turned and started walking back to her apartment, satisfied that she had put Jewel back in her rightful place.

Chapter 7

"So you're the one who owns this bad-ass car?" Romello asked as he approached Lucky, who was in the parking lot spot-cleaning his car. "How much this set you back for?"

"Man, I didn't lay out a dime. My honey picked this up for me."

Romello paused and then started laughing. "Damn, bro, you got it like that? Ya girl got a sister? I need a hookup too!" He made his way around the car, pausing to admire the interior. "Yeah, this mutha is bad as hell. Bro, I can't believe you got it like that."

He walked over and shook Lucky's hand. "Hey, bro, my name's Romello. I stay with my girl over there in one-ten."

"People call me Lucky. Jewel's your girl, right?"

Romello nodded. "Yeah, that's my baby, but she sure ain't putting out a ride like this for me."

He offered Lucky a hit from the blunt he was smoking; without hesitation, Lucky took a few pulls, then passed it back.

"That's some pretty good weed there, man," Lucky said, choking back the cough in his throat.

"Yeah, this shit is some flame." Romello paused to take another hit. "Anytime you want some just come holla at me. My boy keeps me laced with this shit."

Lucky nodded his head, as if to make a mental note. "Anyway, your girl is cool. I met her a few weeks ago, along with some of her friends."

Romello rolled his eyes. "The chatterboxes," he said, shaking his head. "Just about every damn morning they wanna pile up on my porch, gossiping about everyone and everything around here."

Lucky started laughing. "That's what women do, though, man."

Romello looked off in the direction of Peaches's apartment. "I know you met Peaches, right?"

Lucky laughed again. "She's something else, ain't she?"

Romello nodded his head. "My girl is always getting on me about her, complaining I stare a little too hard, but you're a man. You know how it is sometimes. You just can't help but stare when a piece of ass like that is around."

Lucky shrugged his shoulders. "She's definitely nice on the eyes, but the one I wanna know about is that girl Alisha."

"Alisha's fine as hell too, but she's one of those types you'd marry, have kids with. Peaches, on the other hand, is the one you'd have laid out across the backseat every night. You know, the one you'd end up cheating on your wife with."

Romello and Lucky slapped hands as they laughed and nodded in agreement. After they both stopped laughing, Lucky asked, "So what's the deal with her?"

"Who, Alisha?" Romello started laughing again as he shook his head. "Man, if you thinking 'bout trying to creep with that one, don't even waste your time. She is married with a capital *M.* That girl runs around thinking the sun and moon revolve around that husband of hers."

Lucky leaned against his car, folding his arms across his chest. "And what about the husband, is he okay?"

Romello shrugged. "Oh, you haven't met Craig yet? He's good people, but I don't really holla at him too much. He's Mr. White Collar Businessman."

"I think I saw him the other morning, walking with Ladona. He treats her right, though?"

Romello started laughing. "Damn, bro, you wanna know all about the girl, don't you? Well, as far as what my girl tells me he treats that damn woman like a queen. I get sick and tired of hearing my girl talk about '*why can't you be more like Craig? He's so romantic and loving.*' Blah, blah, blah." Romello shook his head in disgust. "I tell ya, man, the way he treats that girl is a little crazy, though. I mean, she must have some good pussy 'cuz my boy acts like he's whipped. It's either the sex is so good, or she's the first piece of tail he's ever had."

Lucky nodded his head as he glanced up towards Alisha's apartment. "Ain't no relationship that damn strong," he mumbled loud enough for Romello to still hear.

"I don't know, man, but hey, if your game is that tight, then I say go for it. I can't imagine that straight-laced muthafucka laying it down right, anyway." Romello leaned in closer. "And if ya hit it, let me know. I'm betting she's a wild one."

Lucky nodded his head, then asked, "What about you? You supposed to be on the low with Peaches?"

Romello threw up his hands in exaggerated frustration. "She's been a tough egg for me to crack. I don't give up easily, though." Romello looked at Lucky with seriousness. "You ain't gonna be going back and telling this shit to my girl, are you?"

Lucky shook his head. "Play on, playa," he said. The two of them slapped hands again.

"I like you, man," Romello said. "We're gonna have to get together sometime, take a ride in the Benz-o, smoke a little weed. You work?"

"Naw," Lucky replied.

Romello grinned. "Let me guess. Your girl is taking care of ya, huh?"

Lucky nodded his head.

"Damn, man! I want your life!" Romello turned and started walking back towards his apartment. "Get at me some time, bro! You do any drinking?"

"Brandy!" Lucky called back to him.

"Aww shit! Good to know I got somebody I can hang with now!"

Romello turned around and started walking again. He saw Peaches step out onto her front porch. "Good afternoon," he called to her, admiring the pink lace camisole set she was wearing.

Peaches waved back. "Was that Lucky you were talking to?" she asked.

"Why?" Romello asked.

"'Cuz I wanna know."

Romello started walking towards her porch. He was not worried about being seen by Jewel. She had taken the kids to go visit her mother for the day.

He walked onto the porch. "That outfit sure looks good on you," he said. "You came out here so I could see you in it?"

Peaches rolled her eyes at him. "Actually, I'm hoping to catch Lucky's eye."

"Wait a minute. You not trying to give him any, are you? If you are, you're gonna make him pay for it, right?"

"Now why the hell would I do something stupid like

that?" Peaches asked, still looking out towards the parking lot to watch Lucky.

"The brotha just moved here and already you trying to throw it at him. Well, what about me? I have been trying to get at you all this time. Why should I have to pay?"

"You've got a girl."

"But so does he."

"You have to pay a penalty for having a *crazy* girl, though."

"So if I move out, would you let me get some for free?" he teased.

Peaches looked at him, not at all in the mood for his humor. "You are such a comedian," she said sarcastically.

Romello tried to touch her arm; Peaches swatted his hand away.

"You shouldn't even be concentrating on him so hard, anyway," he said to her matter-of-factly. "The brotha seems to have his eye on Alisha."

"Stop lying, fool." Peaches went back into her apartment.

Romello followed behind her, admiring the view from the back. "I'm not lying. That's what we were over there talking about. He kept asking me questions about her."

Peaches turned around and looked at him in alarm. "Questions like what?"

"He was asking if Craig was treating her right and shit like that. My man wants to put the moves on little Miss Goody Two-shoes."

"For real?"

Romello walked up on her and cupped her breasts in his hands. "I wouldn't lie to you," he said softly. "I'd be nothing but good to you, if you let me."

"Boy, if you don't get your damn hands off of me, I swear I'll hurt you."

Peaches walked over to the window. She watched as

Lucky picked up his bucket and started walking towards his apartment.

"And you swear you ain't bullshitting me about this?" she asked Romello again.

"Why would I have to lie about this? The nigga don't want you. He wants Alisha." Romello walked over to her and gave her a kiss on her bare shoulder. "Guess you can't have everything you want," he told her before disappearing out the front door.

Peaches was not sure whether to believe him or not. She figured Romello would say anything just to keep her from being with Lucky. The more she gave it some thought, though, the more it sounded believable. If there was one woman in the complex—or on the face of the earth, for that matter—that Peaches felt intimidated by, it was definitely Alisha. While Peaches felt good about her loud, in-your-face personality, she couldn't help but admire the reserved, classy way that Alisha always carried herself, even though she thought the girl was a little too naive to be her age.

When I grow up, I wanna be just like her, Peaches would always tease herself, even though deep down she really meant it. She figured by the time she was forty she would be just as classy as Alisha, but with just a little more sense.

Peaches decided she was not going to sweat it, though. Everyone in the complex knew Alisha was Craig-crazy. There was no way another man was going to make her stray, no matter how fine he was.

As soon as Lucky figures that shit out, he will have no choice but to turn to me, Peaches told herself. When that happened, she promised herself that she would be right there waiting.

* * *

Jewel was shocked to have Romello greet her at the front door with a kiss.

He took the baby from her arms and carried her to the room to put her in the crib. "How was your visit to your mother's?" he asked. "Did you tell her I said hello?"

Jewel watched him with suspicion as he walked back into the living room. "You know how my mother is. She wants to know when you're gonna put a ring on my finger." Jewel dropped down in a chair.

"Well, where are the keys? I was gonna go out for a little while."

Jewel shook her head, knowing something had to be up with him. It was not like him to greet her at the door with a kiss for nothing.

"It's damn near eleven o'clock. Where the hell are you going at this hour?" she barked at him.

"I'm gonna see about making some money."

Jewel reached into her pocket and threw some money on the coffee table. "Mama gave me some money. There's three hundred there, so you don't need to go out."

Romello frowned. Even though that stack of money had ruined his excuse to go see Maria, he did not like the fact that Jewel's mother felt the need to give her money every time she went over there. To Romello, it was like a slap in the face, as if she was constantly reminding him how much of a screwup he was.

"Why do you always take money from your mother like that? You know I don't like that shit, Jewel."

"We need the damn money, Romello! The boys need clothes. The baby needs things. Hell! I need things."

"I'm doing the best I fucking can."

Jewel closed her eyes, not wanting to have the same argument they had every time she came from her mother's house.

"It's not like we have to pay the money back, Romello.

Mama is just trying to help us out a little. She wants to make sure her grandbabies have everything they need."

Romello walked over to the coffee table and threw the money back in her lap. "What she's doing is trying to make me look bad. You know your mama can't stand me."

"Look, there's no way I'm giving Mama back this money, so there's no reason for you to be running the streets at this time of night."

Romello looked around and found the car keys lying on the table. "I'm going to get a drink," he mumbled as he stormed out of the apartment. He had expected to hear Jewel come after him at any moment, but there was silence.

He got to his car and sat down behind the wheel. He was no longer in the mood to see Maria anymore. He just wanted to get out of the house and get away from his situation, not having to worry about Jewel or her mother or the fact that he really was not doing a good job of taking care of his family.

Just then, there was a tap on his car window. Romello jumped at the sight of Peaches standing there.

"What in the world are you doing hiding out in your car?" she asked as soon as he rolled down his window.

"I was about to leave and go get myself some weed or something," he replied.

"No hot date tonight?"

Romello shook his head. "Not in the mood," he sighed. "Where are you on your way to?"

"I'm going to make that money, honey." Peaches looked at Romello with concern. "Are you all right? You look like you got the weight of the world on your shoulders."

"I've got a lot going on in my head right now."

"I'm not the best advice giver in the world, but if you just wanna blow off some steam, I've got a few minutes to spare."

Romello looked up at Peaches. For the first time it did

not matter to him that she was standing in front of him half dressed. Any other time, he would have been all over her trying to cop a feel. Tonight all the sex games were out of his head. Right now he had to deal with the mess he called his life.

"Thanks, but I think I'll be all right," he said.

Peaches started grinning. "I don't like to see you like this," she said, chuckling. "I'm used to the Romello who's always trying to make passes at me. I don't know about this serious Romello."

"I'll be all right once I get some weed in my system."

"Ya know, that stuff is gonna mess up your head. Do you know how many brain cells you kill every time you take a hit? Not to mention what it does to your sperm count, but it's not like you need to be worrying about having any more kids."

Romello looked at Peaches and started to laugh. "Wait a minute. Don't you smoke weed too?"

Peaches smiled. "Well, at least I got you to laugh about something." She reached out and touched his arm through the window. "Whatever your problem is, it's gonna be okay. Like my mother always used to tell me, it's always midnight before the morning comes—or something like that."

"You butchered that one."

"I told you I wasn't good at the advice thing."

Romello started the car. "I'll be fine," he said. "You go on to work so you can work them horny niggas for every dime they got in their pockets."

"Keep your chin up." Peaches turned and started walking away.

"By the way," Romello called after her, sticking his head out of the window, "that damn outfit looks fucking good on you."

Peaches started laughing. "There's the old Romello!"

Chapter 8

Everyone watched as Lucky carried the last few bags of groceries from his car to his apartment. No one bothered to utter a word until Lucky finally disappeared into his apartment.

"The man is even sexy carrying groceries," Alisha was the first to comment.

The other girls started laughing.

"Girl, if only Craig could hear you now," Ladona said to her.

"What? All I did was say he was sexy!" Alisha chuckled. "I'm allowed to look at other guys, just as long as I don't touch."

"Don't you think it's strange that he's been here nearly a month and his girlfriend hasn't been by to visit him?" Peaches asked the group.

"Well, maybe he prefers to go to her," Ladona suggested.

"What do you think, Jewel?" Peaches asked. "You two seem to be all chummy. What's the four-one-one on the girlfriend?"

Jewel shrugged her shoulders. "I don't know. He doesn't talk about her much, and he gets all defensive anytime I try to ask him a question about her."

"Maybe he doesn't even have a girlfriend," Alisha said.

"Yeah," Ladona chimed in. "Maybe that's just a cover story to throw us all off."

Everyone turned to her in shock, but only Peaches bothered to say what everyone else was thinking. "The brotha's gay."

"I sure hope not," Jewel said, lowering her voice so Romello would not hear her. "That would be a waste of a good man."

"He has to be gay," Peaches insisted. "I mean, he hasn't even tried to come on to me yet. Only a gay man could resist a body like this."

Jewel rolled her eyes. "Or maybe he just has taste."

"Well, the man doesn't work, so where would he be getting his money from if the story about the girlfriend isn't true?" Alisha questioned the group.

"His gay lover," Ladona said, giggling.

"Well, I sure hope he isn't gay," Jewel said, lowering her voice again.

"Why would you care?" Ladona asked. "You have Romello."

"For the sake of womankind," Jewel replied.

Peaches scoffed at her. "You're the one who spends the most time with him. Can't you tell if he's gay or not?"

"He doesn't talk gay. He doesn't act gay."

"Like that means anything," Ladona mumbled.

Everyone quickly hushed when Romello walked out onto the porch. Jewel turned and looked up at him.

"What are you doing up?" she asked him.

"Do we have anymore of those enchiladas? I'm starving," Romello said as he waved to the other girls.

"They're in that yellow container on the bottom shelf of the fridge."

"Thanks." Romello turned and went back in the

house. A few seconds later, he came back to the door and poked his head outside.

"Just so you girls know, Lucky ain't gay." He then focused his attention to Jewel and added, "And don't worry, honey, I'm not mad at you for thinking he'd be a waste of a good man."

Jewel poked her head into the kids' room. Angelica was fast asleep in her crib as RJ and Cesar were on the top bunk, too fixated on cartoons to notice her standing there.

"How you boys doing?" she asked them.

Finally, Cesar was the only one to acknowledge her presence. "Hey, Mama," he said, then quickly turned his attention back to the TV.

"I was gonna run a few doors down to drop off some food to my friend. Will you guys be okay here for a few minutes?"

The boys nodded their heads with their eyes still glued to the TV.

"Try not to wake up your sister."

RJ finally looked at her. "Daddy's gone?"

Jewel nodded her head, seeing a hint of sadness in his eyes. She knew that RJ was just as tired as she was about Romello always being gone every night.

"We'll be okay, Mama," he assured her before returning his attention to his show.

Jewel opened her mouth to say something else, but realized there was nothing else that could be said. No matter how many times she tried to make RJ feel better, he would always look at her as if he knew she was telling him a lie.

"I'll be back in a little while."

Jewel went to the kitchen to grab the plate of enchiladas on the table, then went down to Lucky's apartment.

Over the past few weeks, she and Lucky had become very close. Whenever Romello was out for the evening, Lucky was always around to keep her company. Even though she knew it was only a platonic relationship, she still could not help feeling that this was a form of cheating.

While her body was being faithful to Romello, her mind certainly was not. Jewel would often daydream about Lucky coming over one evening and confessing that he was starting to fall in love with her. Then from there, the daydream would progress to the two of them running off with the kids and living happily ever after, leaving Romello's no-good butt behind.

It was all just a fantasy that part of her wished would come true, which is one reason why she had decided to take him some of the dinner she had fixed. The way to a man's heart is through his stomach, was her belief. She believed her cooking was one of the main reasons Romello stayed with her so long—he knew that he would never find another woman to feed him as well as she did.

Jewel stepped onto the porch and was about to knock on the door when she heard Lucky in what sounded like a heated discussion on the telephone. Instead of making her presence known, she moved closer to the kitchen window to hear the conversation better.

"No! I'm tired of this shit!" she heard Lucky say to the person on the other end. "I moved here to be closer to you, but you've barely spent any time with me!"

Jewel assumed he was talking to his girlfriend.

She moved even closer to the window and made herself comfortable because this was one conversation she did not want to miss.

"Well, I'm tired of having a few lunch dates here and there. I expect more time . . . Oh yeah? Well, there are plenty of women around here who would be willing to spend the time if you aren't . . . naw, that ain't no threat . . . fine . . . you do what you gotta do and I'll do what I gotta do . . . yes, that one was a threat."

Jewel heard the phone slam down on the table. She took a moment to soak in everything she had heard. Even though it had only been half of the conversation, Lucky had said enough to tell her everything she needed to know. There was definitely trouble in paradise, and maybe this was the start of making her daydreams become a reality.

She made her way back to the front door and knocked. Lucky answered the door with a scowl on his face that quickly gave way to a smile at the sight of Jewel standing there.

"Did I catch you at a bad time?" she asked him.

Lucky stepped out onto the front porch. "Oh, of course not," he said. "There's never a bad time when it comes to you."

Jewel held out the plate of food to him. "I had cooked extra. I thought you might wanna try my world-famous enchiladas. They're the best this side of the border."

Lucky smiled graciously as he took the plate from her. "I bet they are," he said. "You wanna come in?"

She shook her head. "I can't. The kids are at the house by themselves. I just stopped by to give you the food and see how you were doing."

"I'm good," he replied.

"Well, I hope you enjoy."

Jewel started to turn to walk away, but Lucky reached out and grabbed her arm. "Can I at least thank you for thinking of me?" he asked. Before Jewel had a chance to reply, he had leaned over and gently touched his lips to her cheek.

From the look in his eyes, Jewel knew that was no ordinary kiss. That kiss was more than just a thank-you. It felt more like an invitation—an invitation to pick up where it seemed like his girlfriend was leaving off.

"Uh—well—you're welcome," Jewel stammered.

Lucky grinned as he gave her a lingering glance. "See you tomorrow?" he asked in a low, soft voice that sounded like sweet music to Jewel's ears.

"Yeah," she replied.

Lucky leaned in again, this time with a short, soft kiss on the lips.

If you can't be with the one you love, love the one you're with, he thought.

In the darkness of the parking lot, Peaches sat in her car watching everything that had just transpired.

"That bitch!" she yelled out as she pounded her fist on the steering wheel.

Chapter 9

Alisha walked down the stairs on Craig's arm. "You have a good day at work," she told him.

Craig gave her a peck on the forehead, then glanced in the direction of his SUV. He saw Ladona leaning against the passenger door waiting for his arrival.

"I wonder where she's gotta go this time," he mumbled under his breath.

Standing at the bottom of the stairs, Alisha slipped her arm around his waist. "I told you to be nice, remember?"

Craig gave her a fake smile. "I'll give you a call around lunchtime," he sighed before walking off.

Alisha stood there and waved good-bye as Craig and Ladona got into the truck and pulled out of the parking lot. Out the corner of her eye, she could see Peaches standing on her porch drinking a Coke.

"Girl, I just don't see how you can do it," Peaches said with a chuckle.

Alisha started walking towards her. "You don't see how I can do what?" she asked.

"Let your husband drive some other woman around every morning. I have seen Ladona climbing her butt in that passenger seat almost every day this past week. What's up with that?"

"Oh, Craig's just being nice. Ladona's been having a lot of problems with her car lately."

Peaches looked at her as if she was not buying it. "Honey, I would pay to get the woman's car fixed before I let her use my husband as her personal chauffeur."

Alisha shrugged her shoulders. "It's really no big deal, though. I mean, it would be one thing if he had to go out of his way to take her somewhere, but since he has to go downtown . . ."

Peaches shook her head in amazement, trying to figure out if her naïveté was just an act or truly genuine. "You can't possibly be that damn trusting, girl."

Alisha looked puzzled. "What do you mean? What is there not to trust? I know that Craig would never cheat on me, and Ladona is too good of a friend to even think about messing with my husband."

Peaches started laughing as she took a seat on the top step. "You really are that damn trusting! Honey, I'm not trying to say they've got something going on, but you need to start looking at all the time they are spending with each other."

"All of what time? It's only a forty-five-minute commute—an hour at the most. I hardly think that would be enough quality time to do some cheating."

Peaches snickered. "Whether it's forty-five minutes, an hour, or even ten minutes—that would be too much time for my man to be alone with any female who wasn't me. Hell! I wouldn't even trust my man to be around his own damn mama for too long."

Alisha waved her off with her hand. "Girl, I don't have anything to worry about with Craig."

"Why not?" Peaches snapped at her. "He's a man, ain't

he? You can't trust a man as far as you can throw him, and you certainly don't trust your friends around him."

Alisha shook her head. "Peaches, I think you are just trying to get some mess started." Even as she tried to laugh it off, a tiny part of her wondered if there really was something to what Peaches was trying to tell her.

"Alisha, you're my girl. I would not sit here and try to stir up trouble with you and Mr. Perfect Husband. All I am trying to do is get you to keep your eyes open. If you close your eyes for one second, a man will definitely try to screw you and anything else with a hole. What's worse is that your friends can be even sneakier."

"Sounds like you know all this from personal experience."

Peaches paused before nodding her head. "I guess you could say that," she replied, not wanting to reveal how she had been such a terrible friend in her teenage years. "You just make sure you watch your husband. Most of all, you make sure you watch *her.*"

Alisha stared at her closely, wondering what was behind that distant and regretful look that had come over Peaches's face. She so badly wanted to pry into her business, but before she could open her mouth to speak, Jewel came outside and greeted them.

"So are you two meeting over there this morning?" Jewel called over to them, sounding cheerier than normal.

While Alisha assumed her cheery attitude was the result of a good night's loving, Peaches was stewing, knowing exactly what had Jewel smiling brighter than sunshine.

"Good morning," Alisha said, while Peaches only acknowledged her with a nod.

If looks could kill, Jewel would have dropped dead on the spot as Peaches glared at her with intensity.

"What's your problem?" Jewel asked her. "Wake up on the wrong side of the trick this morning?"

Peaches sucked her teeth, then let out a long, slow breath. "Are you having sex with Lucky?" she blurted out.

Jewel and Alisha looked at each other in shock. Peaches's question had been completely unexpected.

"Peaches!" the two of them gasped.

Peaches stood up and started walking toward Jewel. "No, no, no. Don't you try to hush me. I want to know. Are you fucking Lucky or not?" she asked, her voice getting a little louder.

Jewel turned around to make sure Romello was not standing outside, then turned back to Peaches. "What made you ask something like that?"

"Because I saw you all in his mouth last night," Peaches replied.

Jewel stood there with her mouth wide open, unsure of how she could even begin to deny this one. The last thing she needed was for Peaches to know about her kissing Lucky—it would only be a matter of time before she went blabbing about it to Romello. Despite that fear she had, she still could not help but feel a little happiness because Lucky had kissed her, not Peaches. Lucky wanted her!

"It was an innocent kiss, Peaches. You make it sound like we were groping each other." Jewel looked over her shoulder to check for Romello.

Alisha started laughing. "You kissed Lucky?" she squealed in excitement. "You are such a tramp!"

"Innocent kiss, my ass," Peaches grumbled. "You still haven't answered my question, though. Are you having sex with him or not?"

Jewel gave her a smug look. "It would kill you if I did sleep with him, huh?"

"Actually, it would kill *you*—or at least Romello would kill you if he found out." Peaches turned to Jewel's front door and started calling Romello's name.

Jewel quickly tried to quiet her down. "Stop it!" she

hissed at her. "Okay, we are not having sex. Like I said, though, it was just an innocent kiss. He was thanking me for the dinner I'd brought him."

Alisha started giggling. "You're cooking the man dinner?"

Jewel rolled her eyes at both of them. "You two are making more out of if than it is. Lucky and I are just friends. That's all."

Alisha turned to Peaches and could tell the green-eyed monster had taken her over. "So you're mad that he wasn't kissing on you?" she asked her.

Peaches shot Alisha a nasty look. "I don't get mad; I just get what I want." She turned and went back into her apartment, slamming the door behind her.

Alisha and Jewel exchanged glances. "Sounds to me like she's mad," Jewel said before bursting into a fit of laughter.

The two of them started walking towards Jewel's front porch.

"Okay, Peaches is gone now, so you can tell me the truth," Alisha said, lowering her voice to a whisper. "Do you two really have something going on or what?"

"I am telling the truth, Alisha. There really isn't anything going on between me and Lucky except a friendship," Jewel replied.

She wanted to tell Alisha that part of her wished that there could be more going on, and that his simple kiss did not actually feel so simple. Jewel decided to keep it to herself, though. The less she told, the less she would have to worry about Romello finding out anything.

After talking for a few more minutes, Alisha excused herself, claiming she had to get up to the apartment to finish folding laundry. With Peaches's words of wisdom still heavy on her mind, the only thing she wanted to do was try to reach Craig on his cell phone while he was still on the road with Ladona.

As soon as Craig answered his phone, Alisha could hear Ladona laughing hysterically in the background.

She sounds too damn happy, Alisha thought to herself, wondering what could have been so funny.

Alisha listened hard to the sound of Craig's voice, trying to notice the hint of anything that just did not seem right. "Hey, baby," he greeted her. "Is anything wrong?"

"No, nothing's wrong," Alisha replied, now trying to hear if Ladona was saying anything in the background. She even found herself listening for the sound of traffic to make sure they were still driving and not pulled over in some motel. "I was lonely so I thought I'd give you a call. How's traffic?"

"It's Friday. You know traffic is always heaviest at the end of the week. At least I've got Ladona here cracking jokes, trying to keep me from having road rage."

Alisha tried to smile, but she could not help the feelings of jealousy that had come over her.

"I miss you, Craig."

"Baby, I haven't even been gone thirty minutes."

"Well, maybe you should come on back to the house. Your boss won't be too mad if you call in sick one day, will he? Or maybe you can tell him you're gonna work from home."

"Alisha, are you sure you're okay?"

"I told you that I'm lonely. I want you to come back home."

She heard Ladona mumble something in the background that got Craig to laugh. "What did Ladona just say?"

"Oh, it was nothing," Craig said, chuckling. "But look, baby, I can't turn back now. Ladona's gotta get to her appointment downtown."

Screw Ladona and her damn appointment, she wanted to scream into the phone.

Craig continued talking. "Well, why don't you come meet us downtown for lunch today?"

"Who is 'us'?" Alisha questioned with suspicion.

"Me and Ladona. She said her meeting was going to carry her over to noon so I told her I would treat her to lunch. Why don't you come and join us? We'll probably go to that place that makes those grilled chicken salads you like so much."

Alisha started fuming. *How is he gonna take her to my favorite spot?*

"Craig, you do love me, right?" she asked after calming herself enough to speak.

"Why would you ask me that? Honey, you know I do."

"Well, I just wanted to hear you say it."

"Alisha, I love you more than any other woman on this earth. Why are you acting so strange? Did something happen after I left?"

"Nothing happened," Alisha replied, feeling a little bit better knowing that Ladona had heard him tell her he loved her. "Anyway, that's all I really wanted."

"What? To hear me say I love you?" Craig sounded both annoyed and amused. "Are you sure nothing's wrong with you?"

"I'm fine, Craig, but I wanna hear you tell me you love me again."

"I love you. I love you. I love you. You satisfied?"

Alisha smiled, wondering what was going through Ladona's mind at that moment. "I am definitely satisfied," she answered.

Ladona was glad when Craig finally ended that conversation. It had taken all the strength she had to keep herself from grabbing the steering wheel and running them into a ditch. It made her skin crawl to have to sit and listen to him say *I love you* to that spoiled brat of a wife of his.

"The wifey's checking up on you?" Ladona asked sarcastically.

Craig smiled. "I'm not exactly sure what the hell she was doing. She was just calling to hear me say I loved her. She hasn't done that since we first got married. I wonder if I should go home and check on her," Craig replied.

"I'm sure she's fine," Ladona said, praying that would be enough to keep him from making a U-turn. "If you're that worried, just give her a call when you get to the office. You've come this far; no sense in going all the way back home now."

Craig nodded in agreement. "I guess you're right."

Ladona breathed a sigh of relief. She did not want anything ruining her chance to have lunch with Craig. Even though it was not the big commitment that she was hoping for, at least lunch was a step in the right direction. After all the bogus excuses she'd come up with just to catch a ride downtown with him every morning, it seemed like things were finally starting to pay off, even though she couldn't stand getting up so early in the morning.

This was supposed to be her summer vacation, three months for her to sleep in as long as she wanted. Instead, it was as if she was working another job; at least this one seemed to have the promise of great benefits.

"So did Alisha say whether or not she was gonna come down and meet us for lunch?" Ladona crossed her fingers and her toes, praying that lunch would still be a party of two.

"She didn't say, but I doubt she will," Craig said, sounding a little disappointed. "Alisha can't stand driving downtown by herself."

Thank you, God, Ladona said softly under her breath, letting out a sigh of relief.

Chapter 10

"Seven . . . eight . . . nine . . ."

"Jewel, what in the hell are you doing?" Romello asked as he walked into the room. He went over to the other side of the bed and found Jewel lying on the floor.

"Exercising," she huffed as she squeezed out the last sit-up.

Romello started laughing. "Since when do you exercise?"

"For the past three or four days," she replied, still trying to catch her breath. "I do this every night before I go to bed."

Romello sat down on the edge of the bed. "Oh, so you are trying to lose some weight?"

Jewel rolled over on her stomach and started counting out push-ups. "Yes."

As soon as she got to ten, she jumped up and grabbed her cup of water off the nightstand.

Romello looked at her suspiciously. "You've never been concerned with losing weight before. What's got you all hyped?"

Jewel shrugged her shoulders, then moved to the middle of the room and started counting out her jumping jacks. "You're always saying I should lose some weight, right?"

"But it's not like you've ever listened to me before."

"Well, now I'm listening. Eighteen . . . nineteen . . ."

Romello walked over to the dresser and pulled out a fresh tank top to throw on. "I was gonna go hang out at one of my boys' houses," he said, bracing himself for Jewel's verbal assault.

To his surprise, Jewel did not even look in his direction.

"Twenty-nine . . . thirty." She picked up her cup of water and finished it off.

"Well, did you hear what I said?" Romello asked. "I said I was about to go out for a little while."

Jewel looked at her watch and saw that it was almost 10:30. She shrugged her shoulders then went into the bathroom to run the shower. "Have a nice time," she told him.

Romello stood there, expecting her to come back out and start complaining. When she did not so much as utter a word, he went to the bathroom and stood in the doorway.

"You're not gonna fuss at me?" he asked.

"Why should I?" she asked. "You're a grown man. You can take care of yourself out there this time of night."

He thought this had to be some kind of joke or a trap. "You aren't gonna complain about the time or accuse me of running off to be with one of my girlfriends? Aren't you gonna ask me what time I'll be home?"

Jewel shook her head. "I know what time it is, I know that I'm the only girlfriend you have, and you'll be home whenever you get home."

Romello started laughing. "Okay, okay. I see you're trying to use some reverse psychology shit on me. You've been watching Oprah today, huh?"

Jewel shook her head again. "I'm not trying to use anything, sweetie. If you are going out, then go. But can you do me a favor and just check on the kids on your way out, though? I bet those boys fell asleep with the TV on again."

Romello nodded his head with reservation. "Sure."

Jewel stepped into the shower; she heard Romello's footsteps walk out of the room. By the time she came out of the bathroom a few minutes later, he had already left the apartment.

It did bother her that he was going to hang out in the streets, but she did not waste time dwelling on that. Still dripping wet in her towel, she went over to the phone and dialed Lucky's number.

"I saw your boy leave a few minutes ago," Lucky told her.

"He said he was gonna go hang out with some of his friends."

"So did you want some company for a little while?"

Jewel's heart began to race as she tried to decide how to answer that question. The fact that she had even called him was a big enough sign that she wanted him to come over, but actually having to tell him was more difficult than she had anticipated. In nine years of her relationship with Romello, she had never cheated—never even thought about being with another man, until now.

"Company would be nice," she finally answered.

She could hear Lucky smiling through the phone. "Are you sure? You don't sound too certain," he said.

From somewhere, Jewel built up the courage to say what she really wanted. "I'm sure," she replied.

"I'll see you in about fifteen."

What in the hell am I doing? Jewel asked herself as she made a mad dash around the room looking for something decent to put on.

She tried to calm herself, saying that he was only coming over to sit and have a few laughs, but she knew better—her body knew better. She tried to tell herself that whatever happened would be Romello's fault. She figured that if he were doing more to satisfy her needs then she would not have even been considering going through all this. But the more she thought about how Romello was probably out there giving his loving to someone else, the more she felt justified in letting whatever was about to happen, happen.

Damn you, Romello! she mumbled aloud as she slid on her "special occasion" thong.

On her way to answer the knock at the door, Jewel stopped by the kids' room and found the three of them fast asleep. She let out a sigh of relief, then continued on to the front door. There Lucky stood in what had become his trademark—a white tank top and blue jeans shorts that were two sizes too big.

"You smell good," he said to her as he walked into the apartment.

"Thanks. You do too," Jewel said, feeling nervous. As she always did when Lucky came over, she leaned out the door to see if Peaches was watching. However, tonight she prayed that Peaches was not looking. She did not want any witnesses to the crime.

As soon as Jewel closed the door and turned around, Lucky immediately took her in his arms and kissed her on the lips.

Peaches felt a tap on her shoulder. She spun around and was surprised to see Romello standing there with a smile on his face and a dollar bill in his hand. She quickly snatched the dollar bill from him and started laughing.

"It's bad enough you harass me at home, but now you wanna come to my job," she teased him. "What in the world are you doing here?"

Romello looked around the club. This was the first

time he had ever been in there. "I was bored so I thought I'd come see my favorite fantasy girl in action."

"So you caught my show?" Peaches asked with a smile.

Romello nodded his head. "Now was all that a stage act or can you really do all that in the bedroom?"

Peaches leaned in closer to whisper in his ear. "Nine hundred bucks will buy you the answer to all your questions."

"But I thought you said six! What happened to the good-neighbor discount?"

Peaches threw her head back and laughed. "Boy, I've gotta mingle and make this money 'round here."

"Can I get a free lap dance, at least?"

Peaches put her hand to her chin, as if giving his question some serious consideration. "Maybe," she said, then walked away to continue working the room for her next big-money man.

Romello found a table in the back. For the next hour, he sat there nursing a rum and Coke as he ogled all the girls walking past. However, the only girl he was interested in watching was Peaches.

She worked the club, occasionally disappearing into the private dance room for a few minutes, then coming out with a stack of cash in her hand. Romello prayed that there was only dancing going on in that back room. He did not want to think that she was back there having sex with some other man while he was sitting there waiting on her.

A few times, he had thought about getting up to leave, but then he would see her glance over at him and give him a smile. That was enough to make him want to stay.

Peaches walked over and held out her hand to him. "You got five dollars?" she asked.

Romello went into his wallet and handed her a five-dollar bill.

"Come with me," she said as she grabbed him by the

hand and led him to the back room. She locked the door behind them, then cut on the lights.

"So is this my private dance?" he asked as he took a seat in one of the chairs.

Peaches sat down in a chair across from him. "No, I just want my boss to think I'm in here working. I needed a damn break. These shoes are killing me."

"So you're using me? I should go out there and tell him right now."

Peaches put her feet in Romello's lap. "Rub my feet for me," she insisted as she rested her head on the back of the chair.

Without giving it a second thought, Romello slid off her shoes and began massaging her feet. "This is my first time in here, you know. I'm not really big on strip clubs."

"So what do you think?"

Romello shrugged his shoulders. "How can you do this shit every night?"

"It pays the bills."

"So does a job at McDonald's."

Peaches held her head up. "I know you, of all people, are not trying to preach to me about getting a decent job. How exactly do you make your money?"

Romello smiled. "Okay, okay."

"Isn't Jewel gonna be upset that you're out this late?"

Romello shook his head. "She'll probably bitch when I get home. No different than any other night."

"So, are you feeling any better than you did the other night? Did you get all your issues straightened out?"

"I'm all right now," he replied, surprised that she had remembered.

Peaches relaxed and closed her eyes again, enjoying the feel of Romello's hands kneading her feet like dough. The idea of telling him about the kiss between Jewel and Lucky had crossed her mind, but she decided against being a tattletale. Besides, it was only one little kiss. With all the dirt Romello was into with other girls, she figured Jewel was entitled to have her own little moment of fun—even if it was with the man Peaches wanted for herself.

She opened her eyes and started staring at his profile. Though she would never admit this to him, she thought he was very attractive. If it had not been for the fact that he was practically married with children, Peaches was certain she would have slept with him by now, maybe even dated him.

Romello looked up and caught Peaches staring at him. "What?" he asked.

She shook her head and replied, "I'm just thinking."

"Thinking what?" Romello said with a grin, hoping she was thinking about repaying him for the foot rub with sex.

Peaches grabbed her shoes and started putting them on again. "I was thinking that maybe I should have you come by here every night and rub my feet."

"I'd rather rub something else," Romello said, chuckling as he touched her thigh.

Peaches got to her feet. "Well, time to finish out this last damn hour."

Romello looked at his watch. "I guess I'll take my butt home now."

For a brief moment, their eyes locked in a glance. Peaches felt a chill through her body.

"Thanks for the foot rub," she said.

Romello nodded his head. "If I can make your feet feel that good, just imagine what I could do to the rest of your body."

The moment was over.

Peaches started laughing and gave him a friendly hug before opening the door and walking back out into the club.

Chapter 11

Romello walked into the kitchen and grabbed a beer from the refrigerator. On his way back over to the sofa, he stopped and looked at Jewel.

"Is there something wrong with you?" he asked her.

"No. Why do you ask?"

"You've been sitting here at the table ever since your mother came and picked up the kids two hours ago. Don't tell me you miss them already."

Jewel forced a smile as she shook her head. "I was just sitting here thinking, that's all," she replied.

Romello looked at her with suspicion. "You sure have been acting kinda nutty this past week or so," he said, popping open the beer, then taking a sip.

Jewel swallowed hard. "What do you mean?" she asked, trying to control the shakiness in her voice.

"I don't know. Maybe it's all that exercising you've been doing. All that fitness shit is affecting your brain." Romello went back to the couch and sat down.

No, it's all that sex I've been getting. Jewel chuckled to herself as she went back to staring out the window.

"You sure ain't nothing wrong with you, Jewel? You've barely spoken two words since the kids left."

"I'm fine, Romello."

However, Jewel did not feel fine at all, with her mind filled with guilt. That one evening with Lucky had turned into four other evenings; and while she was sitting there beating herself up for being unfaithful, it made her feel even worse that her body tingled at the thought of there being a fifth.

In all honesty, Jewel did not want to enjoy it so much. She did not want to have to sneak behind Romello's back every time he left the house. While she loved the way Lucky made her feel sexy and wanted, she knew it would feel better if she could get that from Romello.

Jewel watched as Alisha and Craig walked hand in hand across the parking lot to his SUV. She let out a sigh of frustration, wishing that could be her and Romello, such the loving couple.

"They're so damn cute it's disgusting," she said to herself, not realizing she was loud enough for Romello to hear.

Romello pulled his attention away from the TV just long enough to ask her whom she was talking about.

"Craig and Alisha," Jewel replied. "It must be nice to be such a happily married couple, taking the day to spend it with each other."

Romello snickered. "How can you sit there and try to compare us to Mr. and Mrs. Super-couple?"

Jewel continued talking, ignoring his smart comment. "I bet they're going for a picnic in the park, or I bet he rented a boat to take her out on the lake for a few hours. Craig is always doing romantic stuff like that for her, you know. Romello, why don't you ever do anything romantic for me?"

He drank the rest of his beer, then walked to the fridge to grab another one.

"And what exactly would you like me to do that's romantic, Jewel?" he asked on his way back to the couch. "It's not like I have money coming outta my ass to rent a damn boat on the lake."

"Who says you have to rent a boat?"

"Well, you want me to be like Mr. Super-couple, right?" His words were dripping with sarcasm.

"If I wanted you to be Mr. Super-couple I'd have you put a damn ring on my finger." Jewel got up from the table, then took a seat in the living room. "Romello, do you ever plan on marrying me or do you just wanna live in sin for the rest of our lives?"

Romello took a drink of his beer, then gave her a hard, long look. The *m* word was something he hated to hear about, and it seemed that more and more over the last few months Jewel had been bringing it up. He knew her mother was the one who kept pressing the issue, though. Had it not been for her mother, he figured Jewel probably would not make such a big deal about it.

He just was not ready to take that big of a step, though. To him, marriage was the kiss of death. His freedom to sneak around with other women would be over—Jewel would finally own him.

"You keep letting your mother fill your head with all those crazy thoughts of a wedding, huh?"

"My mother isn't filling my head with anything."

"Well, then why do we have to keep having this same damn discussion? Aren't things just fine the way they are now?"

"Who are things fine for? I hope you don't think I'm satisfied. Romello, we have been together nine years. We have three kids. We should have been married years ago."

Romello shook his head and started laughing. "So that's what this whole exercise shit has been about? You trying to slim down so you can squeeze into a wedding dress?"

"What if I am?" Jewel asked defensively, even though that was not the reason.

"Like I said, things are fine the way they are now. If it ain't broke, don't fix it."

"I'm starting to wonder whether or not you really love me, Romello. I mean, if you loved me you would have no problem marrying me. But then again, you don't even wanna have sex with me, so why would you wanna marry me, right?"

"I do wanna have sex with you, Jewel. Unfortunately, you are always wanting sex when I'm tired as hell."

Jewel rolled her eyes at him. Romello did not know it, but he was making it easier for her to consider a fifth time with Lucky.

"Besides," Romello continued, "why should I have to sign a piece of paper just to prove how much I love you, anyway? The simple fact I've been with you for nine years should let you know something."

"Are you cheating on me? Have you *ever* cheated on me?"

Romello groaned in frustration. "You are just determined to cover every single fight-provoking topic in this discussion, huh?"

"Well, since you don't want to marry me or even have sex with me, I'm thinking maybe there's another woman in your life."

"How many times do I have to tell you there's no other woman in my life, Jewel?" Romello lied, as he thought about Latosha, Maria, and Serita.

"So then is it my weight? You don't wanna marry a fat pig, is that right?"

Romello rolled his eyes to the back of his head. He had a feeling the conversation would roll around to this eventually.

Her weight gain *was* an issue to him, though. Even

though she was not fat, he just could not stand being with a "chunky" woman. While all his friends told him he was crazy and that his woman still looked good, Romello argued that he did not like the extra thirty pounds and the stretch marks that had come to appear since they had first met.

Man, that just comes from having a baby, his friends would tell him. None of that made a difference, though. In his eyes, he wished Jewel could be perfect again.

"You're not a fat pig," Romello sighed.

"You may not say it, but you think it. I guess compared to someone like Peaches, I am a fat pig."

"Do you always have to bring her up?"

"Well, you'd marry me if I looked like her, right?"

"No, that wouldn't make a difference," Romello answered honestly. *But it sure would be nice if you did.*

Jewel leaned forward and gave him a serious look. "Romello, do you realize there are guys out there who find me attractive?" she asked. "They wouldn't be bothered with these few extra pounds I have. I wouldn't have to beg them for sex or beg them to put a ring on my finger."

Romello stared back at her, giving an equally serious look. "Just what you trying to say?" he asked.

"I'm not *trying* to say anything. I just wanna make you aware of that." Jewel rose to her feet and went to the bedroom.

Romello was certainly aware of it now.

Lucky took a hit from the blunt, then passed it back to Romello.

Even if he had been sober, Lucky still would have found their topic of discussion to be funny; he concentrated hard to keep a straight face as he gave Romello an answer.

"Naw, man, I haven't seen any guys coming to your door when you ain't there." Lucky took a drink of his beer. "What, you thinking your girl is creepin' on you with some other nigga?"

Romello took a few hits from the blunt. "I don't know, bro," he said, finally exhaling the smoke. "All I know is that she's been acting kinda funny lately. All of a sudden, she is trying to lose weight, and she don't be arguing with me anymore like she used to. I mean, the girl was always trying to knock my head off with something whenever I'd even mention going out at night. Now, it's like she don't care. Like she got her own shit going on when I leave."

Lucky just shook his head. "Damn, man, I can't even sit here and tell ya I've seen something 'cuz I haven't."

Romello threw his head back and downed the rest of his beer. "Then earlier today she starts talking this shit about how other guys find her attractive. Can you believe that shit? Why would she go and say some dumb shit like that to me?"

Lucky shook his head again. "You gotta be careful with females these days, man. They will dog you out in a heartbeat. But what do you care for, anyway? You got your own shit going on."

"It ain't the same." Romello slammed his can of beer down on the table. "How would you feel if you found out some other nigga was giving it to your girl while your back was turned?"

"I feel ya, man."

Romello took a few more hits from the blunt, then passed it back to Lucky. "I'll kill her if I find out she got some other nigga goin' up inside her. And I'll kill his ass too." Romello's voice thundered.

"Is it that serious, man? Pussy is pussy, right?" Lucky took a hit from the blunt.

"That's my baby mama, Lucky. She can't be doing that type of stuff."

Lucky could not hold back his laughter anymore. The irony of the situation was just too much for him to take. Here he was trying to offer words of comfort to the boyfriend of the woman he was sleeping with—a woman he cared nothing about. It gave Lucky such a strong feeling of power to know that at any moment he could tell Jewel he wanted her to leave Romello and she would have her bags packed within the hour.

However, it was not his plan to get Jewel to leave her man. In fact, he really did not like the fact that she was becoming so attached to him. This was all just a game to him—something for him to do since things were not going right in his own relationship, but he knew eventually he'd get things back on track with that, and then Jewel would be history.

"So do you be having any problems like this with your girl?" Romello asked.

Lucky leaned in towards him. "To be honest with you, there's a reason why you don't see my baby around here."

Romello paused to give that some thought, then started laughing when it finally sunk in. "Oohh. So she's married!"

Lucky sat back and smiled. "Something like that."

Chapter 12

"What's all this?"

Craig walked into the candlelit apartment, with the sounds of Freddy Jackson singing softly in the background. Excited and intrigued to walk into such a romantic setting, he quickly set this briefcase down, then shut the door without bothering to lock it.

"Am I in the right apartment?" he called out with a chuckle in his voice. He walked towards the kitchen and found Alisha standing in there wearing nothing but a black lace camisole.

"It's about time you got home," she said to him as she started pouring him a glass of wine.

"Flowers, candles, soft music—are we celebrating something tonight?"

Alisha handed him his glass, then gave him a kiss on the lips. "Just because I love you," she replied.

Craig quickly downed the glass of wine. "Had I known you had all this waiting on me I wouldn't have tried to finish off that last little bit of paperwork."

"It doesn't matter. At least you're here now." Alisha helped him out of his coat, then started undoing his tie. "So how was work?"

Walking in and seeing his wife there half-naked, the last thing Craig wanted to do was talk about his day. In a fit of passion, the two of them made it over to the couch, leaving a trail of clothes behind them. Just as Craig lowered himself onto his wife's naked body, there was a knock at the door.

"Don't you dare get up and open it," Alisha moaned in his ear. "Just put it in. They'll go away."

Anxious to feel the warm, tight folds of her body, he did not intend to get up to answer that door. Instead, he did as she told him to do, easing himself in, enjoying it as if it were his first time. They both let out a collective moan of satisfaction.

"Hey, Alisha, are you in there?" Ladona tried the doorknob and found that it was unlocked. When she opened the door, she was greeted with an eyeful of Craig's bare backside.

"Oh shit! I'm so sorry!" Ladona gasped, quickly covering her eyes.

Craig jumped up and covered himself with a pillow while Alisha grabbed the afghan from a nearby chair.

"What the fuck are you doing?" Alisha howled at her.

Ladona tried hard to fight back the giggles. She knew Craig had come home, and it was her plan to interrupt their evening. She had not expected to walk in on this.

"I'm so sorry," she said again. "The door was open so I figured I'd come on in." No matter how uncomfortable the situation, Ladona did not want to leave that apartment.

Craig managed to slide his underwear back on, then got up to grab his pants. "You have the worst damn timing," he grumbled under his breath.

"What do you want, Ladona?"

Ladona peeked through her fingers and saw they were decently covered. She faked an apologetic smile. "I was hoping I could borrow Craig for a little while. I locked my keys in the car. I was hoping he could help me get them out." She held up a wire hanger.

Craig ran his hand over his head, then looked at Alisha and shrugged his shoulder.

"I guess I can come down there and help," he sighed.

"You couldn't ask Romello or Lucky?" Alisha asked her with suspicion. "You came all the way upstairs just to get Craig?"

Ladona knew that Alisha could see right through her lie, but it did not matter as long as Craig was agreeing to come downstairs. "Well, none of them came to the door when I knocked," Ladona replied. "Besides, I trust Craig more than I trust them. What if they did something to mess up my car?"

"I'll be down there in a second," Craig said. "Just give me a chance to get my shoes on."

Ladona nodded. "Thank you so much," she said. "And I am so sorry to bust in on you guys like this. I really am."

As soon as she closed the door behind her, Alisha shot Craig a nasty look.

"I can't believe you didn't lock that damn door, Craig."

"I know, I know, honey, but I was just so overwhelmed with all the candles and the music," Craig said, silently cursing himself for not having locked the front door as he always did when he came home.

"She came in here on purpose," she whispered to him just in case Ladona was standing near the door. "Who does she think she is just walking into our apartment like that?"

"Don't even sweat it, baby. It won't take me more than five minutes to get that door open for her." Craig gave Alisha a kiss on the forehead. "Your friend seems to have the worst damn timing," he said before walking out the door.

"Yeah, the worst damn timing," she said through clenched teeth.

* * *

Peaches handed Lucky the bottle of Crown Royal, then looked around the apartment, admiring all the nice furniture.

"What did you do, hire an interior decorator? This looks like some shit out of a magazine or something."

"I like nice things," Lucky replied as he went to the kitchen to get some glasses.

Peaches walked around the living room looking for at least one framed picture of Lucky's girlfriend. "Sorry to be coming over unannounced, but I was getting tired of waiting for you to invite me over for that drink."

Lucky walked back in the room carrying the filled glasses. "I hadn't forgotten about you," he said. "I've just been busy with other things."

Peaches took her glass, then sat down on the couch. "Where are the pictures of your girlfriend?" she asked. "I'm starting to think you really don't have a girl."

Lucky grinned at her and was about to answer when he was interrupted by the ring of the phone. "I'll get back to you on that one," he said, chuckling as he went to answer it.

Peaches watched him closely as he stood in the hallway talking on the phone. *He's too damn gorgeous to be gay,* she told herself, then remembered seeing him give Jewel a kiss on the porch. She decided he could not possibly be gay. A gay man would not give a woman a kiss like that.

Peaches's ears perked up as Lucky's phone conversation seemed to grow more intense.

"I sat here and waited for you to come by until two o'clock in the morning . . . what do you mean you got caught up with something else? Look, baby, you wanted me to move here so that we could be closer and we wouldn't have to be driving so far just to see each other. . . . I know, but we saw each other more when I lived further away. . . . I know you have other obligations . . . yes, I know that you put in a lot of time at work, but I have needs. I keep telling you that shit . . . tomorrow? I don't wanna do lunch tomorrow. . . . I'm not gonna sit here and be at your disposal. . . . Fuck it! You do your thing and I'll do mine."

Lucky hung up the phone, then turned to Peaches as if nothing was wrong. "Sorry about that," he said to her.

Peaches smiled, unable to believe her incredible luck. "So was that your girl?" she asked.

Lucky sat back down. "That was the newspaper calling about my subscription," he replied sarcastically.

"Very funny." Peaches took a sip of her drink, then walked over and grabbed Lucky by the hand.

"What's wrong?" he asked.

Peaches didn't say a word as she led him to the bedroom.

If his girlfriend won't do for him, I sure will.

Chapter 13

Peaches watched as Lucky got out of bed to grab his cigarettes from the dresser.

"Can I tell you something without you getting mad?" she asked him.

Lucky turned around, taking a long, hard pull from his cigarette. "You're not gonna tell me I gotta pay for this, are you? Or you better not sit here and tell me you didn't just enjoy that shit."

Peaches emphatically shook her head. There was no way she could ever say she had not enjoyed what had just happened. Thinking she was going to rock his world, he ended up turning the tables on her.

"Are you kidding? The sex was the bomb," she said, ignoring his question about paying.

Lucky got back in the bed. "So what you wanna tell?"

"The girls and I were actually thinking you were gay."

Lucky shot her an evil look. "Why in the fuck would y'all think some dumb shit like that? Do I look like a fucking sissy?"

Peaches shook her head again. "It was the whole girlfriend thing. We thought you might have been making her up since we never see her around."

"So since you haven't laid eyes on my baby y'all wanna think a brotha's funny." Lucky shook his head in disgust. "That's kinda foul."

"You said you wouldn't get mad."

"I never said that. And besides, how you gonna say some crazy shit like that and not expect me to get mad?"

"But what about you asking me if I was gonna make you pay for the sex? Why would you ask me something that foul?"

Lucky put his cigarette out in the ashtray. "Hey. I have heard talk around the complex. I have peeped guys coming outta your place, and don't sit here and insult my intelligence by saying they were family."

Peaches didn't know how to respond to that because "family" is exactly what she had planned to tell him.

"If you don't mind me asking, why do you even do that stuff?"

"Money," Peaches finally answered after a long pause.

Lucky sucked his teeth. "Gimme a break, girl. You don't make enough money just dancing?"

"I make plenty money dancing. It's just that I like very nice things, and very nice things cost a lot of money these days."

"So, you plan on hooking and dancing for the rest of your life, or what? You ain't getting any younger, ya know. That nice-ass body of yours ain't gonna be perfect forever. What will you do then?"

Peaches hadn't really given any of that much thought before. At the age of twenty-three, she really did not feel she had to. As far she was concerned, she was going to be beautiful forever. The plan was never to have kids so that her body would always stay tight and sexy.

"I'm gonna be sexy forever," she replied.

"How old are you?" Lucky asked. He laughed when

she told him her age. "Baby, you need to start thinking about your future. Are you at least putting money away?"

Peaches did not want to hear what he was talking about. This was supposed to have been a time for sex, not a lecture on what she should do with her life.

"I ain't as dumb as you might think. I have a little put away for a rainy day."

"Well, what if some guy comes along wanting to be serious with you? Do you think he'd wanna be with you, knowing you make your fortune on your damn back?"

"I ain't even worried about some man coming along like that," Peaches scoffed. "I'm all about money, money, money. I ain't got time for that love shit."

"You're just a real hard-ass, huh?"

"I'm not a hard-ass. I just don't plan on falling in love. Love hurts and isn't worth all the hassle."

Lucky started to laugh. "You mean to tell me some man hurt you?"

Peaches shook her head to deny it. "Of course not," she said unconvincingly.

"You're a real piece of work, Miss Peaches. You need a man to straighten ya ass out a little."

Peaches smiled as she sat on top of him. "Is that so? So are you offering to straighten me out, Lucky?" She leaned forward and started kissing him on his chest.

Lucky closed his eyes and smiled as he slid himself inside her again. "Enough talking," he groaned. "Go 'head and handle your business."

"Good morning, Mrs. Broward!" Jewel called out to her neighbor who was busy tending to the small garden of flowers she had around her front porch.

Jewel smiled to herself, admiring how well the flowers were holding up in all the summer's heat, and shocked they were still surviving despite her sons' constant trampling.

Mrs. Broward walked over to Jewel and smiled.

"I figured I'd get out here and take care of my flowers before it got too hot out here to even breathe." She looked out and watched RJ and Cesar running around playing tag. "It's something how these kids don't seem to be affected by the heat."

Jewel nodded in agreement. "So how have you been doing?" she asked, not wanting to turn this into a lengthy conversation.

She knew that if she did not keep this short, the elderly woman would talk at her 'til the sun set.

"I can't complain, honey. I am just so glad this has been a quiet summer so far. It seems like every summer there is always some kind of ruckus going on. I certainly thought when that new fella moved in he was going to be some trouble. Just look at the way he wears those pants. They don't make belts anymore?"

Jewel smiled as she thought about Lucky. "He's a nice guy, though."

Mrs. Broward nodded her head as she started giggling like a little girl. "Well, I bet that young girl on the end would say the same thing," she said as she pointed at Peaches's apartment. "Word around the complex is that they been sleeping with each other."

Jewel's mouth dropped to the ground. "What?" she gasped.

The elderly woman nodded her head, excited to be passing along the hot gossip she had been told two days earlier.

"Yeah. You know Ida Mae's daughter in unit two hundred? Well, it seems that young girl went bragging to her about the whole thing. Even talked about how good he made her feel. It seems to me that things that personal shouldn't be spoken of if you want to keep a man around here. The moment you start talking about how good your man is, the girl next to you wants to find out for herself."

Jewel felt like the world was going to come crashing down on her. The man she was cheating with was cheating on her. As she stood there, her emotions spinning with anger and hurt, she did not notice Romello standing in the doorway feeling the same exact way.

He walked outside. Jewel and Mrs. Broward turned their attention to him.

"Hey, Jewel, I'm gonna run down to Lucky's for a little bit." Not waiting for a response, he dashed off towards Lucky's apartment. If the rumor was true, he wanted to hear it from one of the horses' mouths.

"Hey, man," Lucky said as he opened the door to let Romello inside the apartment. "I know you came bearing weed, right?"

Romello stood there staring him down, trying to decide if he should handle the situation rationally or just go off like a maniac. He quickly sized Lucky up and figured he would be able to take him with no problem, but then he thought about Jewel and having to explain to her why he'd gone after Lucky.

He took a deep breath and pulled a half-smoked blunt from behind his ear. "I always come prepared," he said with a half smile.

Lucky graciously took it from him. "That's what I'm talking 'bout," he said. "Hey, man, want a drink? I've got a little Crown Royal, brandy, or some gin."

Romello shook his head. "Naw, bro, I'm cool."

"Well, I'm about to fix myself one. I got a hangover like a sonofabitch. We can go out on the porch and flame up."

Once they were settled on the porch passing the blunt

back and forth and making small talk, Romello finally calmed himself enough to bring it up. He was more hurt than angry now.

"My girl was just outside gossiping with one of the neighbors, bro. Word around the complex is that you got a chance to get you some of that peach."

Lucky took a moment to figure out what Romello was talking about, then started to laugh. "Damn, man, sorry 'bout that. I know how much you were digging her," Lucky replied. "I'm telling ya, though; she was offering, so how could I refuse?"

Romello swallowed hard, still not wanting to believe it was true. "Don't even sweat that shit, bro. Pussy's pussy, right? If she's throwing it at you, you take it."

"You ain't got no beef with me about it, though, do you?"

Romello shook his head. "Naw. I'll still be trying to hit it, though. I mean, unless you two are gonna be hooking up on the regular."

Lucky shrugged his shoulders. "She just seemed to catch me at the right time, that's all. Peaches was over while my baby was on the phone trippin', not wanting to spend no time with me. Then bam! Peaches doesn't say a word; she just takes me to the bedroom and . . ." Lucky started grinning. "That's one bad-ass bitch."

Romello did not want to hear anymore, but he smiled as if he was interested. "I hear ya, bro."

He took another hit of the blunt, then passed it back to Lucky.

As soon as Jewel heard Romello at the door, she quickly dried her tears and went to go meet him.

"Are you okay?" she asked, noticing the serious look on his face.

Romello nodded his head. "I'm fine," he replied. "Lucky and I just got into one of those weed-induced, meaning of life conversations." He went over to the couch and dropped like a brick.

"Well, I'm gonna run up to Alisha's and holler at her for a little while."

Jewel shot out the front door like a torpedo. As she approached Lucky's apartment, she saw him still sitting on the front porch smoking a cigarette. When he looked up and saw her, he started to laugh.

"You here about the rumor too?" he asked.

Jewel put her hands on her hips. "So it's true?"

Lucky shrugged his shoulders. "I can't deny it."

"But I was under the impression we had something going on between us. You told me you were starting to have feelings for me."

"I do have feelings. I think you are a cool friend."

"So do you always go around fucking your *friends*?" Jewel looked around to make sure no one outside had heard her. She had not meant to get so loud.

Lucky shrugged his shoulders. "It all depends on how good the friend looks," he said, laughing.

Jewel smiled to herself, taking that as a compliment.

"Look, Jewel," Lucky sighed, getting serious again. "You're in a relationship. I'm in a relationship. There was nothing serious between us. I mean, how could we be serious?"

"So what did we have then?"

Lucky threw his cigarette in the grass, then stood up. "It was just sex," he replied coldly, then went back into his apartment.

Chapter 14

When 6:00 A.M. came, Ladona was all dressed and ready to go. Today's excuse was a teachers' meeting at the school board headquarters sometime in the afternoon. The only reason she was up this early was that she had talked Craig into having breakfast with her before he went into work.

Even though he only saw it as a casual meal with an acquaintance, Ladona thought of it as more. To her it was a breakthrough—a chance for her to let her personality shine. In her mind, she went over the conversation they would have, and how she would win him over with her charm. She had even stayed up late watching the news so she could be well versed in what was going on in the world.

She had even toyed with the idea of dropping a hint or two to let Craig know she was checking him out, but that did not seem like a good idea—it was still too early to let him know.

Ladona stepped out of the apartment with all the confidence in the world. She looked nice, she felt confident. She was certain today was going to be her day.

"You running late, sleepyhead?" she asked Craig, surprised to see him answering the door looking like he'd just crawled out of bed.

Just then, Alisha showed up in the doorway and gave her a look evil enough to turn someone to stone. "Craig's not gonna be going into work today," she said with a hint of an attitude.

"I'm sorry to cancel on you, Ladona," Craig started to explain before Alisha jabbed him with her elbow.

"I guess you'll have to drive yourself to that meeting today," Alisha interrupted.

Ladona felt like someone had just let all the air out of her balloon, but she refused to let Alisha think she had gotten the best of her.

She looked at Craig and smiled. "Well, that's okay. You'll have to treat me to breakfast some other time, though." She then looked at Alisha and gave her an even bigger smile. "Have a nice morning."

Craig closed the door, then turned to his wife. "What's with the attitude?"

"Is there something going on with you two that I should know about?" she asked. "What's this crap about treating her to breakfast?"

Craig tried to laugh it off despite his wife's icy stare. "Oh, last night when I was down there helping her with the car she kept going on and on about going out to breakfast. I was just gonna stop and get her coffee and a doughnut."

Alisha folded her arms across her chest. "One week you two are doing lunch, now you two are talking about breakfast. It seems to me that you two have been getting pretty chummy lately."

Craig followed behind her as she walked into the kitchen. "What are you talking about? You make it seem like it's some big deal or something."

"Is there something going on with you two that I need to know about?"

"What?"

"All these rides you give her downtown. That's a long time for you two to be alone with each other."

"*You're* the one who insisted I give her a damn ride in the first place!" Craig's voice roared throughout the apartment.

"And are you sure the only thing you're giving her is a ride? You sure did seem eager to go and help her with her car last night. I bet she was lying about having asked Lucky or Romello. She made a special trip up here just to ask you."

"You've lost your damn mind, Alisha. Do you honestly think I would cheat on you with *her*?"

Alisha took a long, hard look at her husband. The words of Peaches kept playing over in her mind. *He's a man, ain't he?*

Craig threw his hands up in frustration. "If it takes you that damn long to answer then you obviously do think I'd cheat on you." He brushed past Alisha and went to the room.

"Where are you going?" Alisha called to him.

"I'm going to work," he replied. "I'm not gonna be sitting around here with you all day arguing over this stupid shit."

Outside the front door, Ladona looked up to the sky and said, "Thank you, Lord." This was the opportunity she'd been waiting for.

"How long are you gonna hold your ear to the door like that?" someone asked.

Ladona turned around and saw that it was Lucky.

She took a few steps away from the door and tried to play it off, but she knew she had been caught red-handed. "How long have you been standing there watching me?" she asked.

Lucky smiled at her. "From about the time you got the door closed in your face."

"Well, you shouldn't be sneaking up on people like that."

"Just like you shouldn't be listening in on other people's conversations. Is this what you go around the complex doing?"

Ladona rolled her eyes at him. "What are you even doing up here? Your apartment is downstairs, isn't it?"

Lucky shook his head at her as he chuckled under his breath. "You've got a thing for the husband, don't you?"

Ladona started walking back to her apartment. "I don't know what you're talking about."

"Yeah, I've seen you jumping in the truck with him in the mornings. Where do you be going? I didn't know they held summer school downtown."

Ladona turned around and looked at him. "You sure do know a lot about my business."

"I'm just a very observant guy, that's all."

"Well, your observations are wrong. I'm not after Alisha's husband or anybody else's husband for that matter." Ladona unlocked her apartment door.

"You know, you and I seem to have a common interest," Lucky said.

Ladona laughed. "Oh? Are you after Alisha's husband too?"

"No, no. I'm talking about trying to stir up a little trouble in the happy couple's marriage."

"Now why on earth would you wanna go and do something like that?"

Lucky shrugged his shoulders. "I have my reasons," he replied.

"Well, your observation is wrong again. We do not have a common interest, and I am offended you would even think about coming at me like this. I should march back over there and let them know the type of person you really are."

"You won't, though. If you did, then I'd have to let Alisha know just the type of person *you* really are."

"Well, I'd love to stand here and chat with you some more, but I've got a lot of things to do this morning."

"Two heads are better than one, ya know."

"Okay." Ladona shut the door in his face, then went to the window and watched as Lucky started back down the stairs.

I don't need anybody helping me. My plan is coming along just fine.

"It was better than good. It was spectacular!"

While the rest of the girls listened to Peaches go on about her sexual encounter with Lucky, Jewel sat off to the side in her own little world, revisiting her own Lucky encounters.

Everything Peaches bragged about was accurate. Lucky was definitely well endowed and he had the stamina of a racehorse. She just couldn't stand the fact that she was no longer the only one in the complex who knew such intimate things about him. And of all people, she hated that she had to share the same experience with Peaches.

"So was this a onetime thing, or is this gonna become a regular event for you two?" Alisha asked.

"Oh, there will definitely be a next time," Peaches said. Nobody saw Jewel roll her eyes.

However, the truth was Peaches really did not know if there would even be a next time. When it was all over with Lucky, she cleaned herself up in the bathroom, then left. That was all there was to it. Lucky had not made any promises to call her the next morning. He hadn't even bothered to give her a kiss or tell her to have a nice day.

What she did not want the girls to know was that Lucky had treated her the exact same way she had treated every man who had walked through her front door. The only difference was that she did not have to leave him money on his nightstand.

"So are you satisfied now?" Jewel asked, finally breaking her silence.

"Hell yeah, I'm satisfied!" Peaches said.

Everyone in the group started laughing except Jewel. Peaches glanced at her out the corner of her eye and figured jealousy was eating her alive.

"Well, look who just stepped outside," Ladona mumbled.

Everyone's head turned in the direction of Lucky's apartment. He looked over at the girls and waved; they all waved back.

Peaches stood up and waved him over.

"The *Mandingo* lover approaches," Alisha said, giggling.

As he walked up to the porch, Peaches rushed over to him and put her arm around his waist.

"How's it going?" she asked, giving him a peck on the cheek.

Everyone noticed how he seemed to shy away from her a bit. "I'm doing all right," he replied. "And how are all you ladies doing?" Even though he spoke to everyone, he seemed to be focusing his attention on Alisha.

Alisha felt his eyes bearing down on her. She looked away in embarrassment.

"So what were you about to get into?" Peaches asked. "You're looking kinda nice this morning."

"I was on my way to meet someone for breakfast," Lucky announced.

"Oh. Running off to see your girl?" Jewel asked with a hint of sarcasm.

Lucky smiled at her. "Trying to work and keep the relationship together."

"Well, why don't you stop by later when you get back?" Peaches suggested, giving his hand a little squeeze.

Lucky seemed to blow her off with a nod, then focused his attention back to Alisha. "So, I guess I'll be seeing you ladies a little bit later," he said.

Alisha started blushing, hoping that no one else noticed all the attention he seemed to be giving her. They did notice, though, and suddenly the air was thick with jealousy and envy from every angle.

As soon as Lucky walked away, Peaches turned to Alisha. "What was all that about?" she asked.

Alisha shrugged her shoulders. "How should I know?"

"Talk about some crazy shit," Jewel said. "He fucks Peaches, but now seems to be more interested in you."

"It is crazy," Alisha mumbled under her breath as she watched Lucky drive away.

Chapter 15

"Hey, Craig!" Romello called out. From Lucky's porch, he waved him over.

Craig did not want to be bothered. Even from a distance, he knew that what Lucky and Romello were smoking on was not a cigarette. He decided to go over there anyway just so no one could accuse him of being too conceited.

Romello handled the introductions. "Craig, I don't think you've met my man here. This is Lucky. Lucky, this is my man Craig."

"Alisha's husband," Lucky said as the two of them shook hands. "She's a very nice woman."

"She's the best," Craig said.

Romello shook his head. "Craig, you can't be stepping up in here with these flowers all the time. You make all us other guys look bad. It's bad enough my girl be complaining that I'm not as loving and romantic as you."

Craig started laughing. "Well, maybe you all should step up your games."

"How long you two been married?" Lucky asked.

"For a little over three years now."

"Y'all happy?" Lucky inquired.

Romello slapped his friend across the arm. "Bro, why you gotta be all in the man's business like that?"

"We're *very* happy," Craig replied, feeling a bit of contention coming from Lucky.

"Well, that's good. It's nice to know there's still a happily married couple out here in the world today." Lucky tossed back another beer, then stood up. "Can I get you a beer, man? Or maybe you'd like to hit the blunt?"

Craig shook his head. "I don't smoke. That stuff will kill you," he said.

"I'm hoping one day me and my honey can be just like you and Alisha," Lucky said, never taking his eyes off Craig. "I want us to one day be married and be *very* happy."

Craig started feeling a little uneasy from the vibe he was getting from Lucky. He wasn't sure if it was because the man was drunk, but there was something about him that just didn't seem right, especially when he mentioned Alisha's name.

"Well, I hope you two have a great relationship." Craig said good-bye to Romello, then headed for the stairs.

"Or maybe I'll get lucky and find my own little Alisha!" Lucky called after him.

Craig turned around in alarm. He was on his way back over when Romello motioned for him to keep on walking.

"Don't mind him, Craig. He's just had too much to drink."

Craig acknowledged him with a nod, then continued up to his apartment.

"Bro, what the hell was that shit?" Romello asked. "Craig's an all-right guy. What's up with the beef you were giving him?"

Lucky sat back down. "All I did was ask the man if he was happily married. What's wrong with that?"

Romello shook his head. "You're a bold-ass sonofabitch.

You should've just come out and told the man you were gonna try and fuck his wife."

Lucky turned and watched Craig as he walked up the stairs. "He doesn't know it, but his wife's about to get lucky," he mumbled under his breath.

Craig stood over Alisha as she slept on the couch, admiring how beautiful and peaceful she looked. He really didn't want to have to wake her, but he was anxious to put an end to their two-day-long fight.

Over the past two days, they had barely spoken a word to each other. Craig made sure he had left the house before she could wake up, then worked overtime and got home late, at a time he was sure she would be in bed.

Today he was home early, though. Armed with a bouquet of her favorite flowers, he was prepared to beg, plead, and stand on his head to get her to forgive him.

Craig bent over and gave her a kiss on the lips. Alisha opened her eyes.

She looked out the window and saw there was still a hint of daylight. "What are you doing home so early?" she asked.

Craig revealed the tulips he had been hiding behind his back. "Alisha, I don't wanna fight anymore. Can we call a truce?"

Alisha's eyes lit up at the sight of the flowers. She stood up and gave him a hug. "I was wondering when your stubborn butt was gonna finally give in," she said, chuckling.

"You're the stubborn one."

"I'm gonna go throw these in some water." Alisha went to walk to the kitchen, but Craig grabbed the flowers and threw them on the couch. "What are you doing?" she gasped.

"I've got something else for you," he said as he swept her off her feet.

As he started carrying her to the bedroom, the doorbell rang. Craig stopped in his tracks.

"You did lock the door, right?" she asked him.

Craig laughed. "Want me to answer it?"

"Not unless you wanna go back to not speaking."

"Not a chance." Craig continued on to the bedroom.

Chapter 16

"I'm home!" Jewel called out as she walked into the apartment with an armful of groceries.

She set them on the table, expecting the boys to come running in the kitchen as they always did, wanting to see what goodies Mama had gotten them. Instead, Romello came strolling in by himself.

"The kids sure are quiet," she said. "What'd you do? Tie them up in the closet?"

"I called your mother and talked her into picking them up for the night," he replied with a grin on his face.

Jewel stopped putting up groceries long enough to give him a look of suspicion. "No, really, what did you do with the kids?"

"I told you, your mother came and got them for the night."

Jewel rolled her eyes. "Don't tell me you've got some of your friends coming over. Romello, I'm not in the mood to deal with a room full of weed-head alcoholics tonight."

"Ain't nobody coming over. I was planning on taking you out tonight."

"And I damn sure don't wanna go to your friend Gino's house. It's a shame a guy so cute can be so damn nasty. Anytime we go over there, I'm afraid to put my purse down. I keep thinking one of those roaches will try and hitch a ride."

Romello started laughing. "Why you gotta dog my boy like that? His place ain't that damn nasty."

Jewel gave him a crazy look. "Romello, if you were nasty like him, I would have left you a long time ago."

"Well, I wasn't talking about going to Gino's crib. I wanted to take you somewhere nice, since you complain I don't ever take you anywhere."

Jewel smiled. "So you mean we're going out on a date?"

Romello nodded his head. "Be ready by six o'clock." He turned and walked out of the room.

Jewel quickly closed the refrigerator and went after him. "Wait a minute, Romello. Tell me where we're going!"

"It's a surprise." Romello walked over and gave her a kiss on the lips. It had been a long time since he had just given her a kiss without there being an ulterior motive.

"Six o'clock," he said as he went back into the bedroom.

For hours, Jewel had been on pins and needles, anxious to find out where Romello planned to take her. When six o'clock finally rolled around and they hopped into the car, she had a hard time calming herself down.

"I'm so nervous," she said to Romello as they drove along the tree-lined streets of the town.

"Why are you nervous?" Romello asked.

"I can't even remember the last time we've been out together. Can you at least give me a hint on where we're going?"

"No hints," he replied.

Romello slowed the car, then came to a stop in front of the high school.

"Why are we stopping? Did you forget something at home?" Jewel questioned.

Romello turned to her with a big grin on his face. "This is it," he replied. "We're here!"

Jewel looked out the window and frowned. "This is the high school. What are we doing here?"

"This is where I wanted to bring you," he said.

"To the damn high school? I thought we were going somewhere special."

"This is special." Romello got out of the car, then walked to the sidewalk and waited for Jewel to get out.

She hesitated a moment, convincing herself that this had to be some type of joke. She was sure Romello was just trying to throw her off from the real surprise he had in store for her.

She finally got out of the car and walked over to Romello. "Okay, Romello, the joke is over. Let's get back in the car and go where we're supposed to be going."

"But this is where we're going." Romello grabbed her hand and started walking. "Just follow me."

"Where are we going now? I can't walk through all this grass. I have on my nice heels!"

Romello started laughing. "Just follow me, woman."

Without another word, the two of them hiked across the large campus to the football field behind the school. As they walked across the dusty track that circled the field, Jewel started cursing, feeling bits of dirt and rocks caught in her toes.

"My damn feet hurt!" she complained to Romello. "I swear I should kill you for this bullshit."

"Stop whining," Romello said, chuckling.

"You have me trekking through dirt and rocks in stiletto

heels. Can you please explain to me how any of this is special? I'd rather pick up a pet roach from Gino's house!"

Romello stopped walking as soon as they were standing in the center of the field. He held out his arms and smiled proudly, as if he were showing her a grand prize.

"*This* is the special place!"

"What's so special about this place?" she asked. "I see grass and dirt and bleachers. Big fucking deal."

"You said you wanted to go someplace romantic, so here we are. What could be more romantic than this?"

"I'm not in the mood to play games with you, Romello. Just take me home."

"Would you just shut up complaining and take a look where we are? You don't know why this is romantic?

"Of all the idiotic things, Romello!"

Romello started laughing. "I can't believe you don't even remember."

"Remember what?"

"Right here! This is the very spot when I first met you. I was a sophomore; you were a freshman. We were both trying out for the track team. You were standing right over there laughing and joking with your friends."

Jewel folded her arms across her chest as the memory came back to her. The anger in her face gave way to a tiny grin. "You had that stupid ponytail," she said.

"Stupid? Girl, that ponytail was the bomb."

"You looked like a sissy. I just never had the heart to tell you."

"The ladies loved it, though."

Jewel looked at him and smiled. "I was standing there with my girl Tessa."

"So are you surprised that I remembered?" Romello asked. "Ya know I should be upset that you didn't remember."

"It was so long ago, Romello. And when you said you

were taking me somewhere special, I was thinking somewhere along the lines of a nice restaurant or someplace without a lot of dirt."

"But do you think this is special?"

Jewel looked around, then rested her eyes on Romello again. "The fact that you remembered makes it special."

"Well, you just hold that thought because it gets even better."

Romello let out a long sigh as he reached into his pocket. In his hand, he held a small white box. He looked at Jewel and smiled as he watched her eyes get big.

"What is that?" she asked.

Romello handed her the box. "What do you think it is?"

Jewel opened the box and began shrieking at the sight of a ring. "Romello . . ." she started to say, but could not quite find the right words to say.

Romello looked down at his feet as he shifted uncomfortably. "I know I don't always do or say the right things sometimes," he mumbled.

Jewel took the ring out to admire it. "Is this an engagement ring?"

Romello shrugged his shoulders, still looking down at his feet. "You've been looking so down lately. I figured you were upset with me, thinking I didn't wanna marry you." He raised his eyes to meet hers. "It'll happen one day, Jewel. I just wanna get shit together."

This was not exactly the marriage proposal she had dreamed of. In her dream, she had envisioned Romello actually getting down on one knee, not standing around kicking rocks, being too embarrassed to look her in the face.

She would take it as it came, though. A proposal was a proposal no matter how it was played out. At least now she had something to show to her family so they would stop saying she was wasting her time with Romello.

"Well, put it on me!" Jewel squealed in excitement.

Romello took the ring from the box, then slipped it on her finger. She held her hand up to get a better look at it.

"So you like it?"

"Are you kidding? I love it! What is this, a karat? Two karats?" she gasped. Jewel was embarrassed to admit she did not know anything about diamond sizes. The only thing she knew was that the rock on her finger was big. "Romello, where did you get the money to pay for something like this?"

"You think I just fuck around when I'm out at night, but I really do be hustling."

"This isn't stolen, is it? I don't wanna be flashing this around, then have someone come up to me saying I've got on their shit."

"Do you honestly think I would put a stolen ring on your finger, Jewel? Please don't insult me like that. I wish you would just be happy that I finally got you a ring."

Jewel nodded her head. "You're right. I'm sorry. The ring is beautiful and I love it."

Romello tried hard to keep a look of happiness on his face; he wondered why Jewel couldn't just enjoy the moment. He was at least thankful that she did not notice how uncomfortable this situation was for him, giving her a ring that he considered to be "borrowed" and giving her a false promise of marriage that he knew he would never go through with. Romello was on edge.

"I still have one more thing to show you," he told her, taking her by the hand and leading her over to the announcer's booth. With a few hard shoves, he managed to get the door open. Once inside, he turned to Jewel and smiled. "Remember this spot?" he asked.

Jewel paused to think about it, then started laughing as the memory came back to her. "This is where you took my damn virginity!"

Romello started laughing. "I took it from you? It's more like you threw it at me!"

Jewel playfully slapped him on the arm. "We had a lot of fun times in here."

Romello nodded his head. "One day I'll bring Romello Jr. back here to show him where he was conceived."

"You are such a fool," Jewel said, chuckling. She looked at him with wonder. "I can't believe you even remembered these spots. I'm supposed to be the sentimental one, not you."

He lowered his eyes to the ground again. "I know it's not a boat ride on the lake or a picnic in the park, but I wanted to do something for you I thought you'd appreciate since you know I'm not all that sentimental."

Jewel nodded her head as she held out her hand to admire the ring some more. "This is beautiful," she sighed.

Romello put his arms around her, giving her a kiss on the top of her head. "I do love you, Jewel," he whispered.

"I know you do, Romello," she said as she rested her head on his chest. "And I wanna tell you I'm sorry."

"Sorry for what?"

"For all the dirty names I was calling you in my head as we were walking."

Romello laughed. "I forgive you."

However, he could not help but wonder if she would ever forgive him if she were to know the truth about this night.

Craig sighed into the phone as he listened to Alisha complain.

"But this is an opportunity for me to shine for my bosses," he managed to get in. "Word around the office is that there's a management spot opening up. This would be a big promotion for me if I can get it."

A promotion meant more money, and that sounded just fine to Alisha, but being deprived of her husband was what was more important to her.

"It still doesn't make sense why all this overtime is gonna make a difference to them, Craig. I mean, what if they give you the promotion, then expect you to keep putting in all these long hours? Am I supposed to just come to the office whenever I wanna see you?"

"Look, there's a lot of work that needs to be done here. I told you a couple of guys quit. I'm taking the initiative to pick up the slack."

"At the expense of our marriage, I see."

Craig imagined Alisha on the other end of the phone pouting like a spoiled child. He had no one to blame but himself for that, though. He gave her just about everything she could ever want, which is why he wished she could give him a break on this.

"Can't someone else in that office pick up some slack?"

"And I should just step aside and let them take the promotion too?"

"Well, I bet they're at home right now with their *happy* wives, though."

"Don't say things like that, Alisha." Craig ran his hand over his head and closed his eyes, trying to figure a way to get her to ease up. Then it came to him. "With this promotion comes more money, baby. If I'm making more money, then who knows? Maybe we can start thinking about having that baby."

Craig felt bad about deceiving her with something he knew she wanted desperately, but it's what he had to do to get her to relax.

"So what time do you think you'll be home?" she asked with her voice noticeably calmer.

"I should be home no later than ten, ten-thirty." Craig felt like giving himself a pat on the back.

"Well, I'll try to wait up for you."

"You don't have to do that," he insisted, knowing that he would be home much later than 10:00.

Alisha took a moment's pause before speaking again. "Well, I'll let you get back to your work," she said.

"I love you, baby." Craig hung up the phone, then sat back in his chair, letting out a groan of frustration before picking up the phone and dialing another number.

"Hey, sexy. I can see you again tonight."

Chapter 17

Ladona held out the box of doughnuts to Alisha. "Good morning, neighbor!"

Alisha took the box of doughnuts and let Ladona inside. "You sure are happy this morning," she said with suspicion.

"Well, I had a great night," Ladona replied. "Do you have some coffee going yet?"

Alisha dropped the box of doughnuts on the table with a thump. "It's still brewing." She watched as Ladona sat down at the table. "So you say you had a nice night, huh?"

Ladona stared off dreamily. "It was the best."

Alisha folded her arms across her chest as she leaned against the kitchen counter. "Well, what was it that made the night so wonderful?"

Ladona flashed a huge grin. "I had a date!"

Alisha's suspicions grew even more. "Oh really?" she mumbled. "I guess that explains why you didn't answer the door when I came by."

"You came by last night? I'm sorry I missed you."

Alisha turned to pretend she was checking on the coffeemaker so Ladona would not notice her rolling her eyes.

"I didn't even know that you had met someone. Does this mystery date have a name?"

Ladona shrugged her shoulders. "We've been talking on the phone for about a week now. I met him one day when I was downtown. I didn't want to talk about him because I wasn't sure if things were going to work out or not. Our date went well, though."

"So you'll be seeing him again?" Alisha inquired.

Ladona nodded her head. "Most definitely."

"What's his name?"

"His name is John."

She could've at least picked a better name than that, Alisha thought to herself.

"Well, tell me about this John guy. Where did he take you?"

Just as Ladona had opened her mouth to answer, Craig walked into the room.

"Good morning, baby," he said as he walked over and gave Alisha a peck on the cheek. He then turned to Ladona and smiled. "Good morning."

Ladona pointed to the box of doughnuts. "I brought doughnuts," she said to him. "Dig in. I made sure they put your favorite in there."

Craig tore into the box. "You got my raspberry jelly–filled?"

Ladona nodded, then turned to Alisha. "You like the glazed, right? I had the guy throw in a couple of those too."

Alisha nodded her head, trying to make sense of what she was just witnessing. Her bullshit meter was going haywire with the terrible performance Craig and Ladona were putting on for her.

Craig bit into a doughnut and smiled. "You are a sweetheart," he said, patting Ladona on the shoulder.

"Did you need a ride downtown this morning or are you two just getting an early start on the gossip?"

Alisha shot him a nasty look. "Ya know, Ladona was just telling me that she's got herself a new man."

"He's not my man. It was only the first date," Ladona said bashfully.

Alisha cringed when she saw Craig touch her shoulder again. "Well, that's great." He turned to Alisha. "I guess there'll be no more matchmaking with the guys from my office then?"

Only he and Ladona found the humor in his question. Alisha stood there with a stone face, still unable to believe that her husband and so-called friend were actually flirting in her face.

"You'll have to bring him by so we can meet him one of these days," Alisha sighed.

Ladona shrugged her shoulders. "I'm gonna give him one or two more dates before I introduce him to the world." She rose to her feet. "Well, I'm not gonna have a cup of coffee after all. I have some phone calls I need to make this morning. Are you going by Jewel's place later?"

"I probably will," Alisha replied.

"Great. I'll see you down there." Ladona turned to look at Craig. "Have a nice day at work, Craig," she said, giving him a little wave.

Craig waved back. "Bye, Ladona."

Was that their little signal to each other? Alisha wondered.

"Did you know she had a new guy?" she asked Craig as soon as Ladona passed by the kitchen window.

"How in the world would I have known?" Craig replied as he poured himself a cup of coffee. "She's *your* friend."

No, she's a backstabbing bitch!

"So are you working late again tonight?"

Craig reached for another doughnut. "Nope. I'm coming home to be with my baby tonight," he said as he gave her a peck on the lips. "Oh, and when you see Ladona later, tell her I said thanks for the doughnuts."

Alisha grabbed his doughnut out of his hand, then tossed it back in the box. "You won't be able to fit out the front door if you keep eating those doughnuts like that," she snapped at him.

Craig patted his stomach. "You wouldn't love me with a few little love handles?"

"Have a good day at work," Alisha said.

As soon as she turned her back, Craig grabbed his doughnut out of the box, then darted out of the door before Alisha could catch him.

Lucky stepped outside on the porch. "I didn't hear you knock," he said, surprised to see her sitting there. "How long you been out here?"

"I didn't knock. I figured I'd just sit around and wait for you to come out sooner or later." Peaches folded her arms across her chest. "I guess you've been spending more time with your girl. I came by a couple of times this week, but you were out."

Lucky nodded his head. "We've been trying to work things out."

"Well, that's nice to know."

"You sound a little annoyed."

"You know what annoys me? The fact that you have sex with me, then barely say two words to me afterwards."

Lucky chuckled. "Isn't that how you get down, though?"

"Yeah, with paying customers," she replied. "You didn't pay, and I certainly didn't consider you a customer."

Lucky smiled unapologetically. "Well, I'm sorry. What can I say?"

"So what was all that talk about finding a man to straighten me out? Weren't you talking about yourself?"

Lucky shook his head. "I really wasn't talking about anyone in particular."

Peaches didn't want to show how embarrassed she felt so she just nodded her head as if she understood.

Lucky sat down next to her. "Peaches, you knew I had somebody."

"Why should it make any difference to me that you have a girlfriend? Hell! I've been known to steal away men before."

"Well, this man can't be stolen."

Peaches shrugged it off. "Do you have a ring on your finger?" she asked.

Lucky held up his hand. "What does that have to do with anything?"

"Then you're fair game, baby, and I ain't done playing yet." Peaches looked around to see if anyone was coming, then slipped her hand inside Lucky's boxers. "Uh-oh. Feels like someone's happy to see me."

"Peaches, what are you doing?" he gasped, wanting to tell her to stop, but it felt too good to end it.

"Now could you imagine what it'd feel like if that were my mouth on there?" Peaches whispered in his ear.

Lucky could imagine it, as he let out a soft moan. "Not out here," he said breathlessly.

Peaches looked around again before leaning over to give it a quick tickle with her tongue. Unfortunately, she did not see Craig coming down the stairway. By the time she lifted her head back up, Craig was standing there looking at them with disgust.

"Can't you go inside with that shit?" he yelled at them.

Lucky's eyes shot open as he quickly tried to get himself back into his boxers. "My bad!" he said, waving his hand at Craig.

Peaches started laughing as soon as Craig continued on to his car. "I can't believe he just saw me do that!"

Lucky started stroking her thigh. "He's right. We should take this inside."

Peaches looked at her watch. "Ya know what? I'm gonna have to take a rain check on that one." She stood up and gave Lucky a kiss on the cheek. "See? At least now I know you'll come running, wanting more."

"So you just gonna leave me hanging like this?"

Peaches looked down at his lap and started laughing. "Actually, that bad boy's not *hanging* at all. You should try sticking him back in."

As Peaches started walking back to her apartment, she saw Alisha running down the stairs, waving at her frantically.

"Peaches!" Alisha called out as she ran towards her.

"Damn, girl. Where's the fire?" Peaches chuckled.

Alisha took a moment to catch her breath. "I need to talk to you. It's an emergency."

Peaches looked puzzled, wondering what could be so urgent. "What?" she asked.

A look of worry came over Alisha's face. "What would you do if you thought your man was cheating on you?"

"The bastard would be history."

Alisha shook her head. "I just can't drop Craig like that."

Peaches looked at her with raised eyebrows. "You caught Craig cheating?" she gasped. "Who's the hussy? Ladona?"

"Shhh!" Alisha looked around to make sure no one else could hear them. "I'm not trying to let the entire complex know about it. I'm not even sure if they are messing around, but there are some awfully strange coincidences."

"When it comes to a cheating man, there are no coincidences. Just signs we knew were there, but chose to ignore."

"Craig could be telling the truth, though. He could just be working late."

"Yeah, and that's probably the same thing Jewel tries to tell herself about the winner she's shacked up with. We all know how he is, though."

Alisha shook her head. "I don't know, girl. I keep telling myself that Craig loves me. He would never cheat on me."

Peaches rolled her eyes, wondering how Alisha could be so naive. "Why not? Just 'cuz he loves you doesn't mean he won't cheat on you. The only way to keep a man from cheating is to shackle yourself to his side twenty-four-seven. Even then you've gotta keep your hand super-glued to his damn dick. It's the *only* way to know he's being faithful."

"So what do I do? Should I confront him?"

"Why? So he can lie about it? Just sit back and play it cool. Do not let him know you know. In the meanwhile, you had better start investigating shit. Start checking the bills for crazy calls or crazy purchases."

"I never see the bills. Craig handles all of that."

Peaches looked at Alisha in awe. "Damn, you've got a good man, even if his ass is out there cheating."

"This is too much shit to be thinking about right now. I think I'll go lay down."

"Now do you see why I don't keep a steady man in my life? They do nothing but bring you heartache and headache, girl."

Just then, Jewel came out her front door and started waving her hand in the air. "You two will never believe this. Come see! Come see!"

Alisha and Peaches exchanged glances, then walked towards her.

"What's got you all worked up?" Peaches asked her.

Jewel held out her hand to show off her ring as she squealed in excitement. "Isn't it gorgeous?" she asked.

"What's that supposed to be, an engagement ring?" Peaches asked.

"Can you believe it? Romello finally asked me to marry him!"

Peaches shook her head. "Nope, I sure *don't* believe it."

"That's a nice ring," Alisha said as she leaned in closer to get a better look. "Romello picked this out?"

Jewel smiled proudly. "He surprised me with it last night. I haven't been able to stop looking at it!"

"Well, you're gonna have an engagement party, right?" Alisha asked.

"I hadn't even thought of that," she mumbled. All of a sudden, she began smiling. "That's a great idea. I can invite all the neighbors and my family. Holy shit! I have to call my mother and tell her the news. She is never gonna believe this!"

Jewel ran back into her apartment without saying good-bye.

"Congrats!" Peaches called after her, then turned to Alisha and rolled her eyes. "Where do you think Romello got the money to get a ring like that?"

The two of them started walking back towards Peaches's apartment.

"Who knows? Maybe he's been saving up."

Peaches laughed. "You know damn well that boy didn't save shit. I mean, that thing has to be at least two karats. Why would a man spend all that money on an engagement ring for a woman he cheats on? It doesn't make sense."

Alisha shrugged her shoulders. "I think he really does love her."

Peaches continued venting. "Oh, that damn thing is probably a fake, anyway. Either that, or he stole it."

Alisha detected a hint of jealousy. "Well, what difference does it make anyway? It's not your finger he put the ring on so why even trip about it? Besides, it's none of our business where the ring came from or how much it cost. As long as Jewel's excited, that's all that really matters."

"It's a nice-ass ring, though."

"Well, with all the shit he has put her through, don't you think she deserves a nice ring? After all, she is the mother of his children."

"He cheats on her, though. I'm telling you, Alisha, it doesn't make any sense," Peaches muttered as she looked back over her shoulder at Jewel's apartment.

Chapter 18

"Damn!" Alisha exclaimed after walking around to the back of her car and finding one of her tires flat.

She looked around the complex, hoping to see someone outside who might be able to help her. It seemed like any other day there was a man standing around doing something. Today, there wasn't an able-bodied man in sight.

Doing the next best thing she could think of, she reached into her purse for her cell phone and dialed Craig at the office.

"My tire is flat," she whined as soon as she heard him pick up.

"Where are you?" Craig asked.

"I'm still here at the house."

"Well, that's what roadside assistance is for, Alisha," he said, sounding a bit annoyed.

"Well, I don't know anything about that, Craig."

"All the information is there in the glove box. You don't expect me to leave work and come down there just to change the damn tire, do you?"

Alisha grinned. "Well, that would be nice. It's been a

while since you came home in the middle of the afternoon. You know I would make it worth your while."

"As tempting as that sounds, I can't leave. I am up to my elbows in paperwork. Besides, this is exactly why I pay the extra ten dollars a month. Just call the tow truck and they will take care of you."

As soon as Alisha hung up the phone, she heard a car pull up behind her.

"Need some help?" she heard someone ask.

She turned around and saw Lucky smiling at her. He looked like a movie star in his shades, sitting behind the wheel of his shiny red Mercedes.

"My damn tire is flat!"

Lucky nodded his head. "So I see," he said, chuckling, looking her over slowly from head to toe.

Alisha folded her arms across her chest, suddenly feeling self-conscious from his heavy stare. "I was just about to call the road service."

"Why? Your man never showed you how to change a simple little tire?" Lucky said mockingly.

"See, that's the thing. I have a man, so why should I learn how to change a tire?"

Lucky nodded his head as he lifted his sunglasses to reveal his eyes. "You're right. I wouldn't have you out here trying to change a tire, either. Let me park my car and I'll come over and give you a hand."

Alisha shook her head. "Oh no," she protested. "I don't wanna bother you."

"For you, it wouldn't be a bother at all."

As Lucky went to park his car, Alisha nervously looked around the complex to see if anyone was watching. Lucky gave her a nervous feeling, as if being around him was something to be guilty about.

He walked back over to her, although it seemed more like a strut. She felt her heart begin to race. She had been in the company of many good-looking guys before who had eyed her as if she were a piece of candy, but none of them had made her feel the way Lucky did.

"So where were you on your way to?" Lucky pulled the spare tire and the jack out of the trunk.

"I was just gonna go to the mall or something. I didn't feel like being locked up in the house all day." Alisha stood off to the side, hating herself for staring so hard at his strong, muscular arms.

When Lucky looked up and caught her staring at him, she quickly diverted her eyes back to the spare tire on the ground.

Lucky started grinning. "You look like you might do a lot of shopping," he said. "I guess your husband has a good job, seeing as you don't work."

"I could say the same about you and your girl."

Lucky went back to working on the tire. "Yeah, I guess you could," he mumbled.

With his back to her again, Alisha found herself staring at his body again. "I really like your car," she said, hoping that talking would keep her mind from wandering.

The two of them made small talk about everything from music to politics. Every time Lucky asked her a question, she almost felt as if she were being interviewed. As soon as he finished and put everything back in the trunk, he turned to her and smiled.

"I should at least pay you for your trouble," Alisha said as she went into her purse for her wallet.

"I don't want your money," Lucky said. "Have lunch with me."

Alisha looked up at him in alarm. "I couldn't do that," she said, chuckling.

"Why not? It's lunchtime. I don't know about you, but I haven't eaten a thing all morning. Besides, it would give you a chance to get out the house."

Alisha shook her head. "I shouldn't," she said, going back into her purse. "Just let me give you a few dollars or something."

Lucky reached out and touched her arm, sending a shock wave through her body. "I said I don't want your money. I'd rather just take you out to lunch."

"Well, if you paid for lunch, then how is that letting me pay you for your help?"

Lucky took a step closer. The scent of his cologne was sweet to her senses. "Your company is payment enough."

The look in his eye made her feel self-conscious again, but it was almost as if his stare was hypnotic. She did not want to go to lunch. She didn't even want him standing that close, but there was a little voice inside her that made her say she'd go.

Lucky took another step closer. This time he was so close she could feel his breath on her face.

"Don't look so worried," he said softly. "I promise to be the perfect gentleman."

Romello rolled over on his back and stared at the ceiling. "You wanna have a what?" he asked.

"An engagement party," Jewel repeated.

"Why in the hell would we need to have an engagement party?"

"That's what people do when they get engaged."

"You mean that's what people who can afford it do. We do not have money for a party. And why do we need to have one, anyway?"

"So we can announce our engagement, Romello."

Romello chuckled. "Why do we need a party to do that? Can't you just call people up on the phone and tell them?"

Jewel playfully smacked him on the arm. "You are so ignorant," she said. "I don't see what the big deal is. We can invite a few people over and grill some hot dogs or something. Hell! If people wanna drink they can bring their own liquor."

"And how many people are you talking about inviting?" Romello inquired.

"Well, there's Alisha and her husband. I would invite Ladona and a few other people around the complex. I'd even invite Peaches."

"Why?"

Jewel held out her hand to admire her ring again. "'Cuz I wanna rub it in her face that you're marrying *me.*"

Romello rolled over on his side with his back to Jewel. He knew no matter how much he protested she was going to pressure him until he gave in.

This definitely was not something he'd planned on when he gave her the ring, though. The ring was supposed to have been a way to get some of the pressure off him so he would not have to listen to her whine about how he did not really love her. Now this ring was bringing yet another thing he would have to hear her go on and on about; he decided to go along with whatever she wanted.

"Fine. We can have the party," Romello sighed.

"You'll have to invite some of your friends, too. What about Gino or Tyrell?"

Romello closed his eyes. "Cut the light off and go to sleep, Jewel," he said.

"Romello, when are we gonna set a date? You know, everyone is gonna be asking us at the party." Jewel cut off the light, then got back into bed. "A winter wedding might be nice with the snow falling around us."

"And we'd freeze our asses off outside," Romello added.

"Okay. What about a fall wedding, with the leaves blowing in the wind?"

"Jewel, we don't have money to get married right now, unless you just wanna go down to the courthouse." Romello held his breath, hoping that wouldn't be acceptable to her.

"So why don't we try to plan something for next year?" Jewel asked.

I would rather plan something for the year 2080. Romello silently let out a sigh of relief. "Yeah, next year would be better."

"Well, what month?"

"Jewel!" Romello groaned.

"What?" Jewel snapped at him. "This is important, Romello. Do you want a spring wedding? What do you think about a summer wedding? Things need to be planned."

"Well, can't we plan it in the morning? Right now, I am tired. I need my sleep."

"Okay. I'll let you get your sleep." Jewel leaned over and gave him a kiss.

"Thank you, baby."

For a few minutes, there was complete silence. Romello closed his eyes, trying not to think of getting married. All of a sudden, Jewel sat up again.

"So when do think we should have the party?"

Chapter 19

Alisha looked out the kitchen window, sipping her morning cup of coffee. She turned to Craig, at the table eating his breakfast and reading the newspaper, then let out a long sigh.

"Craig, I was wondering about something I noticed yesterday," she said to him.

"What's that?" he asked, flipping through the pages.

"Well, I was wondering why none of the credit card bills ever come here to the house anymore."

Craig looked up in alarm. "Why would you worry about something like that?"

"I'm not worried, I was just wondering."

"Okay. Why would you *wonder* about something like that?"

Alisha shrugged her shoulders. "I don't know. What if I purchase something, then need to remember how much I paid for it? You know I always lose my receipts. It would be nice to have a bill to look through for reference."

Craig shook his head as he chuckled under his breath. "I have them sent to the office," he said, looking back down at the paper. "It's just easier for me to handle all the bills there. Besides, you don't need to worry—I mean *wonder*—about some stupid bill. I take care of everything, don't I?"

Alisha looked out the window again, not believing a word of his flimsy excuse. "Well, if you do most of your work at the office, why do you have the second bedroom set up like an office?"

"If I get that promotion, I'll be able to do a lot of work from home."

"Well, I don't understand why you just can't keep the bills in there. Why would you want to keep something as personal as credit card statements in your desk at work? Does your desk have a lock? I bet anyone could come along and go through them and get all our personal information."

Craig looked up again. "Are you really gonna worry me about where I have the credit card bills sent, Alisha? If it is that serious, I will start having them sent here to the house again."

"That would probably be the best thing."

"And since you're so worried about them, would you like to start paying them too?"

"No need for you to get sarcastic about it. I was just asking a question."

Craig pushed his plate away, then wiped his mouth with a napkin. "When we got married, I told you I would handle all the bills, right? I don't bug you about how much you run up your Neiman Marcus account, do I?"

"Well, no," Alisha mumbled.

"Well, then don't worry about how I handle paying the bills or where I even have them sent." He got up from the table and put his plate in the sink. "I'm gonna finish getting ready for work."

"Craig, are you having an affair?" Alisha blurted out.

Craig turned around with a puzzled look on his face. "Are you trying to be funny?" he asked.

Alisha stepped away from the window and walked

towards him. "No, I'm not trying to be funny. I'm asking a serious question. Are you having an affair? Is that why you don't want me to see the credit card statements?"

Craig grabbed his briefcase by the door, then took out two envelopes and handed them to her.

"That's for my American Express and Visa cards," he snapped at her. "Go ahead and pick through each charge with a fine-tooth comb, then come back and tell me whether or not you still think I'm having a damn affair."

"Wait a minute, Craig," Alisha said, suddenly feeling guilty for having asked him such a question.

Craig ignored her and went to the bedroom. Alisha set the envelopes down on the table. As much as she had wanted to get her hands on the statements before, she felt bad about even holding them in her hand. She went and took a seat on the couch, deciding to give Craig a little time to cool off. When he emerged from the room fully dressed in his work clothes, she got up again to plead her case.

"Craig, I'm sorry," she said. "I shouldn't have asked you something like that. I should know better. I know you'd never cheat on me."

"The fact you even asked offends me," he said, sounding genuinely hurt.

Alisha put her arms around his waist. "Don't go to work being mad at me," she begged him. "It's just that you've been spending so much time at the office lately. I'm around here missing you so much."

Craig finally put his arms around her and gave her a squeeze. "And I'm sorry about that," he sighed. "You know I'm just trying to get this promotion. I don't wanna live in this apartment forever. I want us to get a house and raise that family you want."

The two of them went outside and started walking down the stairs towards the parking lot.

Alisha laughed to herself. "I don't know what I was thinking," she said to Craig. "I know you would never cheat on me."

Craig put his arm around her shoulder. "Of course I wouldn't. Do you know how crazy I am about you?"

Alisha spotted Ladona standing, pacing near Craig's truck as if she were waiting on him.

"Is Ladona over there waiting on you?" Alisha asked.

They stopped at the edge of the curb. "Oh yeah," he replied matter-of-factly. "She had caught me when I was coming in last night and said she needed a ride downtown. She'd mentioned something about surprising that new guy of hers for lunch." He gave her a quick kiss on the lips. "I'm gonna have to work late tonight, but I should be home before nine o'clock. Love you, baby."

"Love you too," Alisha mumbled under her breath, feeling all those suspicions coming back again.

She raced back up to the apartment, anxious to get her hands on those credit card statements she had left on the table. When she got back inside, she found that they were gone.

Alisha now had feelings of anger to deal with. When the doorbell rang, she marched to the door, expecting it to be Craig and ready to give him a piece of her mind. Instead, it was Lucky with his sexy dimpled smile.

"Good morning," he said.

"Good morning," Alisha sighed.

"I saw you downstairs. I was calling out to you, but I guess you didn't hear me."

Alisha shook her head. "I'm sorry. I had other things on my mind."

"You look a little stressed out."

"Like I said, I have things on my mind."

"I just wanted to let you know that I enjoyed having

lunch with you yesterday. Maybe we can do that again sometime."

That brought a smile to her face. "I enjoyed lunch too."

"Well, if you aren't busy today . . ."

Alisha was just about to ask him if she could take a rain check when the thought of those credit card statements popped up in her head again.

"You know what? Why don't I cook lunch for you?"

He sure is prompt, Alisha said to herself as she looked at the clock and saw that it was noon.

On her way to answer the door, she stopped in front of the mirror to make sure her hair and makeup were okay.

"Why are you acting like this is a damn date?" she asked her reflection. *This is only lunch—a friendly, purely platonic lunch.*

Lucky knocked again. Alisha took in a few deep breaths before finally opening the door. She had not prepared herself for what she saw. Looking like a heavenly vision in all white, carrying one single red rose, Lucky flashed his million-dollar smile.

"I was starting to think you were gonna stand me up," he said, chuckling.

Trying to keep her emotions and hormones under control, Alisha quickly ushered him into the apartment, praying none of the other neighbors had seen him standing there with a rose. She did not want anyone thinking something foul was going on.

"I just had to make a stop in front of the mirror, that's all," Alisha said, chuckling.

"You look beautiful." Lucky held out the rose to her.

As he stood there examining every inch of her body, Alisha felt herself blushing like a schoolgirl. "Can I get you something to drink?" she asked.

"You don't have any beer, do you?" he asked.

Alisha shook her head. "I have wine or juice or water."

"I can hang with a glass of wine."

As Alisha disappeared to the kitchen, she could still feel Lucky's eyes on her as she walked. "I hope you like chicken salad. It's the only thing I could think to throw together."

"Whatever you fixed is fine with me," Lucky replied.

Alisha walked back out to the living room with the glasses of wine and found Lucky studying the pictures hanging on the wall.

He turned to her and pointed to a picture of Craig. "The luckiest man alive," he said.

Alisha felt herself blushing again as she handed him his glass. "Do you have any pictures of your girlfriend on you?"

Lucky shook his head, then took a sip. "I didn't bring my wallet with me." He went back to looking at the rest of the pictures. "I didn't know you went to Temple."

Alisha saw that he was looking at her degree. She nodded her head.

Lucky chuckled. "Small world," he said. "I went there for a semester. I partied more than I studied. Is that where you met your husband?"

Alisha nodded her head again. "I was in my freshman year; he was already a junior. However, it wasn't until my sophomore year that he finally started noticing me."

Lucky shook his head. "How could he have not noticed someone as fine as you?"

Alisha laughed. "I used to ask him that same thing when we first started dating. He claims he was too into his studies to be worried about having a relationship. Believe it or not, Craig was a bit of a nerd back then—cute as hell, but nerdy."

"And to think we were on the same campus and didn't even know it."

"It's a small world."

Lucky drank the rest of his wine. "Talk about a missed opportunity."

"Are you ready to eat?"

Lucky gave her a look that let her know he had interpreted her question in a way that she hadn't intended.

"More than you know," he said, chuckling.

While his innuendos made her uncomfortable, Alisha rather liked the attention. Worrying about what he would say next helped her keep her mind off her troubles with Craig and the credit card statements. Through lunch, they enjoyed a pleasant conversation about their time in college. Alisha appreciated the fact that Lucky seemed to hang on her every word.

"So what did you plan on doing with an art history degree?" Lucky asked as they made their way to the couch after eating.

Alisha shrugged her shoulders. "Craig asked me to marry him the summer before my junior year. By then he was already making big money at his job. He insisted that he wanted to take care of me, and promised he would give me everything I could ever want. So I dropped my biology major and picked up something that was easy."

"Biology? Sounds like you were a nerd too."

Alisha laughed. "Beauty wasn't the only thing God blessed me with."

"But you gave up what you wanted to do for the sake of a man, though."

"I'm happy where I'm at. I feel like this is what I am supposed to be doing, living the easy life with a man I am absolutely crazy about and shopping 'til I drop. It just wasn't meant for me to be a pediatrician."

"You really love him, don't you?"

Alisha nodded her head. "I do."

"And does he love you? Has he made good on his

promise to take care of you? Has he given you everything you could ever want?"

Alisha thought about the baby. "I guess you could say almost everything."

She had become so relaxed in talking about her husband that she was caught off-guard when Lucky leaned over and kissed her on the lips. She put her arms up to resist him, but the more she pushed him away, the more he fought against her to stay close.

With his lips pressed hard against hers, and his hands beginning to explore the curves of her body, Alisha felt herself give in, returning his kisses with her own.

Finally having a moment of clarity, she tore herself away and jumped up from the couch.

"I think you better leave," she said, trying to control her heavy breathing.

Lucky sat there calmly with a grin on his face. "Are you sure that's what you want me to do?" he asked.

Alisha nodded her head as she walked to the door and held it open for him. "You need to leave now," she insisted.

Lucky took his time standing up, then slowly made his way over to the door. He stopped in front of Alisha.

"I'm sorry about that," he said.

Alisha waved him off with her hand. "We probably shouldn't do lunch anymore."

"And I guess there's no chance of us maybe seeing each other again sometime."

"Lucky, I'm a married woman. I love my husband."

Lucky gently rubbed her cheek with his hand.

"Yeah," he said sarcastically. "I could tell that by the way you kissed me."

Chapter 20

"I was thinking about having the party two weeks from Saturday. Romello and I thought it'd be a good idea to make it a BYOB party so that way we don't go bankrupt trying to buy alcohol."

Alisha could hear Jewel talking, but she wasn't listening to a word that was being said. Her mind was a thousand miles away, thinking about Lucky. While she still had concern about Craig's credit card statements, she just could not get that kiss out of her mind—her guilty little pleasure.

"Alisha, are you paying attention to me?" Jewel asked, giving her a jab with her elbow.

"What'd you say?" Alisha asked, being jarred back to reality.

"Girl, what is wrong with you? For the past couple of days you have been spaced out. You and Craig aren't having problems, are you?"

Alisha looked at Jewel and gave her a half smile. "I'm sorry, girl. I'm just a little distracted. What were you saying about the party?"

"It's in two weeks, and it's gonna be BYOB. You and Craig are gonna come, right?"

"Of course we will."

"So what's wrong with you, Alisha?"

"It's nothing."

"Don't tell me it's nothing. What's wrong with you?"

Alisha let out a long, hard sigh. "Have you ever been tempted?"

"Tempted to do what?"

"Tempted by another man."

A solemn look came over Jewel's face as she shifted uneasily in her chair. "Why do you ask?"

"Has anyone ever made you so curious—so intrigued that you . . ." Alisha turned to Jewel, searching for the right words to say. "I don't know, girl," she exhaled.

"Alisha, what's going on?"

Alisha held her head in her hands. "I don't know, Jewel. I just can't get this man outta my head. It's driving me crazy!"

"Who?"

"It doesn't matter," Alisha groaned. "I'm such a jezebel!"

Jewel laughed. "A jezebel? You must have really did something wrong, getting biblical on me like that. What the hell did you do?"

"I didn't do anything—no, I mean I did do something, but it wasn't that big of a deal, but then again, it was a big deal. Or maybe I'm just making it into a big deal."

"Alisha, you sound a little crazy right now. What did you do that was or wasn't that big of a deal?"

Alisha broke down into tears. "I kissed him, Jewel. I did not mean to, but it just happened. Girl, his lips are so damn soft. And then his hands . . ."

Jewel put her arm around her for comfort. "I take it you're not talking about Craig."

"Don't even get me started on him! One minute the credit card statements were on the table, the next minute they're gone. Ladona supposedly has this new man named John. Would you believe she actually brought him his favorite jelly-filled doughnuts! They were flirting right there in my face!"

Jewel wanted to laugh at her friend's ramblings, but she knew that would make matters even worse.

"Alisha, none of what you said made any sense to me. Something about credit cards and jelly doughnuts. And who the hell is John?"

"Never mind," Alisha said as she dried the tears from her face. "I'm just going through some things right now, but I'll be okay."

Jewel opened her mouth to speak, but was silenced by the sight of Lucky. As much animosity as she still had towards him, she could not help but feel that twinge of attraction and arousal.

"Good morning," he said to both of them, then turned to Alisha as she tried hiding her tear-stained face. "Alisha, you all right?" he asked.

"I'm fine," she replied, too ashamed to look him in the eye.

He walked over and put his hand on her shoulder. Her body trembled under his slight touch. "You look like you've been crying," he said softly. "You sure you're okay?"

Jewel felt a pang of jealousy from all the attention he was giving Alisha. "She's fine," she said to him. "She just got a little bad news, that's all."

Lucky seemed to ignore her, still focusing his attention on Alisha.

She finally managed to raise her eyes to meet his gaze, then forced a smile. "Really, I'm fine, Lucky. Thanks for being concerned."

Lucky winked his eye at her, then turned to Jewel. "Is Romello awake?" he asked.

Jewel pointed to the apartment. Both girls watched as he walked inside.

"Do you like him?" Jewel asked.

Alisha got nervous. "Like him? What do you mean?"

"Do you think he's a nice person?"

"He's okay, I guess. I really don't know him too well. I thought you two were pretty close, though."

Jewel shrugged her shoulders. "No, not really," she sighed.

The two girls sat there in a moment of silence, both of them wanting to tell the other of their Lucky experience, but neither of them having the nerve.

"The way he looks in those tank tops is something else, though," Jewel said as she shook her head.

"Something else," Alisha agreed.

"Have a safe drive, Peaches!"

"I will, CJ!" she said to her bouncer as she walked out the back door of the club. She turned around and started walking towards her car. As she approached, she noticed a man leaning against the side of her car.

"Hey! That's my damn car you're on!" she barked at him.

"I know what your Beamer looks like." Romello turned around and smiled at her.

Peaches started laughing. "Boy, you're a little late if you're here to give me a foot rub. I'm taking off early tonight."

"I was coming from my boy's place. His girl came by so they kicked me out. I ain't in the mood to go home yet."

"Aww. What's wrong? Don't tell me the happy couple's having problems already," Peaches teased.

"Don't start with me." Romello looked her over from head to toe. "Nice outfit."

"You mean this old rag?"

"Old rag or not, you make everything look good."

Peaches playfully pinched his cheek. "You are such a sweetheart, Romey!"

Romello made a face. "Please don't call me that," he said, laughing. "My mother used to call me that. It's embarrassing."

"Aww, that's so cute! Anyway, what is the problem that you don't wanna go home? Hell! You asked the girl to marry you. You bought her that nice-ass ring. Shouldn't you be at home fucking like jackrabbits or something?"

"Between you and me, I only asked her so she'd shut the hell up about it."

Peaches leaned against the side of the car next to him. "Romello, Jewel and I may not exactly be cool with each other, but you shouldn't play with her like that. That's how you niggas end up getting your cars keyed up or your dicks chopped off. Don't play with a woman's heart."

"Well, what else was I supposed to do?"

"Have you men ever heard of this little word called *honesty*?"

"You know what? You've got a smart-ass mouth, girl," Romello said, chortling.

"Now, be honest about this . . . where did you get that ring from, 'cuz I know damn well your ass didn't buy it. That baby's at least two karats."

Romello grinned. "Why you wanna know?"

"Well, if you did buy it, I want the name of that jeweler. It's a nice-ass rock."

"Well, I can't tell you where I got it from."

"What, you think I'm gonna go back and say something to Jewel? It's not like she'd believe me anyway. I just wanna know."

Romello pulled a blunt from behind his ear, then lit it. He took a few hits, then passed it to Peaches. "I took it from this girl I'm messing with. She has a lot of jewelry—some nice-ass shit. I figured she wouldn't miss one little ring so I borrowed it."

"Without her permission," Peaches sighed. "Romello, you are a mess."

"Well, how else was I gonna get her a ring?"

"Get a job, nigga! You act like you are allergic to a real fucking job!" Peaches passed the blunt back. "I'm not saying this to try and blow your head up or nothing, but you could be one hell of a catch, if you wanted to."

Romello grinned. "What do you mean by that?"

Peaches got serious with him. "If you got a real job and stopped all this running around with twenty different women, I honestly think you'd make a good boyfriend—maybe even a husband."

"You think so?" Romello smiled proudly. "I don't think I'd stop the running around, though. I like women too damn much."

"You just need to get you the right one, that's all. You need someone who can handle you. Someone who's gonna call you on your bullshit and put you in your place."

"There's no woman out there like that."

"You need to find yourself a woman like me, Romey. Now, I'm not saying you need *me*, just someone *like* me." Peaches started laughing. "All the shit you be doing to your girl, there's no way in hell you'd be doing that with me. The first time you came to me with some crap about wanting to stay out all night, you would come home and find all your clothes in the front yard cut up and bleached."

"Didn't I tell you not to call me Romey?"

Peaches rested her head on his shoulder. "I'm not Jewel, Romey. I don't jump when you say jump."

Romello playfully pushed her away from him. "What about you? I bet you want a guy who's a real pushover, huh? You probably want a trained nigga to just hand over the check."

Peaches shook her head. "Oh, no," she said with disgust. "A man like that would want to be all up under me, following me around getting all jealous. I'd have to kill his ass. Actually, I want a guy who gives me a challenge—someone who can put me in my place once in a while, but would still hand over the check."

Romello laughed, then suddenly got serious. "Now it's your turn to be honest with me."

Peaches slid her arm around his. "What would you like to know, my dear Romey?"

"Don't call me that unless you want me to call you Peachy."

Peaches held her hands up. "Okay, let's call a truce. So what do you want to know the truth about?"

"Why do you sleep with all those guys? There probably isn't a guy on this earth who wouldn't want to marry you and take care of you for the rest of your life."

"And I'd be another Alisha? No way."

"What's wrong with that? If the guy loves you, why wouldn't you wanna be with him?"

"Because maybe I'm like you. Maybe I'm not ready to settle down. When you think about it, you and I aren't all that different. You sleep with girls to get your rent paid or to get jewelry. I do the same thing with guys."

Romello nodded his head in agreement. "Well, maybe we should make a pact to quit our ho-ish ways."

Peaches started laughing. "I think this weed is fucking with your brain cells."

Romello looked at his watch. "Well, I guess I should head on home now."

"Wow! A whole conversation without you mentioning how much you wanna have sex with me! The end of the world must be coming!"

"Don't think I'm not standing here imagining you with those nice thick legs wrapped around me," Romello said, chuckling. "It's just nice having a normal conversation with you, though."

Peaches nodded. "It's cool," she said.

The two of them exchanged a lingering glance before Peaches turned away and started going through her duffel bag for her keys. "I guess I'll see you tomorrow or something," she said nervously.

Romello leaned over and gave her a kiss on the cheek. "Drive safely," he said before going back to his car.

Peaches turned and watched him as he walked away, putting her hand to her chest as her heart began racing.

Chapter 21

"What are you doing walking out here this time of night?" Lucky asked.

Startled, Ladona stopped in her tracks and turned in the direction of his apartment. "It's too hot to be in the house," she replied.

Lucky threw his cigarette in the grass. "You're welcome to join me on the porch if you want."

"No, thanks. I'll just continue my walk."

"I see you're not one for conversation, are you?"

Ladona exhaled. "I'm a quiet person."

Lucky came off the porch and met her on the sidewalk. "Well, at least I know I shouldn't take it personal," he said, chuckling.

"What are you doing up at this hour?"

"I'm like you, out here enjoying the night air." Lucky lit another cigarette. "Have you been putting your ear to any other apartment doors lately?"

Ladona glared at him, unable to appreciate a joke at her expense. "I guess you think that's funny."

"Actually, I don't. I think it's kinda creepy."

"Well, it's been real nice talking to you, Lucky."

"How are things going with you, though? You make any progress with the husband yet?"

"I don't know why you think I have something going on with Craig. I keep telling you that you're mistaken."

Lucky threw his head back and laughed. "You are actually pretty convincing. I bet you have everyone around here fooled, don't you? You don't fool me one bit, though. Game knows game, baby."

Ladona folded her arms across her chest, careful not to reveal her frustration. "Do you mind if I ask you a question? What exactly is your fascination with Alisha, anyway? I mean, she's a married woman, married to possibly the greatest husband in the world. Then there is the fact that you already have a girlfriend, but she must be crazy to let you mooch off her the way you do. And aren't you sleeping with Peaches too? You're a busy man, Lucky."

Lucky laughed at her again. "Damn. Are you stalking me? You know more about who I'm sleeping with and who's paying bills than I do. What's the problem? You upset that I'm not trying to sleep with you too?"

He had definitely struck a chord with that one, but Ladona still refused to let him see her sweat. "You're a cocky sonofabitch," she said.

Lucky shrugged his shoulders. "Let me fill you in on something, Ladona." Lucky leaned in closer as if he were about to reveal a secret. "If you didn't walk around here looking so mean and evil all the time, you could possibly find a man of your own and stop running behind Craig."

Ladona could not hold back her anger any longer. "Just who in the hell do you think you are telling me what I should do?"

"I'm a man trying to give you some friendly advice, that's all. Men don't like a stalker."

"First of all, I don't need your advice on how to land a man. For your information, I'm dating someone."

Lucky scoffed at her. "Of course you are," he said sarcastically. "If you have a man, why are you so busy chasing after Craig?"

"You are all in my business and you don't even know what's going on. And for your information, I am not a stalker, so go to hell!"

Lucky started laughing as he turned to go back to his house. "Enjoy the rest of your night, honey."

Ladona was too mad to think of something smart to say. Defeated, she went marching back to her apartment, trying to tell herself that what Lucky said about her did not matter, but it did. Especially since it was something she'd heard so many times before.

Why don't you smile more? You always look like you wanna kick somebody's ass. Everyone, especially guys, were always saying the same thing.

As Ladona got ready for bed, she heard a knock at the front door.

"Who is it?" she called out as she walked down the hallway to the door.

"It's Lucky!"

Even though she recognized his voice, she still checked through the peephole.

"Well, what do you want? You come here to hurl a few more insults at me before you got to bed?" she snapped at him.

"Can you please open the door? It's late and I don't wanna have to raise my voice for the entire complex to hear."

"You can talk normal. I'll be able to hear you just fine."

"Ladona, please open the door. I'd like to see your face when I talk to you."

She didn't want to open the door for him, but curiosity got the best of her, wondering what he wanted. Even though she was upset, there was a little part of her that thought he was coming to make a booty call. Since he seemed to be making his rounds with most of the women in the complex, she thought maybe tonight was her night. She hated thinking about it, but it had been such a long time since she had even been with a man.

Ladona finally opened the door. Lucky had an apologetic look on his face.

"What do you want?" she snapped.

"Well, I just wanted to come up and let you know I felt bad about some of the things I said to you a little while ago. I just want to make sure there are no hard feelings between us. I have enough enemies in my life. I don't need one more."

"So is this supposed to be some kind of apology?"

"I'm making sure there are no hard feelings," Lucky repeated, putting an emphasis on every word.

"Your *apology* is accepted," she said with a smile.

"Oh! So you do smile."

"Of course I smile. I'm not the mean ogre you tried to make me sound like."

Lucky smiled back at her. "Well, that's good to know," he said as he turned and started towards the stairs.

"So is that all you wanted?" Ladona called after him, hoping he would turn back around and embrace her with a kiss.

Lucky did turn back around, then asked, "Were you expecting something else?"

Feeling like a fool for even entertaining the idea that he might want to sleep with her, Ladona closed the door without saying another word to him.

Chapter 22

Craig slammed his hand on the steering wheel in aggravation as he cursed the brake-happy Nissan in front of him. It was barely even noon and traffic was unbearably heavy and slow. Any other time this lag in traffic would not have had his nerves on edge, but today he was in a rush to get home. Craig had big news to share with Alisha and it was just too big to say over the phone.

He let out a sigh of relief as he pulled into the parking lot, feeling as if he had just come to the end of a long journey. He smiled to himself, seeing that Alisha's car was there. He would have burst if he had to wait to tell her the news.

Craig walked across the complex with a bottle of wine in one hand and a dozen tulips in the other. On the shoulder strap of his briefcase, he had wrapped the strings of a half-dozen brightly colored balloons. The smile on his face grew wider with each step he took toward the building.

"Looks like a man in love," Craig heard Lucky comment as he walked past his apartment.

Craig acknowledged him with a nod of his head, but did not stop to make conversation.

"Ain't nothing wrong with that, man. I'd probably bring her balloons and flowers every day too, if she were my woman," Lucky commented again.

This time Craig stopped, and without bothering to turn his body, he glanced over his shoulder and replied, "Well, you don't have to worry about that, do you?"

He heard Lucky start howling with laughter, then continued walking toward the stairs. Peaches happened to walk out of her apartment and gawked at him.

"What kind of flowers are those?" she asked him. "They are beautiful!"

This time Craig stopped to say a few words. "They're tulips, Alisha's favorite," he replied.

Peaches walked over to him to smell the flowers. "You two must've had a fight or something. You're coming with flowers and wine—men only do that shit when they know they've done something wrong."

Craig smiled at her. "Maybe I'm just doing it just because."

"You need to be cloned, Craig. Millions of women across America would kill to have a man as good as you."

Just then, Romello stepped out onto his porch. "Damn, man!" he yelled at Craig with a smile on his face. "As if the damn flowers weren't enough, now you gotta come strutting around here with balloons too? I'm gonna have to talk to management about you."

Jewel came to the door and poked her head outside. "Oh my God! Look at all the pretty balloons!" she squealed in excitement. "What's the special occasion?"

Craig laughed to himself, surprised that everyone would make such a big deal over a few balloons and some flowers. He had always assumed a man should do such things for a woman. Part of him felt bad that Jewel and Peaches had not been fortunate enough to have such a man.

"I've got some good news for my baby," Craig replied.

Romello laughed. "You sure you ain't in the doghouse about something?"

Jewel playfully slapped him on the back of the head. "Leave Craig alone," she said to him before turning her attention back to Craig. "Did Alisha mention the party to you? You're gonna come, aren't you?"

"What party?" Craig asked, wondering why Alisha had not said anything.

"Our engagement party," Jewel said, putting her arm around Romello's waist.

"We'll be there," Craig said as he started up the steps to his apartment.

"Bring your own booze!" she called after him.

As Craig walked upstairs, he could see Ladona coming out of her apartment.

What is this shit? Am I gonna have to stop and talk to everybody before I even get to my door? he thought to himself as he prayed that Ladona didn't notice him approaching. What woman could miss a man carrying flowers and a stream of shiny helium balloons? Ladona smiled at him and started walking in his direction.

"Would these be for me?" Ladona chuckled as she leaned in closer to smell the flowers. "What's the big occasion? Is today Alisha's birthday? Is it your anniversary?"

"What's the deal with everybody? Can't a man bring his wife flowers and balloons without there being a reason behind it? I love her; that should be reason enough." Craig let out a long sigh. Seeing the surprised look on Ladona's face made him feel bad for snapping at her. "I'm sorry. It's not her birthday and it's not our anniversary. I've just got some good news for her, that's all."

"I wish I was the lucky one getting all this," Ladona sighed, then gave him an even bigger smile. "My day will be coming soon, though."

Craig smiled back at her. "I'm sure it will."

Ladona continued on with her business as Craig finally managed to make it to the apartment door. With his hands too full to knock on the door, he tapped lightly with his foot.

"Baby, open the door! My hands are full."

Alisha's eyes got as big as saucers when she opened the door and saw him standing there. "What are you doing home this early? And what's with all this stuff?"

Craig stepped inside the apartment and gave her a big kiss on the lips. "Don't people go to work around here?" He chuckled as he set the bottle of wine on the table. "I must've run into damn near everybody wanting to know why I have flowers and balloons."

Alisha looked at him and laughed. "Well, I'm like them. What's all this for?"

"Celebration," Craig said, picking her up and swinging her around the room. "I got the promotion, baby! They gave me the damn promotion!"

Alisha gave him a big kiss on the lips. "Craig, that's wonderful!"

"See! I told you all that overtime was going to pay off! I get a corner office, my own secretary. I even have my own parking space!"

"So I suppose you really were working overtime," Alisha muttered.

Craig looked puzzled. "Come on, baby. You aren't still walking around here thinking I'm cheating, are you?"

Alisha quickly looked in the other direction, not wanting to meet his stare. "Let's not even talk about that now. We should be celebrating, right?"

Craig looked at her in disbelief. He wanted to say something else, but she was right. This was supposed to be a celebration and he didn't want to ruin the moment with an argument.

"And we can't forget about the big salary," he said drily.

"I guess this means we can get a house now?"

"We can get a lot of things."

Alisha squealed in delight. "We've gotta go out and celebrate!" Alisha turned to go to the bedroom. "I'll go throw on some clothes. I have a taste for Jamaican food. What about you?"

Craig reached out to stop her. "We can go out and celebrate another time," he told her as he pulled her into his arms. "I was kinda hoping we could do a little celebrating around here."

Alisha giggled as Craig started kissing her neck. "Craig! It's the middle of the afternoon!"

"What's wrong with that?" He picked her up and carried her into the bedroom. "That just means we have a longer time to celebrate."

Alisha opened her eyes and stared at the ceiling. "Craig, are you up?" she whispered.

"Yeah, baby. What's wrong, you can't sleep?" he asked.

"Not really. I have so many thoughts going through my head right now."

"Well, what's wrong?" Craig asked as he rolled over to face her. He glanced at the alarm clock. "Damn. It's two A.M. already? You really wore me out."

"You were the animal, not me," Alisha said, chuckling. "Anyway, were you serious about us finally being able to move into our own house?" she asked.

"Sure. We can probably start looking at the end of the summer."

Alisha moved closer and snuggled into his chest. "What about starting a family? You said that if you were promoted we could start a family. I mean, now that you have this big, fancy office, you're gonna need finger paintings and family portraits to hang on your wall."

Craig smiled. "Why don't we see about getting a pet first," he sighed. "If we do okay with a dog then maybe we can move up to a human."

"Oh, I want a dog too, but I wanna start having a family, Craig. I wanna have your children."

Craig closed his eyes. "Okay, okay. We can start *talking* about having a family."

Alisha raised her head and kissed him on the lips. "That's good enough for me," she said excitedly as she got out of the bed and slipped on her robe.

"Where are you going?" Craig asked.

"I'm just gonna run to the bathroom, then the kitchen for a glass of water. Want me to get you something?"

Craig rolled over again. "I'm going back to sleep," he said, yawning.

Alisha crept to the bathroom, then quietly closed the door behind her. From the moment Craig had told her the good news about his promotion, she knew exactly what she had to do. Carefully she opened up the medicine cabinet.

"We've done all the talking we're gonna do, Craig," she said to herself. She started popping her birth control pills down the drain.

Chapter 23

Peaches had a grin on her face as she watched William count through the money in his wallet a second time. She knew Mr. 1000 would only count seven twenty-dollar bills—four twenties shy of what he had before he had drifted off to sleep.

"I'm missing money out of my wallet," William grumbled as he started counting his money again.

"You were pretty drunk last night," she said, trying to sound convincing. "You probably just spent more than you remember."

William shook his head. "Uh-uh. I may have been drunk, but I know what I had in my damn wallet. Maybe someone was dipping in there while I was asleep," he said looking at her with suspicion.

"I know you ain't trying to say I took ya damn money." Peaches got out of bed. "I ain't no damn thief, man. You better take that shit somewhere else!"

William looked at her as if she had lost her mind for snapping on him like that. "Wait a minute. Did you hear me *say* you took my money?"

"You didn't say it, but it sure as hell sounded like you were trying to insinuate that I did."

"Well, did you take it?" William asked. "You're sitting here getting all defensive about it. It's making your ass look guilty!"

Peaches started walking up on him. Even though he was almost twice her size, she never let any man intimidate her. She knew her mouth could tear a man down harder and faster than any fist would. Moreover, she never worried about anyone putting his hands on her because she was just too cute to be abused.

"How in the hell are you gonna stand in my damn house and accuse me of being a fucking thief?" She started pushing him out the bedroom towards the front door. "You just need to take your money-losing ass and get the hell outta my house. I ain't got time for this shit! Next time you see me in the club don't even bother to holla. I ain't messing with ya nasty drunk ass anymore!"

Peaches had pushed him one too many times. William turned around and pushed her so hard that she went flying to the floor. "Bitch, you must've lost your damn mind!" he shouted at her. "Don't you ever in your life put your hands on me like that. You understand?"

In her mind, William had just pushed her for the first and last time. The anger in his face scared her, but she refused to let him punk her in her own house. "Get the hell outta my house!" she shouted.

"You took my money, didn't you?" He started walking towards her.

"Why would I take your damn money? Do I look like I need to be stealing money from you? Look at all my shit here! If anything, you need to be borrowing money from me!" Even though he was walking up on her again, she continued to stand her ground. "Now I told ya ass you were drunk as hell last night. No telling how much money you were dropping in the club."

William stood over her, breathing his stale, morning

beer breath in her face. "This is the second damn time I've come up missing money after being with you, bitch. I didn't say shit about it last time 'cuz I thought maybe I had miscounted my money. Not this time, though. This is just too much of a damn coincidence. Now give me my money, Peaches!"

"Nigga, I ain't giving you shit 'cuz I ain't got shit." Peaches started laughing. "Now if you want me to, I can let you borrow eighty dollars, but you're gonna have to pay it back."

William grabbed her by the arms. "You think you so damn funny, huh? Bitch, that's the eighty dollars you took from me. One hundred and forty if you count the sixty you took the last time I was here. I want my money!"

The look of anger in his eyes had turned to something psychotic. Peaches was scared to death now, but she still refused to be meek.

"Fuck you," she said in a soft, stern voice.

William grabbed her by the neck and shoved her into the wall, hitting her head with a loud thump. "Bitch, you don't know who the hell ya fucking with. Don't fuck with my money."

"I ain't got it," Peaches said, gasping for air.

William hit her head against the wall again, then let go of her neck. "Where'd you put my money, Peaches?" He went to her room and started throwing things around, pulling the drawers out and dumping everything on the floor.

Peaches went and stood in the doorway, watching in horror and disbelief. *All this over a few measly dollars,* she thought to herself.

No matter what, she was determined to stand her ground and continue denying that she had taken his money. The last thing she wanted was for guys at the club to know she liked dipping in wallets. It didn't matter if

William went back to the club with a suspicion of her stealing. That was something she could easily dismiss.

Besides, Peaches felt whatever money she took was rightfully deserved. In her mind, she felt she had earned more than the extra money in full. Her body was worth more than the nine hundred dollars he had dropped for a night with her. She considered her time and the fact she had to wash her sheets as being compensable. As far as she was concerned, William should have been grateful that she had not bothered to pick his wallet clean.

After turning out everything in the room, William turned around and glared at her with his bloodshot red eyes.

"Where the hell is the eighty dollars?" he asked. "In fact, just give me back the nine hundred too."

"I don't have your funky little eighty bucks. And if I can't take my pussy back from you, what makes you think you can get that nine back from me? I more than earned that having to sleep with your ugly ass."

Peaches smiled to herself, knowing that her money was so well hidden underneath the carpet that lifted up in the corner of the bedroom. She did not take chances when it came to putting money away. It had only taken one time for her to get burned before learning that tricks couldn't be trusted.

Without warning, William came charging after her again. Peaches screamed and tried to run back to the living room, but he was quick in grabbing her by her long red braids, then dragging her into the living room.

"Give me my money!" William yelled each time he raised his fist to hit her. Peaches screamed for help, trying to crawl away.

She finally managed to get away by giving him a kick to the groin. Peaches ran for the door, but he managed to catch her at the door. Grabbing her by the hair again, he threw her into the wall.

"Give me my money!" he yelled.

"I ain't got your damn money!"

William grabbed her again, this time throwing her to the floor. He stood over her as he started unzipping his pants.

"Well if you aren't gonna give me my money, I'm about to get payment in another way."

William towered over her as he unzipped his pants. Peaches tried to kick him but he moved out of the way, only making him angrier.

"William, you better not put a hand on me," she commanded.

William dropped his pants to the floor. "And just what the hell are you gonna do about it?"

Just as he went to pull down his underwear, a man's voice boomed through the apartment.

"What the hell is going on?" Everyone turned around to see Romello standing at the front door. To Peaches, he looked like an angel sent from the heavens. Jewel stood behind him, peeking over his shoulder.

Romello came rushing in and grabbed William by the back of his shirt. "Man, you've got three seconds to get the fuck outta here."

"Look, I don't want no problems, man. You just need to tell this bitch to give me my money!" William said, trying to pull his pants back up to his waist.

Romello threw him against the wall, shoving his elbow into William's neck. "You need to watch who you calling a bitch, man."

William started gasping for air. Jewel rushed over and grabbed Romello's arm. "Romello, you're choking him. Let him go," she said.

Romello loosened his grip on the man. "Get away from me, Jewel," he hissed at her.

Jewel quickly backed away from him, never having seen Romello this upset. Both girls watched in shock as the two men continued to struggle against the wall. Even though William had Romello in size, Romello overpowered him in strength.

"I said I don't want no trouble, man," William said, trying to plead with Romello. "Just give me my money and I'll be gone."

"I heard Peaches tell you she didn't have your damn money, so I think you need to leave."

William pushed Romello off him, then started walking towards the door. He turned back around and looked at Peaches again. "You shouldn't have crossed me, bitch," he said, unaware that Lucky had walked up behind him.

Lucky grabbed him by the shoulder. "Did you just call her a bitch?"

Before anyone even had a chance to take a breath, Romello and Lucky pounced on William like two madmen. The room was astir with Jewel and Peaches yelling and screaming for them to stop.

"Romello, stop! You're gonna kill him!" Jewel cried out.

Peaches continued watching, hoping that's exactly what would happen. William needed to learn he couldn't just come into her castle and bully her around like that.

"That's enough!" Jewel cried out, unable to take the sight of blood. "Lucky! Romello! Let the man go."

Romello kicked him one last time. "Don't you ever put your hands on her again," he said.

Lucky threw in one last punch before allowing William to get up from the floor. With blood dripping from his face, he looked at everyone in the room, finally resting his eyes on Peaches.

He opened his mouth to say something, but Lucky took a small step towards him and started shaking his head. "Don't even say it, man. Just pick your shirt up and get the hell out of here," he said with so much calmness in his voice that it made everyone in the room a little nervous.

William paused to look at Lucky again. Not wanting to take his chances on receiving any more punishment, he turned and walked out the front door. Romello and Lucky walked to the front door to make sure he got into his car and drove away. Then all eyes turned to Peaches, still sitting on the floor naked with blood coming from her nose and mouth.

Jewel rushed over to her and helped her to her feet. "Girl, are you okay? You don't need to go to the hospital, do you?" Jewel asked.

Romello took off his tank top and handed it to Peaches. "Put this on," he said.

Peaches slipped the shirt on over her head. "I don't need to go to no hospital. I'm fine," she said.

"Let me help you to the bathroom to help you clean up your face," Jewel said.

"I'm fine," Peaches snapped at her. "Look, I appreciate you guys coming over to help me out, but really, I'll be okay."

"I could hear you screaming all the way from my apartment," Lucky said. "Who was that guy?"

"My *cousin*," Peaches said, chuckling.

"You think he's gonna come back?" Lucky asked.

"After that ass-whippin' y'all just gave him? He'd be a fool," Jewel said.

"Mama!" one of the kids yelled from next door.

"Go see what they want," Romello said. "Lucky and I will stay here for a bit to make sure the guy doesn't try to come back."

"You don't need to stay," Peaches said, looking at all of them. "I keep telling you I'll be fine."

Jewel left to go check on the children.

"Well, if you need me, you better call." Lucky turned and walked out the house.

Romello walked over to Peaches and touched her face. "So that was your *cousin*, huh?"

Peaches looked down at the floor, too embarrassed to look him in the face. "Thank you for defending me like that. I don't know who that nigga thought he was."

Romello wanted to put his arms around her and comfort her, but he knew Peaches would resist. Instead, he reached out to touch her hand. "I'm not gonna let no nigga come over here and disrespect you like that," he said softly. "Are you sure you're gonna be okay? It's not a problem for me to sit here with you if you don't wanna be alone."

Peaches laughed nervously. "You act like I'm some delicate little flower or something. I am fine. It's just a little blood. Stop looking all worried like that."

"It's okay to cry, Peaches."

She finally looked up at him, determined to show him that she was a rock. "I ain't got no reason to cry. I can take a lickin' and keep on trickin'." She laughed at her own joke, but Romello did not see the humor in it.

"Well, you'll call me if you need me, right?"

Peaches nodded her head. "Yes, I will call," she sighed.

As the two of them stood there staring at each other, she wished that he would at least put his arms around her. More than anything in the world, she wanted to feel his comfort.

Romello touched her hand again before turning to leave. As soon as he was gone, Peaches went to the bathroom to check out her face. Any other woman would have been an emotional wreck, but not Peaches. Yes, it had scared her that William had gone crazy on her like that; it was the first time any man had ever treated her that way.

Peaches refused to dwell on that, though. The only thing that mattered to her now was her money. She knew the club was going to be busy tonight. It was important to make sure her face would not be too swollen.

Chapter 24

With an ice pack on her face the entire day, Peaches managed to keep down the swelling enough to throw on some extra makeup and make it into the club.

Nothing was going to keep her from making her money. While it stayed on her mind that William would show up to the club and try to seek revenge, she still wasn't going to let that stop her. She laughed to herself, thinking that even if she had a broken leg, she would have thrown some glitter on the cast and the crutches and still hobbled up on the stage.

"You're looking pretty rough tonight," many of the girls had commented throughout the night.

Peaches just laughed it off, telling everyone she hadn't seen that wall jump in her way. Despite how rough they thought she looked, all that mattered were the men. They still thought she was the finest piece in the house. As always, she was the golden girl, bringing in the most tips of any other girl.

For the first time in a long time, Peaches wasn't up for mingling after the club closed down. Even though there were plenty of big-money men sitting in the audience who would have easily dropped the money to spend the night with her, she just wasn't up for having company. Especially since her room still looked like a cyclone had passed through it.

Peaches waved good-bye to the bouncer, then turned to walk to her car. A smile spread across her face when she saw Romello sitting on her hood.

"Now you're gonna have an ass print on the Beamer," she fussed at him jokingly. "Let me guess. You were on your way home," she said, laughing.

Romello jumped to the ground and inspected the hood of her car. "Looks good to me," he said, caressing the hood. "For your information, Miss Smarty-Pants, I came here from home. I figured I'd ride over here and make sure you were okay."

"Why wouldn't I be okay? I told you there is nothing to worry about. That guy isn't gonna be back."

Romello stepped closer to get a better look at her face. "At least you aren't all swollen up," he said. "You're still beautiful even after all that."

A chill went through her body. "Nobody can stop the Peach."

Romello leaned against the side of the car. "You got a friend coming over tonight?"

Peaches shook her head. "I'm not up for company tonight," she replied. "Besides, my place is in no condition to be inviting someone over."

"You should stop that, you know."

"Stop what?"

"After the shit that happened this morning, you shouldn't be having these crazy-ass guys coming over to your place anymore. The money ain't worth your life, Peaches."

She waved him off with her hand. "I'm a big girl, Romello. I can handle myself."

Romello laughed at her. "Do you really think you're fooling anybody with this tough girl act?"

"It's not an act."

Romello nodded his head and gave her a look to say that he knew better. "Well, I'm gonna follow you back to the complex to make sure you get there okay."

Peaches smiled. "So are we Kevin Costner and Whitney Houston now? You wanna be my bodyguard?"

"I checked around before I left the complex, but who's to say that guy isn't lurking around the corner waiting to follow you home or something?"

Peaches put her hand on his shoulder. "I'm not worried about him," she lied.

"One of us has to be worried. Anyway, I wouldn't feel right unless I knew you got home okay."

Peaches opened her car door and threw her purse on the passenger seat. She loved the attention he was giving her, but she tried not to show it. "I'm fine, Romello. I think it's great of you to stand vigil here in the parking lot, but I don't need you to be my babysitter."

She got in her car and quickly took off. She smiled when she looked in the rearview mirror and saw Romello getting into his car to follow her. Peaches picked up speed and took a detour home. She didn't want Romello following her, but most of all, she wanted to make sure William wasn't following her, either.

Peaches breathed a sigh of relief as soon as she pulled into the complex. She noticed Romello's car already parked. She knew he'd be upset that she hadn't come straight home, but she was certain he was in his apartment watching out the window to make sure she made it back.

Dreading that long walk from her car to her front door, she took a few moments to sit behind the wheel. She took a few deep breaths, trying to calm herself down.

"There's no boogeyman out there waiting to get you,

Peaches," she said aloud. "Romello has to be watching. He's not gonna let anything happen you."

On the count of three, she finally jumped out of the car and made a dash to her front door. Even in three-inch heels, she was able to move like Carl Lewis. Track was one of the things she had loved during her days of high school—that was before her life seemed to take a sour turn.

"Shit!" Peaches said as soon as she reached the porch. She took a moment to catch her breath, then put her key in the lock and quickly opened the front door. Before stepping inside, she took one last look around to make sure no one was coming up behind her.

"What took you so long?" Romello said, coming from around the side of her apartment.

Peaches jumped in fright as she dropped her keys on the porch. "Damn it, Romello," she said in a loud whisper. "What in the hell are you doing around there?"

"I was securing the perimeter, Whitney," he said, putting his hand to his head as if to salute.

With her apartment being at the end, Romello had walked around to the back to make sure no one was hiding. "What took you so long to get home? Did you take a scenic route or something?"

Peaches put her hand over her chest. "You scared the crap out of me, Romello! Don't ever do that shit again!"

Romello walked onto the porch and picked up her keys for her.

"There you go, playing hero again," she said as she walked in the house.

"I told you I wanted to make sure you were okay," he whispered.

Peaches cut on the lights and closed the door. "And yes, I did take a detour home. I just wanted to make sure I wasn't being followed by you."

Romello walked over and picked up an end table that had been knocked over. "Peaches," he said with a serious look on his face, "if you don't feel safe here by yourself, I'm quite sure Jewel wouldn't have a problem with you spending the night at our place on the couch."

Peaches shook her head. "You'd like that, wouldn't you? Wife in the bedroom . . . fantasy girl on the couch. Honestly, Romello, I wish you wouldn't make such a big deal over me. I keep telling you I'll be fine."

Romello looked around at all the mess still on the floor. "That nigga fucked your place up, huh?"

Peaches gave a halfhearted laugh. "If you think this is bad, you should see my bedroom."

The two of them stood there looking at each other, unsure of what to say next.

"Well, since you say you're okay, I should probably get home now, unless you're too scared to be alone."

"I'll be okay. If I need anything I'll just bang on the wall."

Romello nodded his head, searching for something he could say just so he could stay a little longer. Peaches put her hand on his shoulder.

"Stop looking so serious," she told him. "I'm gonna be fine."

"You're not going to work tomorrow, are you?" he asked.

"Why wouldn't I? Romello, I can't let that man stop me from making money."

"Well, I'll be in the parking lot waiting for you afterwards."

Peaches shook her head at him. "You know, you really don't have to do that."

"I know you walk around here like you're all tough, but somebody needs to have your back."

"You're taking this bodyguard shit to the extreme, don't you think? I hope you don't think this little show of valor is gonna get you any closer to getting in my pants."

Romello shook his head. "That's not even what I'm trying to do."

"So you're not interested in having sex with me anymore?" Peaches asked.

Romello started laughing. "Did you hear me say that? I mean that if you were to offer, I certainly wouldn't turn it down. I just wanna be respectful."

Peaches scoffed at him. "Respectful? Since when do you respect women?"

"Since I saw that man disrespecting you."

"So now you're Mr. Sensitive?"

Romello took her hand in his. "Naw, I'm just someone who cares a hell of a lot about you."

Peaches looked away, feeling a bit uncomfortable. "Uh, thanks again for this morning," she said.

Romello nodded his head as he left. On his way back to the apartment, he saw Lucky running towards him.

"Where are you on your way to?" Romello inquired.

"I was up, so I figured I'd go see how Peaches was doing."

"Oh . . . well, she's doing fine. I just came from over there."

Lucky grinned. "You used that moment of being a hero to ease into them pants, huh?"

"Naw, bro, I'm not trying to push up on her like that right now."

Lucky started to grin. "Well, I was just wondering," he said before walking away.

"Where are you going?" Romello asked, even though he could see Lucky was heading in the direction of Peaches's apartment.

"If you aren't gonna use the hero thing, then I sure will."

"Oh, so you two are still messing around?"

Lucky's laugh echoed. "Ask me that again in the morning, man!"

Romello stood on the porch and watched as Lucky knocked on Peaches's door. He found himself holding his breath when he saw her come to the door, then step out and give him a hug.

Please don't let him in the house. Please don't let him in, he chanted in his mind.

Peaches looked over in his direction. She seemed to pause, then raised her hand to wave.

"You okay over there, Romey?" she yelled to him with a grin.

It didn't even matter to him that she had called him by that silly nickname. He just wanted her to turn Lucky away. Romello waved back. "I'm fine."

His heart sank when he saw her hold the door open and let Lucky inside. Not once did she take her eyes from Romello. "Well, I guess I'll see you in the morning," she said with some reservation.

"Sure," he said, unable to hide the disappointment in his voice. "You have a nice night."

Peaches continued standing on the porch, looking as if she wanted to say something else. She thought that maybe Romello would say something to her, but he turned and went back into the apartment.

"I thought maybe you could use a little help cleaning up," Lucky said, bringing her attention back to him. "I know you said that body of yours isn't meant for hard labor."

Peaches smiled at him. "It sure isn't," she replied, closing the front door behind her.

As soon as Peaches opened the door, Jewel shoved a plate of food at her.

"Good morning," Jewel greeted her.

"What the hell is this?" Peaches asked, rubbing sleep from her eyes.

"I'd fixed some pancakes, bacon, and sausage patties for breakfast this morning. There was some left over, so I figured you might be hungry."

Peaches looked at her strangely. "This is the stuff that fell on the floor, right? Why would you be concerned whether or not I'm hungry? Are you trying to poison me?"

Jewel ignored her questions of suspicion and held a bright smile on her face. "Don't be silly. I did not drop anything on the floor, nor did I put poison in it. I just thought I'd try to do something nice for you."

"So you're doing this out of pity because of what happened yesterday?"

"Why do you have to be so suspicious? Can't I just wanna do something nice for you?"

"Why would you? You never have before."

"I wanted to see if you were feeling all right after yesterday. I see your face doesn't look too bad."

Peaches held the door open for Jewel to come in. "You know you really didn't have to do this," she said.

Jewel let out a long breath, preparing to swallow a bitter pill.

"Look," she said, "I know over the years we've been pretty nasty to each other."

Peaches shook her head. "No, you're the one who's been nasty."

"Okay, okay. Maybe I have been the nasty one over the years, but when Romello came in last night, he and I had a long talk. He said some things that made me realize I've really been unfair to you. So, we both agreed that I should come over and apologize to you."

Peaches put her hands on her hips. "You mean he forced you to do it?" she said with a chuckle.

"No, I mean it was a mutual decision. I am now convinced that you aren't trying to sleep with my man. I'm sorry for having accused you of it all this time."

"Well, I'm so glad you've finally realized that," Peaches said with sarcasm.

Jewel nodded her head. "I would hope that we could make a truce and be civil with each other. Maybe even try to be friends."

Peaches nodded her head. "A truce is fine," she replied.

Jewel smiled as she looked around the disheveled living room. "If you need any help cleaning up, or if you need someone to talk to, I'm always home."

"Lucky came by and helped me straighten up a little bit. My bedroom was a disaster."

Jewel felt a wave of jealousy hit her like a brick wall. "Well, that was nice of him," she mumbled. "Well, enjoy your breakfast."

Jewel walked back out the door, then turned around to say one last thing. "When you're done with the plate, could you please return it? It belongs to a set my mother bought me when Romello and I moved in here. It's a little expensive; she'd kill me if she came over and found a piece missing."

Peaches laughed. "Girl, I'll return your damn plate, and thanks for the food."

"Oh! One more thing before I go! Our engagement party is gonna be in two weeks. It's BYOB."

Peaches smiled politely. "I'll be there."

Chapter 25

Alisha tiptoed into the living room and knelt down in front of Craig's briefcase. Listening for the sound of him still in the shower, she quickly checked each pocket and flap of the bag hoping to find the disappearing credit card statements.

Even though she had convinced herself that Craig could not possibly be cheating with Ladona, she still had that little voice in her head nagging her about finding out whether or not he had something to hide. That same little voice inside her head kept up drama in regard to Lucky, as well.

Alisha had managed to do a good job at avoiding contact with him, though. She did not need anything or anyone coming along to mess up her perfect life.

Damn! Alisha cursed after going through the last pocket of the briefcase and not finding so much as a parking receipt. Feeling silly for even having looked, she got up from the floor and went to the kitchen to get started on Craig's breakfast.

As she started up the coffeemaker, she heard Ladona's voice calling her from the front door.

"Girl, did you hear what happened to Peaches a

couple of days ago?" Ladona brushed past her and sat down at the table.

"I hadn't been to Jewel's in a few days, so I'm a little behind on the complex rumors."

"One of her tricks beat her up. From what I heard, there was blood everywhere. Lucky and Romello got there just in time. The guy was about to stab her with a knife!"

Alisha looked horrified. "But I just saw her standing out in the parking lot yesterday afternoon. I saw her at a distance, but she didn't look like anything was wrong."

Ladona shrugged her shoulders. "All I know is that the guy beat her up pretty bad. Lucky and Romello ended up beating the guy up. I heard the guy had to go to the hospital."

Alisha shook her head in pity. "Well, what happened? Why did the guy go off on her like that?"

Ladona shrugged her shoulders. "People say it had something to do with drugs, but I don't know. I thought Peaches was only into tricking. I didn't know she was dealing too."

Alisha watched as Ladona walked over and poured herself a cup of coffee. Although she loved to hear all the gossip around the complex, she knew better than to believe everything she heard. Even though she wasn't that close to Peaches, she couldn't believe Peaches was dealing drugs. There was something about her that didn't scream "drug dealer," but Alisha shrugged it off.

"I guess you never really do know your neighbors," she sighed. "Anyway, on a lighter note, Craig got a promotion the other day. All that overtime he was putting in paid off. And here I was worrying that he was out doing other things when he really did have his butt at the job."

"Doing other things like what?" Ladona asked with a grin on her face.

Craig walked in the room and gave Alisha a kiss on the lips that made Ladona turn away in embarrassment.

"Get a room, lovebirds," Ladona joked.

Craig laughed as he walked into the kitchen to fix himself a cup of coffee. "Good morning, Ladona," he said. "Ya know it's too early in the morning for you ladies to be gossiping."

"Alisha just told me about your promotion. I take it you two won't be living around here too much longer."

Craig shook his head. "Nope. I'm gonna be packing my queen up and moving her into her own little castle."

"And filling that castle with little princes and princesses," Alisha mumbled under her breath.

Craig shot her a look as Ladona started feeling sick to her stomach. "Well, with all this love in the air, I think I should probably go," Ladona said, trying not to sound too upset. She rose to her feet. "Alisha, are you going out today?"

Alisha smiled. "I don't know. I was thinking about going to the mall to get in some shopping. Did you wanna go with me?"

The one thing Ladona could not stand was going to the mall with Alisha. To Ladona, it was bad enough going shopping when you did not have much to spend, but then to go with someone who seemed to have an open line of credit at every major department store made things even worse.

"I'll have to pass on that one." Ladona turned and headed for the front door. "Well, you two have a good day."

Ladona did not wait for anyone to say good-bye.

"Hey, Alisha, I have to tell you something else about the promotion," Craig said as he took a seat at the table.

Alisha went to the fridge. "You mean there's more good news? What do you want for breakfast?"

"No breakfast," Craig replied, "and you might not think of this as good news."

Alisha turned to her husband. "What? Don't tell me they changed their minds."

Craig chuckled. "No, no. Do you think I would be this calm if they tried to take the promotion back? No, the thing is that I'm gonna have to do some traveling once or twice a month."

"You mean like Japan or London?" Alisha started giggling. "Oh my God! We could go to Italy! Think of all the designer shoes and purses I'd get for next to nothing!"

"Calm down, baby. I'm gonna be domestic most of the time, but there's a chance I may have to go abroad."

"Well, that doesn't sound too bad."

"My first trip is tomorrow. I've gotta go to Ann Arbor, Michigan."

"Tomorrow? On such short notice?"

"I know it's short notice, but I have to meet with some of the bosses out there. I will only be gone two nights. You won't even have time to miss me."

"I spoke too soon. This traveling crap is starting to sound bad."

"You aren't mad, are you?"

Alisha looked at him suspiciously. "How can I be mad? You say you're doing it for your job, right?"

"Hey, Romello, is Jewel here?" Alisha asked as she walked up to the porch.

Romello pointed towards the front door. "She's in there getting the kids dressed to go to her mom's. You can go on in." He took a drink of his beer. "How you been doing?"

"I've been doing okay. I heard about the scuffle that

went on at Peaches's place the other morning. Is everything okay?"

Romello looked at her with a scowl. "Things are fine," he mumbled.

"Oh, okay." Alisha stepped past him to get to the front door.

"How's the husband?"

"He's fine. He just went out of town this morning."

"Oh really? Where'd he go?"

"Michigan," Alisha replied.

Romello nodded his head. "Hey, I've got some people who stay out there."

Thanks for that useless piece of information, she thought to herself. "Well that's nice," she told him before going inside. "Jewel! It's me, Alisha!" she called out.

"I'm in the bathroom giving the boys a bath! I'll be out in a few minutes. Just kick Romello and Lucky out the living room and have a seat."

Lucky? Alisha turned around, and there he was coming out of the kitchen carrying a beer. Her pulse began to quicken.

"Well, hey there, stranger," he said with a grin on his face. "I haven't seen you around lately. I've been thinking you've been trying to avoid me."

"Uh—no. I've just been busy."

"How's Craig?"

"He's doing just fine."

Lucky walked over to her and whispered in her ear, "I haven't been able to stop thinking about you ever since that day."

Alisha felt her heart begin to flutter as they stared at each other, his face just inches away from hers. *I've been thinking about you too,* her body screamed.

"Things got a little out of hand that day," she said to him.

Lucky's face moved a little closer. "You were feeling it, though. I could tell."

"I'm happily married, Lucky."

"That's what you keep telling me, but who are you trying to convince, me or yourself?"

"I think I better wait for Jewel outside."

Alisha turned to walk away, but Lucky grabbed her wrist and pulled her into him. "What's wrong? Do I make you nervous?" he whispered softly.

"Why would I be nervous?" she said, unable to control the shakiness in her voice.

"There comes a time when you've gotta be honest with yourself, Alisha. If you feel it, you should just do it," he whispered, breathing heavily on her neck.

The way he said her name made her body quiver. "I—I—I don't feel anything," she stammered.

"Well then, why are you breathing so hard? Why do I feel your body shaking?"

Alisha realized her chest was heaving up and down, and she could feel her pulse pounding in her fingertips. She wanted to move away—she knew that she had to move away, but she couldn't. "Lucky, I'm not sure what you want from me, but you're not gonna get it."

"You know exactly what I want from you, and yes I will get it." He leaned in closer to give her a kiss, but she turned her head away.

"Please let me go so I can leave."

Lucky let go of her wrist, but before she could back away from him, he leaned in to kiss her again, pressing his lips hard against hers.

"Oh shit!" Jewel cried out.

Alisha ran out the house, leaving Lucky standing there with an evil grin on his face. Jewel stood there glaring at him.

"What in the hell were you doing?" she hissed at him.

Lucky shrugged his shoulders. "I was just talking to my neighbor," he replied callously.

Romello came rushing into the house. "What happened?" he asked Jewel.

Lucky started laughing. "Alisha had slipped and I was just helping her up," he answered. "I guess your girl got the wrong idea."

Jewel and Romello exchanged glances. The look on her face told him she had walked in on a lot more than Lucky was willing to reveal.

Chapter 26

"You look like you've lost some weight," Romello said as he watched Jewel change into her nightgown.

Her face lit up. "You can tell?" she asked excitedly as she ran over to the mirror. "My clothes have definitely been fitting a lot looser, but I wasn't gonna say anything; I wanted to see if you would notice."

Romello climbed in the bed. "Well, you're looking good."

Jewel turned to face him. "I am gonna look so good in that wedding dress. I was thinking I could go looking at some next month." She cut off the light and got into the bed. "I'm so excited about the party this weekend. Your friends said they are gonna come, right? Mother already said she'd keep the kids for the weekend."

Romello sighed. "Gino's coming with his girl. I don't know about Lamont and Terrance."

"Did you invite that nice guy Raymond? I think he would be a good guy to introduce to Peaches. He's got a job and he's respectable. I think she needs a guy like that in her life."

Romello did not want to talk about fixing Peaches up with another man, even though he was a little annoyed with her. "You two sure have become buddy-buddy these last couple of weeks."

"Well, now that I'm starting to get to know her a little bit, she really isn't all that bad of a person."

"At least now I won't have to sit and listen to you accusing me of sleeping with her," he said, chuckling.

"Okay, so maybe you didn't sleep with her, but you sure did want to."

Romello kept silent, fearing he would say something to incriminate himself.

"I feel bad for her, though."

"Why's that?"

Jewel rolled over on her side and looked at him. "Underneath all that loud mouth is someone with a heart. I think her problem is that she needs a good man in her life."

She doesn't need a man in her life when she keeps screwing around with Lucky, he wanted to say, but he knew he wouldn't have been able to keep himself from sounding too jealous.

"You've talked to the girl for two weeks, Jewel. Now all of a sudden you know what she needs?"

"I think she's lonely. Whenever I talk about you, it's like she gets this sad look on her face. She may talk all that crap about she don't want a man unless he's got big bucks and can buy her all this material shit, but she's not all that shallow. She wants to be loved. That's why I think your boy Raymond would be perfect."

"Jewel, why do you wanna be with me?" Romello blurted out.

"What kind of question is that?" Jewel chuckled.

"I don't have a job. I have to go out damn near every night to hustle just to get the bills paid. I hear you talking all this stuff about what Peaches needs, but what about you? Don't you need the same?"

"I have that," Jewel said as she rested her head on his chest. "I mean sure, I wish you would go and get a regular job with a regular paycheck, but I know one day it'll happen."

"Well, what if it doesn't? Won't you feel like you've wasted your time?"

"But I love you, Romello, and I know that you love me. Outside of that, I know that everything else will be okay."

"Do you ever think that your life could be better off without me? Maybe I'm not the one you're supposed to spend the rest of your life with."

Jewel lifted her head and looked at him with concern. "Why would you say something like that?"

"I'm just asking a question, that's all."

She rested her head again. "Good night, Romello," she said, not bothering to answer his question.

Her answer would not have made a difference anyway. Romello had already made up his mind that she was not the one for him.

Alisha set Craig's cup of coffee in front of him. "They're sending you on *another* trip? You just took one two weeks ago!"

"I know, honey, but there are a lot of divisions of this company all over the U.S. It's important I get acquainted with the heads of those divisions."

"Well, where are you going this time? When are you leaving?"

"I leave for Salt Lake City on Thursday."

"You're going to Utah?" Alisha said as if he were being shipped off to a third world country.

Craig laughed. "You make it sound like it's the worst place in the world to be. I hear it's pretty nice out there."

"Well, when are you coming back? Friday?"

"I'll be there 'til Monday," Craig replied, bracing himself for Alisha's reaction.

"Monday?" she shrieked. "You're going for a weekend? I've never heard of a damn business trip on a weekend."

Craig shrugged his shoulders. "The fat cats out there want to wine me and dine me."

"But Jewel and Romello's engagement party is this weekend."

"So what, I'm supposed to tell my boss I can't do my job because I have to go to some stupid engagement party?"

Alisha glared at him. "Well, I don't wanna miss the party."

"Why would you miss the party?"

"Well, if you're going somewhere for the weekend then I'm going with you."

"Don't be silly, Alisha. You can't go with me. I am going to be working. I don't want you stuck in the hotel, mad at me because I don't have time to spend with you."

"If you're gonna be wined and dined then I don't see the problem with me going. They can wine and dine me too."

"We're gonna be talking business."

"It's not like you all deal with matters of national security."

"Maybe the next trip." Craig glanced at his watch, then stood up. "I'd better be leaving for work."

Alisha didn't continue to argue the point. She really hadn't wanted to go on the trip anyway; she just wanted to see if Craig would object to taking her.

She watched as he grabbed his briefcase by the door. He came back over to her and tried to give her a kiss, but she moved her head away from him.

"So now you're gonna have an attitude with me?" he asked.

"I don't have an attitude with you."

"Well then, why are you standing there with your arms crossed, pouting like a spoiled brat? Come give me a kiss."

Alisha kissed the air in front of him, then walked back to the bedroom. "Have a great day at work," she said sarcastically.

"I love you, honey." Craig opened the front door and looked outside. He saw Ladona scurrying back to her apartment.

Alisha turned the knob and found Ladona had left her front door unlocked. She stepped into the apartment, but did not see her standing around.

"Ladona, it's me!" she called out. "You left your front door open!"

When she got no response, Alisha slowly crept towards the bedroom. Behind the closed door, she could hear Ladona talking on the phone. Alisha put her ear closer to the door to hear the conversation.

"Is that the only flight you have that leaves out on Friday?" she heard Ladona ask. "No, that one leaves too late. I'll take the morning flight . . . two tickets . . . I'd like to put them on my Visa. . . ."

Alisha covered her mouth to keep from screaming. She slowly backed away from the door about to run out of the apartment when Ladona came out of the room. The two girls screamed at the sight of each other.

"Oh my God!" Ladona gasped.

"I'm sorry, but your door was open. I tried calling but you didn't answer." Alisha fought hard to keep herself from crying.

"Well, I was just on the phone."

Alisha nodded her head. "I know. I think I'm gonna go now."

"But I'm off the phone now, girl."

"Yeah, but I think I need to lie down for a little while. I'm feeling a little light-headed." Alisha quickly turned her face away from Ladona so she could not see the tears that were starting to fall.

"Well, let me walk you back to the apartment," Ladona said.

Alisha waved her hand at her. "I'll be okay," she said, rushing for the door. "I'll just talk to you later."

A giant grin spread across Ladona's face.

Chapter 27

Jewel was not sure what to expect before she walked into Peaches's room. She expected to walk into a sex chamber, with chains and whips all over the place and a swing hanging from the ceiling. However, she was relieved to see her room was as normal as any other normal room, complete with expensive satin sheets and a collection of stuffed animals in the corner.

"I've had those ever since I was a little girl," Peaches said when she saw Jewel staring at them.

"And you kept them all this time?"

Peaches nodded her head and smiled proudly. "Believe it or not, I'm very sentimental. Would you believe I still have the movie ticket stub from my first date when I was thirteen? Don't ask me his name, though. I can never remember guys' names."

Jewel continued looking around, admiring the chalk drawings hanging on the wall. "You drew those?"

Peaches nodded again. "I did those in high school. I don't draw too much anymore, though."

Jewel looked at her. "You're pretty good."

Peaches shrugged her shoulders. "Thanks."

"Look, I hope this doesn't offend you, but your room isn't anything like I expected."

Peaches chuckled. "Well, what were you expecting to find, some guy chained in the corner as my sex slave?"

Jewel laughed. "Something along those lines."

Peaches opened the closet door that revealed the biggest collection of clothes and shoes Jewel had ever laid eyes on. Hanging on hooks on the inside of the door was a collection of wigs Whitney Houston would have envied. They were arranged by color and length. Jewel walked over to admire them.

"I've never seen you in any of these," she said to Peaches.

"I wear those to the club. They're part of my costume," Peaches replied. "Some people wear hats to accessorize an outfit; I wear wigs."

"So each wig has an outfit?"

"And shoes to match." Peaches went into the closet and pulled out an outfit that looked like a few pieces of red and orange material held together by string. "This is my firegirl costume," she said, laughing. "I usually wear it with that long red wig."

"Girl, I could only dream of having the body to fit into something like that." Jewel picked up the wig, then walked over to the mirror. "Mind if I try this one on?"

"Girl, try on anything you like."

"If only I could fit in your clothes." Jewel stood in the mirror putting on the wig, making sure there was no trace of her own jet-black hair showing. "What do you think?" she asked turning to Peaches.

"It actually looks good on you. Have you ever thought about coloring your hair?"

"Romello would have a fit if he saw me like this." Jewel started laughing. "I should wear it to the party tonight to make everyone think I colored my hair."

"We'd look like twins," Peaches said, referring to her own fire-red braids.

Jewel continued primping in the mirror as Peaches went searching through the closet for an outfit. "How about this?" she asked, holding up a cute little tube top dress.

"Now see, I wanna be able to wear cute stuff like that."

"Why don't you?"

"I don't have the body for it."

"There's nothing wrong with your body. You think you're too fat or something?"

"Compared to you I am."

"Well then, stop comparing yourself to me. You aren't fat, though." Peaches threw the outfit on the bed, then went back into the closet to find something else. "What are you wearing tonight?"

"T-shirt and shorts—my usual."

Peaches looked over her shoulder. "Jewel, it's your engagement party! You are supposed to be the sharpest girl there. This is your chance to show all those niggas the good thing Romello's getting ready to take off the market." She pulled out another dress, then held it out to her. "This one will fit you. Honestly, girl, you really aren't that much bigger than me."

Jewel took the dress from her. "Okay, I'll try it on. Where's your bathroom?"

"Bathroom? Girl, just slip into it right here. It's no big deal. We're both girls. You don't have anything I don't have."

"I can't undress in front of you," Jewel said, gasping.

"Well, it's not like I'm gonna be sitting here gawking at you while you try the thing on. Don't you know I get undressed around women every single night? It's really no big deal."

Jewel shifted uncomfortably. "Peaches, can I ask you a personal question?"

Peaches smiled. "I already know what you wanna ask me and the answer is yes."

Jewel looked at her as if she had horns growing out of her head. "Well, how many girls have you been with?"

"I don't know, maybe two or three."

"So you're bisexual?"

Peaches got down on her knees to search through her shoes in her closet. "I'm definitely not bi," she replied. "I love dick too much. A few years ago, I got drunk at a party. There were some girls who approached me and I was curious. But like I said, I was drunk, so that's why I'm not too sure if there were two or three. That's the only time I've been with women."

Peaches finally found the pair of shoes she was looking for, then stood up to face Jewel again. "So are you gonna try the dress on or not?" she asked her.

Jewel took in a deep breath, then went ahead and tried the dress on. She let out a squeal of delight when the sundress fit her just fine.

"I have lost a lot of weight," Jewel said as she admired herself in the mirror.

"New hair, new outfit. Romello won't even know who you are."

"Peaches, I know I've said this to you at least a dozen times over the last couple of weeks, but I really am sorry for being so mean to you these past years."

"Girl, you don't have to apologize."

"But I feel like I do. I feel really bad about it."

"I'm not even trippin' on that, girl."

Jewel looked at her watch. "I've gotta get home and start getting things ready." She took off the wig. "Do you really think I should wear this thing tonight?"

Peaches laughed. "Why not? We'll look like twins!

* * *

"Hey, honey," Craig said, "you missing me yet?"

"Yeah," Alisha said, trying to sound enthusiastic about his call. She took a pause before speaking again, listening for someone else in the room with him. "So how is your trip going so far?"

"It's okay, but I miss you already."

"Well, you wouldn't have to miss me if you had just let me come with you. In fact, why don't you call and reserve a ticket for me? I'm sure there's a red-eye I can catch."

"A ticket on this short of a notice would cost an arm and a leg, Alisha. Like I told you, on my next business trip you can come with me."

Alisha rolled her eyes. "So what are your plans for the evening? You just gonna hang out at the hotel?"

"Actually, I hit it off with a guy at the office out here. He offered to take me to a sports bar for a couple of drinks."

"No picking up women," Alisha warned him.

Craig started laughing. "You'd be embarrassed if I told you just how many times I've pulled your picture out of my wallet, showing you off to all the guys. There's no reason for me to cheat when I have someone as fine as you waiting on me at home."

Alisha wanted to believe what he was saying, but not when she knew Ladona was out there with him.

"Well, I've gotta get dressed for this party," Alisha said, wanting to get him off the phone.

"Baby, are you okay? You sound a little distracted."

"I'm fine."

"Well, do you want me to give you a call when I get back to the room?" Craig asked.

"No, no. I'll just give you a call," Alisha replied, wanting to call him when he'd least expect it.

"I love you, Alisha."

Alisha hung up the phone without saying the same. Her blood began boiling with anger. "Lying sonofabitch," she grumbled under her breath. "They both think they have me so fooled."

Jewel walked into the living room, sporting her new look. "So how do you like it?" she asked Romello.

Romello looked up and nearly choked on the beer he had just swallowed. "You look like Peaches," he snapped at her. "Go take that shit off."

"Why? I think I look pretty good." Jewel walked over to the mirror and started playing with her hair. "I love this color."

Romello looked away, not wanting his facial expression to reveal how he really felt about her new look. He loved it, and for the first time in a long time, he wanted to drag her into the room and pretend like they were in high school—back when he couldn't get enough of her. However, seeing her in that red hair made him think of Peaches; and while Peaches was still the sexiest woman in the world to him, she was also the source of his anger and resentment.

I can't believe she went and had sex with Lucky, Romello thought repeatedly. It had hurt him to see Peaches invite him into the house that night, a few weeks ago. *What in the hell is so special about him? It should have been me.*

"Romello, did you hear a word I just said?" Jewel said as she shook his shoulder.

He looked up at her, not realizing his mind had drifted off. "What?" he snapped at her.

"I asked you if you wanted me to take the outfit off."

Romello got up and went to the kitchen to grab himself another beer. "You do what you want to," he huffed.

"You have had such a shitty attitude these past couple of weeks, Romello. I hope you don't act like this at the party."

"I didn't even wanna have this stupid thing," he mumbled under his breath.

"What did you say?"

Romello sat back down on the couch. "Nothing."

"Well, are you pissed at me about something?"

"No, I'm not pissed at you. You've been asking me that for the past couple of weeks, and for the past couple of weeks I've been telling you the same thing. Nothing is wrong with me. I just wanna be left alone, okay?"

Romello got up from the couch again, then stormed out the front door, leaving Jewel standing in the middle of the room looking confused. She wasn't sure what had just happened, but she refused to let it spoil her night. She was determined to put on a show and let everyone see a happily engaged couple, even if it killed her.

As Romello took a seat on the front porch, he could see some of the neighbors start to straggle over in the direction of the apartment. He let out a long sigh.

Lord, just help me get through this crap tonight.

Chapter 28

Jewel's short invitation list of just a few friends had somehow grown into a small mob of barely recognizable faces that spilled out into the front and backyards. This is what Jewel had wanted, though, walking around from group to group, smiling and laughing, playing the role of the perfect host. This was her moment to shine and show everyone she had finally landed her man. However, while Jewel was busy putting on the performance of a lifetime, Romello's only performance was making cans of malt liquor disappear.

Nestled away in a corner of the backyard by himself, Romello brooded over the idea of being a good man. He knew a good man would never lie and cheat on his woman, and a good man would be able to provide for her the things she needed.

A good man would not give his woman a ring he'd stolen from his lover. A good man would not be sitting here knowing he was in love with someone else.

"Romello!" a familiar voice called out over the chatter of the crowd.

He looked up and saw Jewel standing at the back door waving at him. He waved back and watched as she made her way over to him, stopping briefly to greet well-wishers who wanted to look at her ring.

"I've been looking all over for you," she said when she finally made it to him. "Why are stuck back here all by yourself?"

"I ain't much for socializing today," he said, finishing off his third can of beer.

"Well, we're gonna need some more plastic cups. Can you drive to the store or should I send someone else to go get them?"

Romello shook his head. "I can go," he said, looking forward to getting away from the party for a little while.

Jewel leaned over and gave him a kiss. "I know you're tired of me asking, but are you sure you're okay?"

Romello rose to his feet. "I'm fine," he said, trying not to sound too annoyed with her.

Jewel disappeared back into the crowd to mingle some more. As Romello began working his way towards the back door, he heard Peaches's loud voice laughing and joking with someone in the house. Then, like a scene right out of a movie, with her braids blowing in the wind and a white glow around her while violins played in the background, she appeared in the doorway with a big, bright smile.

"Hey Romello," she said as he approached the doorway.

"Hi," he mumbled under his breath.

Peaches smiled at him. "So what did you think of your girl's new look?"

"You made her into your clone."

His tone of disgust caught Peaches off-guard. "You make it sound like it's such a terrible thing."

"Do you think I want my girl walking around looking like you?"

"Well, I'd think you'd be happy with the way you've run around here trying to have sex with me all this time."

"But it's not like you were willing to gimme any, though. But then maybe I could've got it if I walked around here looking like Lucky."

Peaches shot him a nasty look. "I see you have an attitude problem. What did I do to you?"

"You didn't do anything to me, and I guess that's the problem. The only one you've done anything to is Lucky." Romello went into the house to get his car keys.

Peaches followed him. "Where are you going?"

"I've gotta run to the store for Jewel," Romello said as he walked out the front door to the parking lot.

"Well, what exactly is your problem? Why are you tripping on Lucky?"

"Just leave me alone, Peaches."

"What, you call yourself being mad because I slept with Lucky? Why should you care?"

Romello finally turned around to look at her when he got to his car. "You're right. Why should I care?"

Peaches laughed at him. "You have a lot of nerve trying to cop an attitude with me about who I fuck. In case you haven't noticed, we're here at your damn engagement party."

"You're right. You fuck who you wanna fuck. So what if Lucky or any of those other niggas don't care about you? All that matters is that you're happy, right?" He got into his car and drove away. In his rearview mirror, he could still see Peaches standing there.

Alisha turned her back as she saw Jewel approaching. She hadn't talked to her since the day she'd run out of her kitchen, too embarrassed to face her.

"I wasn't sure if you were coming," she heard Jewel say.

Alisha turned around and smiled nervously. "Well, of course I'd be here," she replied. "Nice turnout."

Jewel nodded her head in agreement. "Where's Craig?"

"Oh, he's out of town on business. He won't be back until Monday."

Jewel's eyes darted around the room, then finally came back to rest on Alisha. "Alisha, about the other morning—" she started out saying.

"It's not what you think, Jewel."

Jewel pulled Alisha away from the crowd. "I saw you kissing him!"

"What you saw was Lucky kissing me. I didn't want him to do it!" Alisha insisted.

Jewel shook her head. "How long have you two had something going on?"

"There's nothing going on between us. Lucky has been coming on to me for weeks. What you saw, that wasn't the first time he'd pulled something like that."

Jewel sighed, not sure whether to believe what she was hearing. In her mind, she asked herself why it even mattered. Lucky was not her man; she was getting married to Romello. She just could not help but feel a little bit of jealousy, wishing she had been the one Lucky locked lips with.

"So where is Ladona?" she asked, wanting to change the subject before her emotions could show on her face and betray her secret. "I thought she said she was gonna be here, but I haven't seen her around."

Alisha lowered her head and mumbled, "I don't know where she is."

Jewel knew Alisha was lying.

Lucky came up behind Peaches and put his arms around her waist.

"It's the funniest thing," he whispered in her ear.

"There's another girl walking around this party who could almost be your twin. You fixin' girls up, starting a legion of redheads?"

Peaches turned around and smiled at him. "That's Jewel. She looks cute, huh?"

Lucky shrugged his shoulders. "Doesn't matter how much weight she loses or what kind of wig she throws on, she'll never be as fine as you."

"My dear, no one can ever be as fine as me, but the least I can do is help a sistah get a little closer to perfection."

Lucky laughed. Her confidence was one of the things he liked most about Peaches. "Have you seen my boy Romello around here? I got some weed I wanna smoke with him."

"Who cares where his ass is," Peaches said with an attitude.

Lucky smirked at her. "You sound upset with him. What's the matter? You tired of him following you around like a little lapdog?"

"I don't know what his problem is. He's just tripping today, that's all."

"The nigga likes you. What do you expect?" Lucky pulled Peaches into his arms. "The man's jealous that I got to pick fruit from the peach tree and he couldn't."

"Lucky, you are a fool," Peaches said, chuckling.

"I'm a horny fool. Let's go into the bathroom right quick and take care of some business. You owe me from that morning on your porch a few weeks ago."

Peaches shook her head. "Boy, you better go to your girlfriend for loving. I told you I'm not trying to get down with you like that anymore."

"And why is that?"

"'Cuz I'm just not."

Peaches tried to push away from him, but Lucky tightened his grip around her waist.

"Now I know you're not gonna pass on a chance to get lucky tonight, are you?" he asked.

Out of a room full of people, Romello managed to spot Lucky with his arms around Peaches. As if his heart could not sink any lower, he heard a thud the moment he watched Lucky lean in and give Peaches a kiss on the lips.

He stomped his way through the crowd of people, then threw the bag of plastic cups on the kitchen table. Peaches caught a glimpse of him as he was walking out the front door.

"Stop it," she told Lucky, pushing him away.

Chapter 29

Romello walked over and tapped Jewel on the shoulder. "I'm back," he whispered in her ear. "I left the cups in the kitchen."

As soon as Jewel turned around and smiled at him, he knew she had managed to get drunk within the hour he had been gone.

"Here's my baby!" Jewel announced to the group of people that surrounded her. She got up from her chair and gave him a big kiss on the lips. "Everybody, I'd just like to say that even though it has taken me nine long years to get this man to do this, I finally got his sexy ass to put this ring on my finger!" She held out her hand for everyone to see the ring.

"So when's the big day?" someone in the group asked.

Romello looked at Jewel, waiting for her to give a response. He didn't think his answer of "never" would have been appropriate.

"We haven't decided yet," Jewel said, giving him another hug. "So far my baby has told me we could plan something for next year."

Romello looked up and saw Peaches watching them

from a distance. He quickly looked away from her and gave Jewel a kiss on the cheek.

"I'm gonna go grab myself a beer," he whispered to her.

"I love you so much, Romello!" Jewel said in a loud, drunken tone before sitting back down to finish entertaining her group of friends.

Romello walked to the backyard to grab a beer from the ice chest. He spotted Lucky and Alisha sitting off by themselves.

That brotha is relentless, Romello chuckled to himself before heading back into the house to hide out in his bedroom.

He sat on the bed and turned on the TV, planning to sit out the rest of the evening in there without being bothered. As he surfed through the channels looking for a good movie, the bedroom door opened.

"Are you decent?" Peaches chuckled as she poked her head through the door.

"What, are you following me around?" Romello said with a nasty tone.

"I was wondering if I could talk to you for a second."

Romello turned his attention back to the TV. "About what?" he asked.

Peaches stepped into the room, gently closing the door behind her. "Well, I was hoping we could talk about what's bothering you. I didn't appreciate the way you snapped on me in the parking lot earlier."

"Ain't nothing bothering me."

"Well, what's all this lip you keep giving me about Lucky? Why are you so worried about what I'm doing with him?"

"Look, I thought we had already discussed this. You do whoever you wanna do. I don't care."

"Well, if you don't care, why are you being such an asshole about this?"

"I saw you and your boy Lucky kissing in the living room a little while ago."

"He kissed me."

"Well, now he's out back with Alisha. You should be keeping a shorter leash on his ass."

"Lucky was acting stupid. I wasn't kissing on him. I still don't see why you keep riding me about Lucky."

"Seems to me you're the one who keeps riding Lucky."

Peaches started laughing. "Lucky was right about you. You're jealous."

Romello cut the TV off, then got up and started for the door. "I ain't got time for this bullshit," he huffed.

Peaches blocked the door with her body. "Aww, poor Romello's mad because I wouldn't have sex with him."

"How can you keep fucking that guy?" he roared, his heart full of anger and hurt. "One day he's running to you, then the next day he's running behind Alisha. What the fuck? Is that the kind of guy you like? I mean, what in the hell is so damn special about him?"

"What do you mean? I don't keep fucking him."

"All that brotha wants is to have sex with you, nothing more. You're nothing more than a piece of ass to him, and you're just all too willing to give it up to him. You don't see he ain't about shit, or is it that you don't care?"

Peaches stared at him blankly. "I know what Lucky is about," she muttered.

"What about that night he came over right after I left? He wasn't coming over there to make sure you were okay. He wasn't concerned about how you were doing or if you felt safe. I know for a fact he was only going over there to try and have sex with you, and you let him in!"

"Just because I let him in my house doesn't mean I had sex with him. Besides, why do you even care if I did? What I do is my own damn business, not yours. You seem to forget you put a ring on Jewel's finger, not mine. I'm not your woman, so if I wanna fuck the entire Dallas Cowboys defensive line, it would still be none of your business."

"You're right. It's none of my business if you wanna run around with guys who don't give a crap about you 'cuz you obviously don't give a crap about yourself."

"You can't sit and talk about me running around with a whole bunch of people. Look at the shit you do!"

Romello moved Peaches from in front of the door, then stormed out of the room.

Alisha looked down and realized she had knocked her drink over. She looked at Lucky and laughed hysterically. "I think I need another drink!" she said to him.

"I think you've had enough already," he told her.

Alisha held up her empty cup. "I know my limits, and I haven't had enough yet."

"What were you drinking?"

"Vodka and fruit punch."

"You should slow down on the vodka. It can sneak up on you sometimes."

Alisha shoved her cup in his hand. "Are you gonna fill me up or not?"

Lucky gave her a wink. "I'd love to fill you up," he said.

The two of them walked into the house.

"So where's your husband? He decided to skip out on the party?"

"He's in Utah on business, or at least that's what he claims. What about you? You didn't bring your girl to the party?"

"Oh, well, you aren't the only one who's with a workaholic."

"I'm sorry to hear that."

Lucky shrugged his shoulders. "It's no big deal. We're gonna hook up tomorrow, and besides, that just means I get to spend the evening getting to know you a little better." Lucky finished fixing the drink, then handed it to Alisha.

"Well, here's to our workaholics," Alisha said, holding her glass up for a toast. "They may have left us lonely tonight, but we still love 'em."

Lucky grinned. "You really should slow down on those."

"I can handle my liquor," Alisha assured him. "In college I could drink the best of those frat boys under the table."

"So you were a wild one in college, huh?"

Alisha leaned in closer as if she was about to reveal a secret. "Beauty, brains, and a high tolerance for alcohol—I was definitely a popular girl."

"But Craig was the lucky one to snag you."

Alisha nodded her head. "I wonder what would've happened if our paths had crossed at Temple."

The two of them went outside to the backyard. Everyone had taken all of the chairs to sit down, so they found a spot of grass where they could sit.

"It wouldn't have taken me a whole year just to notice you," Lucky said, chuckling.

Alisha threw her head back and laughed. "I'm sure the ladies were all over you back then. You wouldn't have noticed me."

"Or maybe you wouldn't have noticed me. Back then, I was going through an experimental phase. You know, going through different looks, hanging with a different crowd. I was not the fine specimen of man you see before you now."

Alisha caught herself looking at Lucky's perfectly defined biceps. "Well, no one can accuse you of being modest."

"I guess not," he said after taking a drink. "Oh well, I

guess it was for the best that we didn't meet up. Things have worked out well for you, right? You and Craig are living the perfect life, and I can't really complain about what I've got."

"Oh sure, up until today everything seemed to be perfect." Alisha took a sip of her drink, then gave Lucky a somber look. "He's cheating on me."

"He is?"

Alisha nodded her head. "He's cheating with Ladona. Can you believe it?"

"Well, what makes you think the man is cheating?"

Alisha threw her hands up in the air. "Look around. Do you see Ladona around anywhere? It just so happens that I overheard her buying their tickets to Utah. Can you believe it? He's got her making the reservations for them!" Alisha took another drink. "I mean really, Lucky. If you were my husband, would you choose her over me?"

"I wouldn't even have to be your husband to make that decision," he replied.

Alisha quickly finished the rest of her drink. "You are such a sweetheart, even if you are a big flirt and you can't keep your hands or lips to yourself. If your girl doesn't already know it, she should feel lucky to have you." Alisha doubled over in laughter. "Did you hear what I said? She should be lucky to have you—lucky to have Lucky."

Lucky shook his head and started laughing too.

This is gonna be too easy, he thought to himself.

"Hey, Alisha, you're about to be empty. Want me to refill that drink for you?" he asked.

Chapter 30

Alisha finished off the last of her drink, then shook her head when Lucky asked if she wanted another one. She knew he was trying to get her drunk, making sure her cup never stayed empty for too long.

"I think I should go on home now," Alisha sighed, as she stood in the doorway watching the dance contest in the backyard. "What time are you leaving to go see your girl tomorrow?"

"Not 'til the afternoon," Lucky answered. "And you shouldn't run off to the house so soon. The night is still young. Who am I gonna hang out with if you go?"

"Didn't I see Peaches around here earlier?"

"I'd rather be around you, though."

"I'm sorry, but I promised Craig I'd give him a call tonight. You can be a gentleman and walk me to my apartment, though."

Lucky smiled. "I'd love to," he said.

"I'm sorry ma'am, there's no answer in that room," the hotel clerk said. "Would you like to leave a message?"

Alisha felt her face hot with anger. "No, that's okay.

Thanks anyway." She hung up the phone, then took a drink from the cup she had brought from the party.

She sat on the couch and waited another thirty minutes before calling Craig's hotel room again. Even after the third try, forty minutes later, there was still no answer in his room.

I bet she's in there with him now, she kept thinking to herself as she paced around the living room.

Just then, there was a knock at the door. Alisha opened it up to find Lucky standing there with a couple of wine coolers.

"No sense in the two of us sitting around being lonely on a Saturday night while our lovers are out there doing God knows what," he said.

Alisha's face lit up with a smile. "If you don't mind listening to me vent my frustrations, then you're welcome to come on in," she said.

"No sitting here being down," Lucky said as he walked in. "We're supposed to do what we can to make each other feel better."

There was something in the way he said it that gave Alisha the chills. In the back of her mind, she knew being there alone with Lucky probably wasn't a good idea, but when she thought of what Craig was doing with Ladona at that very moment, that not-so-good idea didn't matter.

Alisha went over to the stereo to start up a CD. Johnny Gill came blasting through the speakers singing about rubbing somebody the right way. Lucky started laughing.

"I ain't heard that brotha in ages," he said.

"That's my boy." Alisha giggled. "If Craig hadn't come along, I probably would've searched the globe for Johnny."

Lucky laughed as he watched Alisha pop open a wine cooler. "You really can hold your liquor," he said. "I thought I was gonna come up here and find you passed out or something. Instead of Romello, you might have to be my new drinking buddy."

"Craig's not much of a drinker, so I don't drink too much around him. But when I get a chance to drink, I let loose."

"Same here. My baby doesn't drink much either and is always getting on me about my drinking and smoking. It's a drag sometimes, but I can't complain. I'm well taken care of."

Alisha quickly finished off the wine cooler, which was like water to her. She set the bottle down on the table, then grabbed Lucky's hand. "Let's dance," she said, moving around like a wild woman.

Lucky grabbed her by the waist and pulled her into his arms. "I prefer a slower pace," he said.

"But this is a fast song, silly."

Lucky looked deep into Alisha's eyes, holding her face close to his. "Pretend," he whispered softly.

Alisha felt her body tremble in his arms as her heart began to race. The two of them swayed to an imaginary slow song playing in the background. Alisha closed her eyes, feeling warm and secure.

"If your husband is out there with another woman, he's a damn fool," Lucky whispered. "He should be here right now, holding you in his arms, wanting to make love to you all night long."

All Alisha could do was nod her head in agreement. The sound of Lucky's voice and the feel of his warm breath against her ear felt better than anything she could imagine. That was until she felt that first kiss on her neck. Lucky's lips were soft and warm, followed by the wetness of his tongue on her ear. She wanted to stop him, but she couldn't. Every nerve in her body was extra sensitive to his touch. She did not want such a good feeling to go away.

"You are so beautiful," he whispered, as she felt his hands under her shirt, touching her bare skin.

"Lucky," she heard herself moan, tilting her head towards his to receive him for a kiss.

"Alisha, are you sure you wanna do this?" Lucky asked.

"Don't ask me stupid questions," she snapped at him as she worked feverishly to unbutton his shirt.

"Let's go in the bedroom," Lucky said between kisses.

"I want you right here," Alisha moaned.

Lucky had no problem with that as he eased her shirt over her head. "You are so damn beautiful," he said.

Alisha didn't say a word. She didn't want to hold a conversation. All she wanted was to have this man inside her, as if it would make her feel better while thinking that her husband was inside another woman.

"Do you want me to be gentle?" Lucky asked.

Alisha shook her head. "I want it rough," she answered, something Craig wasn't very good with.

"Bitch, I'm about to fuck you 'til you beg for mercy," Lucky whispered in her ear.

Just hearing it made her even more excited. Suddenly Salt Lake City was gone from her mind.

Romello felt more at ease now that most the party had thinned out and had moved out to the front yard. Jewel was still going strong, playing the perfect host. To him, it seemed as if her new identity had made her become more alive.

The party had definitely been more for her than it was for him, something he really did not mind. For Romello, the party was nothing but a sham. The engagement was a sham; moreover, their relationship was a sham. In his heart, he really did love Jewel, but he knew he would always love her since she was the mother of his kids.

Romello sat down on the back porch and lit up a blunt. As soon as he took a few hits, he heard footsteps walking behind him.

"Who's that?" he asked. "Speak up if you wanna hit this shit."

"Sure," he heard Peaches say. She sat down next to him and took the blunt from him, taking a few hits before passing it back.

"I thought you were out front with the rest of the party," Romello said.

"I'm not in much of a partying mood," Peaches replied.

"Look, I'm sorry for saying all that shit to you earlier."

"Which time? You pretty much snapped on me twice tonight."

Romello let out a deep sigh. "I've got a lot of stuff on my mind."

"Like me and Lucky."

"There's other shit too."

"Anything you wanna share?"

"I'm not happy, Peaches. I don't want to be engaged to Jewel. In fact, I don't even want a relationship with Jewel. I'm 'bout ready to just pack up my shit and push the hell on. Don't get me wrong. I love her and I will always love her 'cuz she's the mother of my kids, but that's as far as it goes. I wanna be happy right now and I just don't see myself ever being happy with her."

"You should've thought about that before throwing this party, don't you think? And I don't even understand why you would even bother to give her a ring if you don't want to be with her."

"Okay, okay. I am a dumb-ass for all that, but how in the hell am I just supposed to tell her I don't wanna be with her no more?" Romello held his head in his hands.

"And then there's you. I keep thinking about you, trying to figure out what you think is so special about Lucky. Is it his car? Do you think he has money? Everything he has is because of his girl."

Peaches sat back and smiled. "The brotha looks good."

Romello looked up at her as if she was crazy. "That's all it is? 'Cuz he looks good? Are you really that shallow?"

"Am I that shallow? What about you?"

Romello shook his head. "We ain't talking about me."

"I know, 'cuz if we were, we'd be talking about how much of a hypocrite you are."

"Well, maybe I've seen the error of my ways. Maybe I'm not looking to run around with all these different women."

"And what miracle came along to bring about this new and improved Romello?" Peaches asked sarcastically.

"You," Romello said softly.

Peaches didn't say a word.

Romello turned his body towards her. "Look, I may not have the expensive cars or the flashy clothes or money just falling outta my pockets, but I think I could be a good man for you. All the other women, I am willing to give 'em up. A steady job—I will get it. I will do what I have to do to 'cuz I wanna be with you, and I don't just mean sleep with you. I wanna be able to call you my girl."

Peaches stood up. "I've gotta go to the bathroom," she said.

"Well, damn. Don't you at least have something to say about something I said?"

"What exactly do you want me to say, Romello?"

"I don't know. Anything would be better than nothing."

"Okay, well let me say that I am not gonna be a home wrecker. You say you don't wanna be with Jewel, but giving her an engagement ring was kinda backwards, don't you think?"

Romello stood up and grabbed her hand. "This whole engagement thing is a bunch of bullshit, and I've told you that before. If you said the word, I would leave her for you in a heartbeat."

"So you want me to say we can go running off together, like it's no big deal? Like I said, I ain't no home wrecker."

"But you do wanna be with me, right? You've been feeling what I'm feeling, haven't you?"

Peaches looked away from him. "No," she said in almost a whisper so she would not have to hear her own lie. She turned and went into the apartment.

Feeling as though she had just shattered his heart in a thousand pieces, Romello sat there continuing to smoke his blunt. When he finally finished, he jumped up, marched to the bathroom, and knocked on the door. He still had more to say.

"Someone's in here," Peaches called out from behind the door.

"Peaches, was I wrong for telling you all that shit?" Romello asked her.

The bathroom door opened. There stood Peaches, her face wet with tears. Romello walked in and closed the door behind himself.

"You weren't wrong, you were just saying how you feel," she said just before walking up on him and smothering him with a kiss.

Whether it was emotion or hormones, something took over to embrace them in each other's passion. This was going to be their moment.

Romello easily slipped out of his shorts, then picked Peaches up and wrapped her legs around his waist.

"We shouldn't be doing this in here," she moaned in his ear as she felt him ease himself inside her.

Romello held her steady as he made slow, deliberate strokes, concentrating hard to keep himself from exploding right then.

"Oh, you feel so good," Romello moaned. With each stroke, it was getting harder and harder to control things.

Peaches let out a soft moan to let him know he was hitting all the right spots.

"Open your eyes," Romello told her. When Peaches opened her eyes, he gave her a kiss on the lips. "I love you," he whispered.

He could feel Peaches tighten around him, as if hearing that excited her even more. In his ear, she begged for it harder and faster.

"I don't wanna be with Jewel. I wanna be with you," Romello grunted in her ear. "We can make this work. Tell me you wanna make this work."

Peaches moaned, "I do!"

As they continued enjoying their moment of passion, they both heard a man's voice yelling from outside in front of the apartment.

Jewel sat in the lawn chair with her back to the parking lot, talking with a group of friends she had known since high school.

"No one ever thought that asshole would finally put a ring on your finger," one of her friends said.

Jewel held up her hand to admire her ring once again. "To be honest with you, I never thought so either," she said. "I really do love him, though. No matter what he has done or said in the past, I love him and I know he loves me."

As she talked, William walked up to the apartment unnoticed. To everyone around, he was just another well-wisher from the complex coming to pay his respects and grab a drink. Therefore, no one thought anything of it as he made a beeline to the redhead sitting in the lawn chair until he raised his arm and revealed a handgun that was loaded and cocked.

"Peaches, I want my money, you bitch!" he yelled out before firing three rounds at Jewel.

She never saw it coming. She never knew what hit her.

If it hadn't been for that wig . . .

Chapter 31

"What the hell was that?" Peaches asked.

Romello rushed to pull up his shorts. He looked at Peaches, and they both knew those three explosions sounded nothing like fireworks. Someone was out there shooting.

Before running out to the porch, Romello went to the bedroom and grabbed his gun from under the bed. Once outside, he ran over to his friends, who had someone wrestled to the ground.

"What's going on out here? Who is that nigga on the ground?" Romello came out yelling.

Gino got up from the ground and put Romello in a bear hug. "Come on, Ro. Let's just walk over to your car," he said as he started pushing him towards the parking lot.

"Wait a minute, Gino. Just hold the fuck up. What in the hell is going on, man? Who's out here shooting? Where's Jewel?"

"Look, Ro, I don't even know who that nigga is. He just came outta nowhere shooting. You don't wanna see the shit, Ro. It's bad. It's really bad."

Romello turned around and saw a group of people standing around someone slumped over in one of the lawn chairs. "Jewel!" he screamed as soon as he recognized the blue sundress. He tried running back towards her, but Gino was bigger and stronger.

"You don't wanna see that shit, Ro. She's gone. That nigga smoked her."

Romello looked at the guy who was on the ground and saw that it was William. That's when he realized that Jewel had been mistaken for Peaches.

"I'm 'bout to kill that nigga!" Romello growled.

Everyone could hear the sound of sirens coming in the distance. Gino wrenched the gun out of Romello's hand. "The cops are coming, man. You can't be waving that piece around like that."

The two of them went back over to William and stomped him until the police came to take him away.

Peaches stood on the porch watching everything.

"Those were gunshots!" Lucky jumped out of the bed, then hurried to the living room to grab his pants from the floor.

Alisha sat up in the bed, her head swimming from all the alcohol. "Black folks can't do anything without some kind of violence jumping off," she mumbled under her breath.

She was in no rush to get out of bed to see what was going on. Hearing all the screaming and yelling downstairs, she figured that one of Romello's ignorant friends from the hood was trying to be cute, firing his gun into the air.

She continued to sit there, cursing them for having ruined what had so far been one of the most intense sexual experiences of her life. This was not how she'd wanted the night to end for them. She had expected to fall asleep in his arms, and then wake up to coffee at the first sign of dawn.

"Alisha!" she heard Lucky call to her. He appeared in the doorway with a troubled look on his face.

"Did you see what's going on down there?" she asked him.

"You might wanna get dressed and come out there. Somebody just shot Jewel."

Lucky disappeared again, leaving Alisha to scramble around the dark room for her robe. By the time she made it downstairs to the party, the police and paramedics were swarming the area.

Alisha found Peaches standing on the front porch looking horrified. She walked over and put her arm around Peaches for comfort.

"Peaches, what happened?" Alisha asked.

Peaches just shook her head. "He thought she was me," she said before finally breaking down.

"Let me see her! I wanna see her!" Romello was yelling.

By now, a few officers had stepped in to hold him back from where the paramedics were covering Jewel's body.

"Hey! You're gonna have to calm down!" one of the officers ordered him. "We're gonna need to get a statement from you. What went on here?"

"We were having an engagement party. I was in the apartment when I heard the shots." Romello broke down and started crying again.

Alisha watched as Peaches stepped off the porch and made her way over to Romello. She reached out her arms to comfort him, but he stared at her with so much hate and contempt.

"He thought she was you!" Romello yelled at her. "If you hadn't given her that damn wig she'd still be here!"

Peaches took a step back and gave him a confused look. "But it's not my fault, Romello," she said softly.

Romello continued to struggle to get away from everyone so he could see Jewel. "Let me go! I wanna see her!"

Peaches tried to comfort him again, this time reaching out to hold his hand.

"Get away from me!" he lashed out at her.

Lucky came over and put his arm around Peaches's shoulder, then led her away. "Peaches, why don't you go on back to your apartment? Romello is going through a thing, right now. You should just let him be," he whispered to her.

"But it wasn't my fault, Lucky," Peaches started raving. "I didn't do anything wrong! Why is he blaming me?"

"He's just upset. He knows you didn't do anything."

Alisha ran off the front porch and joined Peaches and Lucky. Peaches turned to her and started crying even harder.

"Alisha, it's not my fault. You understand it's not my fault, right?"

Alisha nodded her head. "I know, girl."

The three of them stood in silence as they watched Romello screaming like a madman, still trying to make it over to Jewel's body.

Peaches finally turned away, unable to watch Romello in so much pain.

Chapter 32

"Mama Rivera, why don't you go have a seat? I'll take care of these dishes later. You should be out there with the family," Romello insisted as he led Jewel's mother out of the kitchen.

Mrs. Rivera looked at him with annoyance. "You were never Mr. Helpful when my Jewel was alive," she snapped at him, going against the promise she had made to herself to be civil with the man she faulted for her daughter's death.

It may not have been Romello who had pulled that trigger, but she was sure that he had a fault in it somehow. Part of her felt that if her daughter had just listened to her and left Romello years ago, she would still be alive.

Romello smiled politely at his almost-mother-in-law, not wanting to cause a scene in front of all the guests gathered in his living room. Even though it had not been said, everyone in the room knew Mrs. Rivera blamed him for Jewel's death. In his own mind, he felt as if maybe he did play a part in it.

If I had been out there, maybe I could've prevented it from happening, he had told himself over and over since that night. *If I hadn't been in the bathroom with Peaches, maybe she'd still be here. I would've seen him and stopped him.*

One of Jewel's relatives came over to give Mrs. Rivera a hug. "It was such a lovely funeral," she told her, pausing to acknowledge Romello's presence with a slight nod.

Mrs. Rivera wiped a tear from her cheek. "I never thought I'd have to bury my own child," she sighed. "I kept telling her to get away from here, though. I just knew there was nothing but mess going on around here."

Romello continued to smile, even though he felt both women's evil stare burning through him. As if on cue, Alisha came over and gave him a hug, then turned to Mrs. Rivera and offered her condolences.

"I just wanted to come over and say how sorry I am about all this," Alisha said to the both of them. "Jewel was such a sweet girl."

Romello nodded his head in agreement. "She didn't deserve this."

"Did you get you some of the enchiladas?" Mrs. Rivera asked her. "They were Jewel's favorite. Romello, why don't you go fix her a plate?"

Happy that he finally had an excuse to get away from her damning stare, Romello turned to walk back to the kitchen.

"You really don't have to fix me a plate," Alisha said. "I don't want to put you through the trouble."

"It's no trouble," he said. "I'm just glad to get out of that room with all her family staring me down like I was the one who shot her."

From the kitchen, the two of them could hear the sudden silence that fell over the small crowd in the living room. Alisha went to see what was going on and saw Peaches standing just inside the front door.

"Peaches is here," she said to Romello.

He glanced over his shoulder to look at Peaches. Instantly he felt sorry for her as she made her way through the room of Jewel's relatives' stares.

"I can't believe she had the nerve to show up," Romello heard one of the relatives say.

Looking more conservative than she ever had before, in a simple black dress that was more material than skin, Peaches walked toward the kitchen carrying a foil-covered dish. Alisha gave her a hug, then excused herself from the room.

"I hope you don't mind me coming by to pay my respects," Peaches said in a soft voice.

Romello couldn't bring himself to look at her. "I don't mind," he replied.

Peaches walked over to him and set her dish on the counter. "I figured I should bring something," she said, pulling back the foil to reveal a bowl of cherry gelatin.

Romello smiled. "You went all out on the cooking, huh?"

Peaches laughed nervously. "Well, cooking isn't exactly one of my better talents," she said. "Besides, I didn't wanna slave over a hot-ass stove to make something, only to be turned away at the front door."

Romello finally looked up at her. "I didn't see you at the funeral," he said.

Peaches held her head down in shame. "I wanted to go, but—"

Romello cut her off. "I understand."

"You blame me, don't you?"

Romello looked over his shoulder to see if anyone was watching them, then turned back to Peaches. "Look, we haven't really had a chance to talk since that night. I know I had said some crazy shit to you and I really am sorry about that. I was just upset. You understand, don't ya?"

Peaches nodded her head. "I understand," she replied.

Romello reached over and touched her hand. "So how have you been?" he asked.

Peaches shrugged her shoulders. "I've been okay. How about you?"

"Well, to be honest, I can't wait to get her family out of here. They all keep looking at me like I ain't shit."

Peaches chuckled. "I experienced a little bit of that when I walked in the door. Do they know about us? I mean, do they know we were together?"

"Jewel told her mother about you, that's all."

"Romello, that whole thing that went on in the bathroom. Are we supposed to forget it ever happened or what?"

"Peaches, I can't even think about that now."

"Romello, what are you—" Mrs. Rivera's sentence was cut short at the sight of seeing Peaches and Romello standing there.

"Mama Rivera, this is my neighbor. She came by to drop off some dessert."

Mrs. Rivera walked over and extended her hand to Peaches. "It was nice of you to come."

After a brief moment of awkward silence, Peaches leaned over and gave Romello a kiss on the cheek. He wished Peaches had not done that because out the corner of his eye, he could see a look of disgust come over Mrs. Rivera's face.

"I should be going," Peaches said. "Call me if you need anything," she said to Romello before walking out the kitchen.

Romello quickly turned his back to Mrs. Rivera, hoping she would not have a thing to say.

"*Aye dios miyo!*" Mrs. Rivera exclaimed just before letting out a long string of obscenities spoken in Spanish. "Jewel told me all about your tramp neighbor. How dare you parade your filthy whore around here in front of my family."

"She's not a whore, Mama Rivera," Romello said calmly.

"I saw how you were looking at that girl, with lust in your eyes. My baby hasn't even been in the ground two hours and already you're in here undressing her with your eyeballs."

With his back still to her, Romello was able to hide the grin on his face. The thought of Peaches undressed had not crossed his mind until she had said something about it, but he quickly shook his head to get rid of that thought. He needed to be concentrating on Jewel's memory, not Peaches.

"I wasn't undressing her with anything. She came to drop off the dessert," he replied, pointing towards the bowl Peaches had left behind.

Mrs. Rivera came over and looked in the bowl. "Jell-O?" She snickered. "She couldn't do any better than that?"

"Not everyone one can be a great cook, Mama."

"Well, I suppose her cooking wasn't why you were creeping around with her anyway. You had my baby to be your cook and your maid. That black bitch was just your whore."

Romello turned around and glared at her. All day he had blown off all her smart remarks, but he refused to listen to them anymore, especially in his own house.

"She is not a whore, and don't start with me, Mama."

Lucky came up behind Alisha and slid his arms around her waist. "Where's your husband?" he whispered in her ear.

Alisha quickly moved away from him, looking around to make sure no one had noticed. "He went to the bathroom," she snapped at him. "You can't be walking up on me like that, Lucky. What if my husband had seen you?"

"The risk of it all makes it even better." Lucky reached out to grab Alisha's hand but she quickly moved it away.

"Look, Lucky, the other night was nice, but that's all it was. One nice night."

"You say that as if you wouldn't want another nice night . . . or another day."

The expression on Lucky's face sent a chill throughout her body. Even though her mind was telling her he was a thrill she needed to leave alone, her body was screaming to be touched by him again.

"Lucky, I'm a married woman. I'm not going to leave my husband."

Lucky leaned in closer to whisper in her ear. Alisha felt the warmth of his breath on her skin and wanted to melt.

"I never said anything about you leaving your husband. Don't forget that I'm in a relationship too. I have no intention of leaving my boo. I know what I like, though. There's no reason we can't share with each other."

"Share?" Alisha gasped.

Lucky brushed his hand against her sleeveless arm and gave her a seductive smile that almost made her want to sneak him into one of the bedrooms.

"I want what your husband has," he whispered softly in her ear.

"It's too risky. We live in the same apartment building. Sooner or later someone would see something and start talking."

"So what if people talk? I think you're worth the risk, though."

As soon as Alisha opened her mouth to respond, she spotted Craig walking out of the bathroom, then stopping to speak with one of Jewel's family members. She breathed a sigh of relief that he had not seen her standing a little too close for comfort with Lucky, but she knew it was time for their conversation to end.

"We should talk later," Alisha said.

Lucky nodded his head. "We should do more than talk."

Alisha looked up at him one last time. She wished he wasn't so damn good-looking. She wished he did not have those inviting, deep brown eyes and those irresistible dimples. Deciding she finally needed to tear herself away, she turned to disappear in the crowd, but Lucky reached out and touched her arm again.

Alisha stopped walking, and without even looking back in his direction, she nodded her head and said softly, "I'll come by later."

Lucky smiled proudly as he watched her walk off into the crowd again. In the opposite direction, he saw Craig walking around, and that made him smile even harder. For him, it was all about the thrill of the chase.

Craig planted a kiss on Alisha's cheek. "Hey, baby," he said, "you doing okay?"

Alisha nodded her head, though still a little flushed from her conversation with Lucky. "I'm fine," she sighed.

"Well, it looks like people are starting to clear out. Are you about ready to go on home?" he asked.

Alisha thought of Lucky. "Umm . . . I was gonna hang around here and help Romello clean up. You don't mind, do you?"

Craig smiled. "My sweet Alisha," he said, chuckling. "I swear when you die you should be a saint."

If you only knew, Alisha thought to herself as she caught a glimpse of Lucky leaving out the front door.

"You go on without me," Alisha urged her husband, walking him towards the front door.

"If there are any leftovers of those enchiladas, can you bring some up? I swear they are the best."

Alisha impatiently nodded her head. "Sure, baby," she replied.

She gave Craig a quick kiss on the lips, then nearly shoved him out the front door, eager to get him out of the way so she could get to Lucky.

"You two look so sweet together," Alisha heard someone behind her say.

Alisha turned around and saw Mrs. Rivera standing there with a smile on her face.

"Thank you," she told her. "How are you holding up?"

Mrs. Rivera shrugged her shoulders. "As good as any parent who just buried her child."

Alisha gave her a hug. "Well, if there's anything I can do for you, you just let me know. If you need me to stay behind and clean up, I will."

Mrs. Rivera shook her head and said, "No, no. Romello is an able-bodied young man. He can clean up when all the guests leave. Besides, he and I have some things to discuss when everyone is gone. You go on home to that husband of yours. Jewel told me how good he is to you. I wish she had found someone as nice as him."

Her words seemed to erase all the excitement and anxiety Alisha was feeling. It was as if Mrs. Rivera was acting as her conscience; Alisha did not like that.

Yes, Craig is a good man, but Lucky is just damn good, she thought to herself, bringing a smile to her own face.

"Well, I can see you're anxious to get to him," Mrs. Rivera said. "You go on now. Be sure to thank your husband for coming."

Alisha gave her a hug, then quickly dashed out the front door. Like a schoolgirl late for class, she rushed to Lucky's apartment, not wanting to be marked tardy.

From the kitchen window, Ladona watched her, shaking her head. "Now just where in the hell is Little Miss Perfect running off to?" she spoke aloud to herself. *Her apartment is upstairs. . . .*

Chapter 33

"Damn, baby. I like the way you say hello," Lucky said with amusement as he watched Alisha slip out of her dress inside the front door.

Alisha smiled. "No time for small talk," she said with seriousness in her voice. "You want it. I want it. Let's do this."

Without giving him a chance to respond, she was all over him, smothering him with kisses, pressing her half-naked body against his. Lucky definitely wanted it, and it excited him that Alisha was so anxious and willing to give. Deciding that he would let her take control of the situation, he obediently followed as she led him to the couch and pushed him down.

"I like this," he mumbled as he slid out of his pants while watching her come out the rest of her clothes.

"We haven't even gotten to the best part yet." Alisha smirked as she straddled him, slowly easing him into her body.

She closed her eyes and began stroking him, unaware of him sitting there, smiling at her in amusement. While thoughts of how good it felt raced through her mind, Lucky could only think of how good it felt to be him. His life was filled with beautiful women. He had proven to himself that he could have any woman he wanted and that he could make them desire him as much as they did their own lives.

Alisha was by far his most prized conquest, though. Not only was she beautiful and smart, but he had been able to snag Mr. Perfect's wife. The thought of having Craig walk in and see his wife riding him like a jockey excited Lucky even more. He thrust himself into Alisha even harder, making her cry out in passion.

"Oh yes!" Alisha moaned.

Get louder, baby, Lucky thought in his head. *Let the entire complex hear you. Scream until that husband of yours comes knocking.*

As if she could read his mind, Alisha's moans grew louder; Lucky became even more excited, but he paced himself, wanting to climax with her. He knew that would drive her crazy. She would think of him as being sensitive and want to come back for more. For Lucky, it was all about keeping her coming back. He did not want to take Alisha away from her man. He just wanted to know he had that kind of pull.

Lucky finally rested his head back and closed his eyes, ready to enjoy Alisha's enthusiasm. He felt her walls tighten around him as her breathing and moans became louder and heavier.

"Come on, girl," he grunted. "Come on!"

"Yes!" Alisha screamed as she felt a fiery explosion go off within her body.

At the same time, Lucky released himself. He opened his eyes and looked at Alisha in wonder. "You give it to your husband like this all the time?" he asked.

Alisha rested her head on his shoulder. "Don't talk about him right now," she mumbled.

Just then, the phone rang. Alisha insisted he let it

go to voice mail, but Lucky reached over and picked it up anyway.

"Hey, baby," he said into the receiver with a big smile spreading across his face. "I wasn't doing anything but sitting around watching TV . . . well, you know I would love to see you. You have some time to get away? Well, why don't we meet in an hour . . . okay . . . love you too."

Lucky hung up the phone.

"So was that your girl?" Alisha asked.

He nodded his head. "We've got a lunch date."

"But we aren't finished."

"I'm sorry, but I'll have to take a rain check. You know how it is when your honey calls." Lucky stood up, then slipped his boxers on.

Alisha folded her arms across her chest and pouted like a little girl. "Well, you could have told her you were busy."

"If that had been Craig, would you have told him you were busy?"

Without any hesitation, Alisha nodded her head and responded, "Yes."

Lucky smiled to himself. *Gotcha!*

Romello ushered the last few guests out the front door. He was tired of the hugs and condolences. He just wanted time to himself. He wanted to lie on the couch with a couple of beers and a bag of weed, then sleep the next few days away.

From the kitchen, he could hear footsteps. He cringed, knowing he was alone with Jewel's mother. Bracing himself for what he was sure would be more insults, he took in a deep breath, then let it out slowly.

Mrs. Rivera stepped out of the kitchen. "I thank you for

having everyone come over here," she said. "My house is just so cramped with all the remodeling going on."

Romello nodded his head. "It was no problem," he replied.

"And I wanna thank you for letting the kids stay at the house with me this past week."

Romello nodded his head again. "I figured it would be too much for them to be around here."

Mrs. Rivera walked toward the couch and looked as if she was about to take a seat. Instead, she turned back to Romello and gave him a nervous smile.

"My husband and I have been talking. We think it'd be best if the kids stayed with us on a permanent basis."

"Well, you don't have to do that."

Mrs. Rivera cut him off, waving her hand in protest. "I'm not really asking your permission. I'm just letting you know what the plan is," she said sternly. "Let's be real, Romello. How in the world are you going to manage taking care of three young children? You don't have a job. How in the hell are you gonna afford to even keep this apartment?"

"I've been doing a damn good job of it these past two years. Your daughter was never homeless."

Mrs. Rivera nodded her head in agreement. "Maybe so, but I still don't think you can take care of those kids the way they need to be taken care of." She finally sat down on the couch with a smug look on her face. "Now, I'm not saying I'd cut the kids out of your life forever. You'd be more than welcome to come visit them and take them for the weekends."

"They are my kids, Mama."

"And that's why you'd be welcome at my house at anytime to spend time with them. I just think my husband and I can offer them the love and stability they need right now. They just lost their mother, for heaven's sake."

"And I just lost my girl. She was practically my wife."

Mrs. Rivera snickered. "Oh spare me the loving and concerned act, Romello. You are a terrible actor. You should look at this as a blessing. You'll be able to continue running after your whores without having to be tied down with three kids."

"I don't need you doing me any favors."

"Well, you may not need a favor, but I'm giving you one anyway." Mrs. Rivera started for the front door. "Don't try and fight me on this, Romello. My grandkids are better off with me. Any judge in the country would agree with me on that one. The kids love you. I would not want to have to paint the picture of the unfit, womanizing, drug-addicted sonofabitch you really are. When I get done with you, you'd be lucky if the judge even allowed you to carry their pictures in your wallet."

"Why do you hate me so much?"

Mrs. Rivera laughed. "Because you ruined my baby's life," she replied coldly. "You may not have been the one that shot her, but you had killed her a long time ago. My baby had potential to be something great and make something of her life. All you did was keep her knocked up, living as your damn maid while you ran around with all these different women."

"Your daughter had a choice. I didn't make her stay."

"She loved you, Romello. She was so sure you would change. You don't love anybody but yourself, though. That's why the kids will stay with me."

"I'm not gonna let you stand here and talk this shit in my own damn house, woman. I've been respectful to you, letting you dog me out all day, but not anymore."

Mrs. Rivera shrugged her shoulders and muttered something in Spanish, then started laughing. "Now you wanna talk to me like you're a man. I told you, you aren't a very good actor."

Romello watched her walk out the front door without saying another word to her. He didn't know what else to say because he knew there was nothing else he could say that would make any difference to her. She had his kids, and as much as he hated to admit it, she could provide a better home for them.

Hustling and sleeping around had been the only way he had managed to pay for the apartment and keep food in the refrigerator. He knew he could not have raised three kids still trying to do that.

Romello walked to the front door and was just about to close it when Peaches walked in.

"I was waiting until she left," she said to Romello. "I don't think she liked me very much."

Romello didn't respond. He walked over to the couch and sat down.

Peaches took a seat next to him. "You okay?" she asked.

Romello shook his head, trying to get out the naughty images that had crept into his mind about Peaches. Gone was her conservative black dress. She was back to her normal attire, leaving not much to the imagination. Any other time, Romello would have been all over her, anxious to get to what was underneath such a pretty wrapper. He just could not bring himself to do it, though. Her sexiness was not enough to tear him from the more pressing issues he had going on.

"That woman hates my guts," Romello said, trying not to look at Peaches.

She put her arm around his shoulder to comfort him. "It'll be okay," she whispered.

"I need to find a job, Peaches. It's about time I grew up and took some responsibilities like a grown man."

Peaches chuckled. "Damn! What did that woman say to you?"

"She's keeping the kids. She doesn't think I can handle raising them."

Romello paused, expecting to hear Peaches come to his defense, but when she said nothing, he finally turned to her with a look of hurt and anger in his eyes.

"You agree with her, or something?" he said, gasping.

Peaches shrugged her shoulders. "Well, I'm sorry, Romello. What do you want me to say?"

"Well, you could say that she is wrong. Say that the kids would be just fine right here with me."

Peaches gave him a look of disbelief. "Now do you honestly believe that? You don't have a job. You smoke weed like you need it to live."

Romello jumped up from the couch. "Fuck you," he snapped at her. "You can take that shit somewhere else."

Peaches got up and went over to him, throwing her arms around him. "I don't mean to hurt your feelings, Romello. I think her taking the kids is a good idea until you can get yourself together." Peaches gave him a peck on the lips. "They don't have to be with her forever."

As Peaches pressed her body against his, Romello felt himself getting excited. Despite how mad he was, the softness of her body soothed him. As if he had lost control of his own body, he found his hands rubbing all over her body as his mouth sought the caress of her tongue.

This isn't right, he thought to himself. *We just buried Jewel. It isn't right.*

While his mind was protesting, his body was aching for more of Peaches.

"Peaches, we shouldn't be doing this," he moaned softly as he felt her hands ease down into the front of his pants.

"You need this," Peaches moaned back.

"Romello, I need to get some of the kids' things." Mrs.

Rivera burst into the front door, then let out a shrill cry. *"Dios miyo! Dios miyo!"* she cried out repeatedly.

Peaches and Romello quickly pulled apart, both embarrassed and ashamed. Even though she couldn't understand much Spanish, Peaches knew exactly what *puta* meant, as Mrs. Rivera paced around the living room, ranting and raving in a Spanish-obscenity tirade.

"Hijo de puta!" she kept screaming as she waved her fist at the two of them. "*Bastardos!* You and your nasty *puta!*"

"I'm gonna go," Peaches said to Romello.

"My baby's not even cold in the ground!" Peaches heard the angry woman rant as she walked back to her apartment.

"I should have locked that damn door," Peaches said, chuckling under her breath, feeling sorry for the hysterics she had left Romello in.

One Month Later

Chapter 34

As Romello parked his car, he saw Peaches peeking out of her kitchen window. He knew that she was waiting for him to get home. Part of him felt relieved, but another part of him was not ready for a confrontation. He had done his best to avoid seeing her for the past month. Mama Rivera had worked him over to the point that he felt guilty just thinking about Peaches, or any other woman for that matter.

His heart wanted her, and even more, his body wanted her, but there was so much guilt. If it had not been for Peaches and that stupid wig, Jewel would still be alive. And even though he knew he would've left Jewel by now, he hadn't wanted her dead. He had not wanted to be in the bathroom enjoying another woman while Jewel sat outside having her life taken by some crazy man.

Romello sat in the car and watched as Peaches's front door opened. His heart began to race as he watched her step outside looking as sexy as ever.

Damn. Why does she have to look so damn good? he asked himself, wishing that she'd gained weight or done something else to let herself go over the past month. Deep down, he knew a few extra pounds on her would not have made a difference to him, though—not the way it made a difference with Jewel. He would have still wanted Peaches all the same. For that, he felt even more guilt.

Peaches walked out to his car and tapped on the window. Romello unlocked the door and Peaches jumped into the passenger seat.

She smells so good, Romello thought in his head as he tried not to look at her. There was just too much flesh to ignore, though. His eyes slowly moved up from her thighs to her face.

She smiled at him. "It's been hard catching up with you," she said.

Romello sighed. "I've been busy working," he replied. "Working a legit job takes a lot out of a brotha."

Peaches nodded her head as if she understood, but she knew work was not the only reason he had been so hard to catch. "Have you been doing okay?" she asked him. "You haven't been returning any of my calls, and I guess you're asleep whenever I knock on the door."

Romello chuckled. "I'm sorry. I've been meaning to get back to you."

"It's almost like you've been avoiding me."

"I'm sorry, Peaches. I've just been busy."

Peaches leaned over and rested her head on his shoulder. "Well, at least we've finally made contact," she sighed. "I've missed talking to you."

Romello agreed. He had definitely missed talking to her as well. "I'm real sorry about what went down that day with Jewel's mother."

"Don't sweat it. I have had people say worse. Besides, she had a right to be upset. We were in there like a couple of dogs in heat. The dust hadn't even settled on her grave."

Romello cringed. "You make it sound so morbid."

"I'm sorry."

Romello shifted in his seat uneasily. His pants seemed to be getting tighter as he felt her hand caressing his.

"Well, I need to get inside and get a shower," he said, chuckling. "I probably smell like dirt and sweat."

"You smell like a hardworking man," Peaches replied. "I don't mind at all, unless you want me to come in and wash your back for you."

Romello shifted again, but there was no way of getting his pants any looser. He needed a cold shower immediately.

"Uh . . . not tonight. I'm pretty tired."

"Romello, we need to sit down and have a talk."

"A talk about what?"

Peaches rolled her eyes at him. "Don't sit there and try to act like you don't know. We need to talk about us and our future."

"What future?"

"Whether or not we're gonna be together. All that stuff you were saying to me that night in the bathroom. You were serious, right? You wanna be with me, and I wanna be with you."

Romello held his head down and spoke in a soft voice. "I don't know," he answered.

"What do you mean you don't know?"

Romello shrugged his shoulders. "I just don't know anymore. Right now, I just need to concentrate on getting my life together. I would like to have my kids back one day."

Peaches sat up straight and looked at him in shock. "You blame me for what happened, don't you?"

"No, no. I don't blame you."

Peaches folded her arms across her chest. "Yes, you do. If I hadn't given her that damn wig, she'd still be here, right?"

That is exactly how Romello felt, but he didn't want to

admit it. He cared a lot about her and did not want to run the risk of hurting her any more than he had.

"It was just a freak accident," he tried reassuring her, but Peaches was not buying it.

Peaches sat back and closed her eyes. "Well, I think that sometimes," she admitted. "I feel bad, like there was something I could've done to prevent it, but at the same time I keep thinking that I'm glad I was in that bathroom. It could've been my funeral."

Romello sighed. "I have a lot of guilt too," he was willing to admit. "If we hadn't been in that bathroom I might have been able to save her, though. If I had just insisted she take off that stupid wig, she'd still be here."

Peaches looked puzzled. "You didn't want to be with her anyway. You said you wanted to be with me."

"Well, now I don't know anymore."

"You don't know?" Peaches shrieked. "While you had your dick up inside me you were pretty sure about what you wanted. Why the change now? So what, you got you some and now you don't wanna be bothered?"

Romello shook his head. "That's not it, Peaches. You just have no idea what I'm going through right now."

Peaches reached for the door handle to get out of the car, but Romello grabbed her arm to stop her.

"Let me go!" she barked at him.

Romello didn't want to let her go. He didn't want her to be mad at him or think that he didn't care about her. He did the only thing he could think to do. He leaned over and gave her a kiss, something he knew would be like asking for trouble. He wanted to put some distance between them while he got his head straight, but a kiss was only going to bridge the gap even more.

Peaches responded back with her warm, sensuous lips, making it harder for him to pull away. Before he knew it, they were in each other's arms. Peaches's shirt had somehow managed to end up in the backseat while Romello's pants were undone.

"I want you," Peaches moaned in his ear.

Romello could not answer. He could only respond with a nod as he felt Peaches lean forward and take him into her mouth.

"Oh, Peaches," he moaned as he stroked her hair, feeling both pleasure and guilt at the same time.

Peaches sat up again. Romello opened his eyes and saw her smiling at him.

"Why did you stop?" he said, trying to catch his breath.

"Because I just wanted to make sure that you did want me. Now I'm convinced that you do. So when you're able to cut some time out for me in your busy schedule, you'll know exactly what I've got waiting for you." Peaches reached in the backseat and grabbed her shirt.

Romello started laughing. "Uh-uh. Don't do this to me, Peaches. You can't just leave me hanging."

"You've left me hanging for the past month."

"It's not on purpose, though. You know I'm going through some shit, girl."

"Good night, Romello." Peaches got out and started walking back to her apartment.

It killed her to leave him like that. It killed her to leave herself hanging like that, but she felt she needed to do something to wake Romello up a little. There was nothing stopping the two of them from being together anymore. Even with all the guilt the two of them had between them, she was certain they could work everything out.

Back in the car, Romello fixed himself, then got out and went into his apartment. As bad as he wanted to go after Peaches, he figured it was best if he just left it alone.

* * *

With a beer in his hand, he sat down on the couch, propping his feet up on the coffee table. Even after a month, it still felt strange coming home to an empty apartment. There were no kids running around and no smell of dinner warming in the oven. He missed Jewel more than he was willing to admit, but as he tried to push all thoughts of her out of his head, his mind kept creeping back to Peaches.

This was the perfect time for the two of them to be together. He was a bachelor again. No kids, no nagging girlfriend—he could be with the girl he was in love with, with no problems. It just was not that easy for him, though.

Romello heard a knock at the door. "Come on in! The door's unlocked!" he called out, too tired to get up.

Peaches walked in carrying a plate of food. "I figured you might be too tired to fix yourself something to eat, so I thought I'd bring something over for you," she said.

Romello looked up and started to laugh. "It's not a plate of Jell-O, is it?"

Peaches smiled as she walked over and revealed a roast beef sandwich. "Oh, come on. I can do a little more than that."

She sat down next to him and handed him the plate. Romello took a bite of the sandwich and nodded.

"Not bad," he said.

"It's pretty hard to fuck up cold cuts. Hope you aren't too sore with me for leaving you like that."

Romello set the plate on the coffee table, then sat back, putting his arm around her and pulling her closer.

"It wouldn't be the first time you left me hanging like that."

Peaches rested her head on his shoulder. "Mind if I sit here with you for a while?"

"I'm not gonna be much for conversation."

"We don't have to talk," she replied. "We can just watch some TV. I'd like the company."

Romello closed his eyes and smiled. "Me too," he sighed.

Craig opened the front door, pausing to look back at Alisha, who was too busy reading her magazine to notice him.

Over the past few weeks, she always seemed to be preoccupied. The days of her fawning over him seemed to be long gone. He could not help but wonder if he needed to do be doing more to hold her attention.

"I'm getting ready to leave for work," Craig announced.

Alisha did not look up or even seem to care. "Okay, dear," she replied. "Have a nice day."

"Well, aren't you gonna at least give me a hug or a kiss to send me off?" he asked.

Alisha seemed to force a smile. "You don't really need me to do that every morning, do you?" she asked, still not looking up and noticing that what she said had hurt his feelings.

"But I like it when you do that," Craig whined.

Alisha set her magazine down on the table, then walked over to him and gave him a kiss on the cheek. "Have a wonderful day at work, my sweet," she said, faking her enthusiasm.

That was enough to make Craig feel a little better. "Alisha, is there something going on that I should know about?"

"What do you mean?"

Craig closed the front door again. "Well, you seem so cold and distant lately. For the past month or so you've been acting like you don't want to be bothered with me."

Alisha waved him off with her hand as she went back

to the table to sit down again. "Don't be silly, Craig. Of course, I want to be bothered with you. You're my husband."

"Well, you don't meet me at the door when I come home. You don't see me off with a kiss. It's like you don't care anymore."

"I'm still trying to get over the fact that Jewel is gone. For something like that to happen around here to someone I knew pretty well is a little jolting, Craig."

Craig nodded his head, feeling guilty for voicing what he now thought were childish concerns. "I'm sorry to even come at you like that," he sighed.

Alisha smiled, then went back to reading her magazine. "It's okay, honey. Just give me some time. I'll get over it," she replied. "Anyway, shouldn't you be heading off to work now? I wouldn't want you to be late."

"Screw work." Craig set his briefcase on the floor, then walked over to Alisha. "I tell you what. Why don't I call off from work today? We can ride out to the lake and rent a boat. Getting out in the sun might do you some good."

Craig was certain that Alisha wouldn't resist an afternoon out on the lake, but to his surprise, she looked up from her magazine and shook her head.

"I'm sorry, baby, but I have so many errands to run today. I've been putting them off for so long that I can't put them off any longer." She went back to reading her magazine.

Craig snatched the magazine out of her hands. "It's a little annoying trying to talk to you while you have your nose stuck in that damn thing."

Alisha sucked her teeth. "What do you want, Craig? I told you I'm not going to be able to hang out with you today. Besides, you shouldn't blow off work. Every time you blow off work, you end up having to put in even more overtime. You know I can't stand it when you have to work late."

"It seems like you don't wanna do too much with me these days. Do you have a problem with me?"

"I don't have a problem with you, honey." Alisha stood up and gave her husband a kiss, then went into the kitchen to pour herself some coffee. "I don't know, maybe we can do something on Friday."

"Sure. Friday," Craig grumbled in frustration. Before walking out the door, he reached down and picked up his briefcase. "Want me to call you later?" he asked.

Alisha smiled pleasantly. "I'll be in and out most of the day, but you can reach me on my cell phone."

Craig turned and walked out, slamming the front door behind him. She waited until she heard his footsteps going down the stairs, then rushed to the window to watch him pull off in his truck.

As soon as he was out of sight, she rushed to the phone and dialed Lucky's number. Her heart fluttered at the sound of his seductive baritone voice saying hello. "I swear, I thought that man would never leave," she sighed into the phone. "I'll be down there in about another hour or so, unless you wanted to come up here."

Lucky wanted to kick himself for not having checked the caller ID before answering.

The novelty of being with Alisha had since worn off. There was no longer that thrill of being with another man's wife, disrupting his perfect world. He felt as if he had created a monster, with Alisha wanting to be with him more than she wanted her own husband. He had toyed with the idea of telling her to back off, but he figured that would cause more trouble than it was worth.

Instead, he humored her, offering up his body to the sex-crazed woman just to keep peace in his own life.

"Good morning, sexy," he said to her. "Actually, I'm not

gonna be able to see you today. I made plans with my baby. It's such a nice day, we're gonna go hang out at the beach."

"The beach?" Alisha mumbled.

"Why not? The weather's nice. We can lay in the sand for a couple of hours."

"Sounds lovely," Alisha said, her voice dripping with sarcasm.

She and Lucky made small talk for a little longer, then finally said their good-byes. Alisha hung up and immediately called Craig to let him know she'd had a change of heart. After two tries, she gave up, realizing he was probably too upset with her to answer his cell phone.

Asshole, she mumbled under her breath as she went back to the couch to watch TV. She didn't know whether to be more upset with Lucky or Craig at this point. All she knew was that her daily afternoon rendezvous was going to have to be put on hold because Lucky wanted to be with his girlfriend.

Alisha laughed at herself for actually getting jealous over Lucky wanting to be with his girlfriend, but she couldn't help but wish she could be his only one.

Craig looked at the display and saw his home number appear again. Ignoring her, he went back to talking.

"That was her again, but I'm not answering. All I wanna do is spend the afternoon with you on the boat. It's been a while since we've spent some quality time together. Not since Salt Lake . . ."

Ladona giggled with delight into the phone. "This is such short notice, but I'd love to go. I can't even tell you the last time I've been out to the lake. What time do you want me to meet you there?"

Chapter 35

Ladona stepped out of the apartment feeling like a million bucks, or at least three hundred and fifty, which is what she had spent on her hair, nails, and outfit so that she could look this good.

Peaches looked across the courtyard and started laughing. "Holy mother of God . . . is that Ladona?" she asked Alisha as the two of them sat on her front porch.

Alisha looked up to see Ladona slowing walking down the stairs, using the rail as a way to steady herself in three-inch heels. In all the time she had known Ladona, this was the first time she had ever seen her look this nice. Even on the many dates she'd set up for her, Ladona's look would always have something that was a little off. Tonight, however, she had herself all together, looking like she was fresh from the salon.

Alisha rose to her feet, feeling a wave of anger come over her. Here Ladona was looking like she was ready for the date of her life, and Craig was working late again.

Peaches and Alisha waved for Ladona to come over. They watched as the new and improved Ladona strutted her way across the complex to them.

"Where are you going dressed like that?" Peaches asked.

"I have a date," Ladona announced, then twirled around to model her new outfit. "Do I look okay?"

"I am loving that outfit," Peaches said, "even if it is a little too conservative for my taste. Girl, who knew you had legs like that? You should come down to the club on amateur night!"

Ladona started laughing as she turned to Alisha for her approval.

"I've never seen you get all fancied up like this for a date. I thought you were into the casual, all-natural look," Alisha said, being spiteful.

"I figured that it might be time for me to make a change." Ladona stroked her freshly permed hair. "Can you believe I actually got a perm? No more press and curl for me."

"Well, you look really nice," Peaches said.

"Who's the guy?" Alisha wanted to know. She couldn't wait to hear the name Ladona was going to make up this time.

"I'm going out with John."

"Is he the same guy from a month ago?" Alisha said with sarcasm.

Ladona nodded her head. "We've been hitting it off really well. Tonight he says he's got something special he wants to ask me."

"Well, how come you haven't brought this John person around so we could meet him? Why don't we ever hear you talk about him that much?" Alisha inquired.

Peaches nudged Alisha on the arm. "Damn. What is with the first degree, girl? Just tell Ladona to have a good night so she can be on her way to her date with John."

"I didn't wanna talk about him too much in case things didn't work out," Ladona offered as an explanation.

Peaches waved her hand. "Girl, you don't have to explain anything to Alisha. She is just being silly. You go on and have a nice evening." Peaches shot Alisha an evil look.

Alisha was hardly finished talking, though. "But you run off to Vegas to spend a weekend with a man you hardly even know, without saying anything to your friends? He could have been a murderer or a rapist. Where did you say you met him?"

She could have gone on and on with the interrogation, but Peaches nudged her again.

Ladona smiled. "Well, you will definitely hear all about him tomorrow, but right now I've gotta get going so I'm not late." Ladona started walking away but then stopped to look back at Peaches again. "Girl, how do you dance in shoes this high, let alone walk in them?"

Peaches laughed. "It just takes practice, honey. You should have got yourself two-inches or something. Save the big heels for the professionals."

Ladona giggled as she went on to her car. Alisha turned to Peaches and shot her an angry look.

"You know she was lying, right?" Alisha hissed at her.

"Lying about what? Having a date?" Peaches said, chuckling.

Alisha nodded her head. "That girl doesn't have a date. She is about to go meet my husband somewhere. It seems like damn near every time he works late, she's running off to go meet with some made-up brotha named John. How unoriginal is that?"

Peaches shrugged her shoulders. "You still think she's messing with Craig? I thought you had investigated that shit already, nipped it in the bud."

Alisha rose to her feet and pulled her keys out of her pocket. "I haven't had proof, but tonight I'm gonna get it. You're coming with me, right?"

"Coming with you where?"

"I'm gonna follow her." Alisha turned around and saw that Ladona was still struggling to make it to her car.

"Girl, I'm going to work tonight."

"I need someone to go with me. I don't wanna do this by myself."

Peaches really did need to go to the club to make some money. For the past month, she hadn't been going that often; she was too depressed over what had happened to Jewel. However, at the same time, she hated the idea of missing out on some drama, especially since it was happening to someone else.

"I'll go. Just let me lock up my house."

Alisha turned around and saw that Ladona was almost to her car. "Well, hurry up! She's about to leave."

Just as Ladona was getting into her car, Peaches and Alisha started heading for the parking lot.

"I can't believe we're actually gonna follow this girl," Peaches said. "And have you thought about what you're gonna do or say if you do see her with Craig?"

"No matter what happens, my lawyer will plead justifiable homicide," Alisha said as she got into the car.

Alisha followed Ladona's car into the hotel parking lot, then found a spot as far away from the front door as she could get without losing sight of Ladona. She cut off the engine, then sat and waited to see what would happen next.

"She's at the hotel," Alisha sighed. "What kind of date would you meet at a hotel?"

"I hear there's a five-star restaurant here, though. Would you believe William would always talk about taking me here? As if I would actually be seen on a date with him!" Peaches chuckled under her breath. "I'm surprised Craig hasn't brought you here. You two seem to do all that other fancy, lovey-dovey shit."

Alisha kept her eyes glued to the front entrance. "We'd talked about coming here, but just never got around to it."

"Girl, do you honestly think Craig is cheating on you? If you ask me, I think you are just being paranoid. For Christ's sake, the man is in love with you."

Alisha sighed and looked at Peaches. "Well, would you say that I was in love with him?" she asked.

"You two are so in love with each other it's sickening."

"How would you feel if I told you I'd slept with another man?" Alisha didn't know why she wanted to reveal this to Peaches but she was dying to tell somebody about what was going on with her and Lucky.

Peaches laughed. "Yeah, right. *You* slept with another man? The world must be coming to an end."

"I was with another man the night of Jewel and Romello's party." Alisha turned back to the front entrance of the hotel.

"Who the hell would you have slept with? Everyone there knows how you and Craig are. No one would have been—" Peaches slapped Alisha on the arm as she started laughing hysterically. "You didn't! Please tell me you didn't sleep with Lucky!"

"Craig was in Salt Lake City. I'd overheard Ladona on the phone making flight reservations for them. I was angry. I was drunk."

Peaches sat back and stared out the window towards the front entrance. The initial humor of it had passed away; she now felt a little bit of jealousy. After a few moments of silence, Alisha turned to her.

"You aren't upset about it, are you?" Alisha asked. "I didn't think that you and Lucky were serious."

Peaches looked at Alisha. "I'm just shocked."

"Why?"

"Well, you come across as this sweet and innocent, naive person," Peaches said, chuckling. "You know that feeling you got when you found out there really was no Santa Claus or that there is no such thing as a tooth fairy?"

Alisha nodded her head.

"Well, that's kinda how I feel. It's like finding out that the one person you thought was perfect really isn't."

Perfect? Alisha said in her head.

Peaches turned and looked out her window again. "There she is! I see her walking towards the entrance!"

"Come on." Alisha unlocked the doors, then started getting out of the car.

"Where are you going?" Peaches asked.

"Well, we've gotta go in there. I'm telling you, I am gonna find out what's going on once and for all."

"So you're just gonna march in there and make a scene?"

"I'll decide that when I get in there." Alisha got out and started walking towards the front entrance, but stopped when she saw a man approach Ladona and give her a hug.

"That damn sure isn't Craig," she heard Peaches say.

Alisha shook her head, feeling both relieved and disappointed. She watched as Ladona and the man stood there talking. After a few minutes, arm in arm, the two of them walked into the hotel's restaurant entrance.

Peaches started laughing. "I can't believe the girl went white on us!"

Alisha turned around and got back into her car.

"Ladona's got her a white boy named John!" Peaches started laughing again.

"I feel so stupid," Alisha mumbled as she stared out the window.

"Girl, you should feel relieved. At least now, you know that Craig's not cheating. You should be happy!"

Alisha shook her head. "It doesn't make any sense, though. I heard her making plans to go out of town. She was making travel arrangements to go to Utah. I heard it as plain as I hear myself talking right now."

"Girl, let's go home. Craig's not here."

Alisha pulled out her cell phone and dialed Craig's work number, but no one answered. She then tried him on his cell phone. Again, no one answered.

"He's not answering either phone," Alisha said.

"Well, there are a thousand reasons why he's not answering, but one thing is for sure: he's not here with Ladona."

"Well, then where the hell is he?"

The ride back to the apartment complex was silent.

Not only was Alisha trying to figure out what was going on with Craig and Ladona, but what Peaches had said was weighing heavily on her mind too.

"So are you still gonna go into work tonight?" Alisha asked as she pulled her car into her parking space.

Peaches looked toward Romello's apartment and saw that he had made it home. "No. I'll probably just stay up and watch some TV or something. You can come hang out if you want."

"I see you looking over at his apartment. What's going on with you and Romello?"

Peaches shrugged her shoulders. "Nothing, girl. I guess you could say we're just friends."

"Just friends, my ass. I have seen the way you two look at each other. And now that he's got himself a decent, legitimate job, he's a damn good catch."

Peaches shook her head. "We're just friends," she repeated.

Alisha reached over and touched her hand. "If you

feel any guilt about what happened to Jewel, you shouldn't. You didn't do anything wrong."

Peaches turned to Alisha. "You don't know why I feel guilty, do you?"

"It's because of the wig, right?

Peaches shook her head. "That's not it." She took in a deep breath then let it out slowly as she said, "Romello and I had sex."

"So he finally wore you down or was it sympathy sex?"

"It happened the night of the party. Romello and I were in the apartment—in the bathroom—when it happened."

Alisha's jaw dropped open. "Oh," was all she could say.

"I keep thinking what would've happened if we hadn't been in there together. That probably would've been me laying there dead." Peaches shook her head. "Romello was in there telling me how he didn't want to be with Jewel anymore. The next thing you know, I'm kissing him and then it happened. We heard the shots, then came running out."

"Wow," Alisha said.

Peaches continued talking. "Ain't it funny the way life is sometimes? I mean one minute, I'm telling Romello we can't be together because he has Jewel and the kids, and that I don't wanna be a home wrecker. The next minute some guy comes along and takes her life. Was this a sign from God that we were supposed to be together?"

Suddenly, her problems with Craig did not seem so important anymore. Alisha realized Peaches was going through something way more tragic and life-changing. She leaned over and gave Peaches a hug, searching for the right words to tell her.

"You'd think he'd be all over me, insisting that we be together, right?" Peaches shook her head. "The boy will barely even talk to me. I try to come at him, but all he does is shut me out. He says he doesn't, but I think he blames me for what happened."

"Well, damn, Peaches, the man just lost his wife. Try to be a little more understanding. I'd hope Craig wouldn't be ready to hop in another woman's bed the moment I die." Alisha stopped to laugh at herself. "What am I saying? He's already in another woman's bed and I'm still alive!"

"She wasn't his wife. They weren't married."

"Nine years is a long-ass time. You might as well say they were common-law."

Peaches rolled her eyes. "Thanks a lot for trying to cheer me up."

"I'm sorry, girl."

"Yeah, well it's not like he wanted to be with her anymore. He was talking about leaving her for me."

"I had always figured you had a thing for him. Even though you would talk mess to him, I just got this vibe that you were kinda feeling him. So what, are you in love with him?"

Peaches ignored her question. "Do you think I'm bad for what I did, though? Was it wrong for me to have been in that bathroom with Romello?"

Alisha laughed. "Who am I to judge what's wrong or right? While you were in the bathroom with him, I was in my marital bed with Lucky."

Peaches started laughing too. "He was good, wasn't he?"

Alisha started blushing. "He is awesome!"

"What do you mean, he *is* awesome? You've been with him more than once?"

Alisha didn't have to answer. Her grin was enough to give her away.

Peaches shook her head. "Ain't that some shit," she said with a chuckle. "You're a lot naughtier than anyone ever imagined."

"You have to swear you won't tell anybody, though."

"Girl, I won't say a word."

Alisha started giggling. "I guess that means we have something in common. We both got Lucky, huh?"

Peaches started laughing again. "We have more than that in common. We're both some badass girls. He is one fine-ass man, though. He'd make a nun wanna do wrong."

"*Fine* isn't even the word for him."

"Would you leave him for Craig?"

Alisha looked at her as if she was losing her mind, but that was a question she had to pause and think about. "No," she finally answered, not sure if she could believe that herself.

Just then, there was a knock on Alisha's back window. Both girls turned around and saw Craig standing there waving at them.

"Well, I guess I'll see you later." Peaches got out of the car and started walking back to her apartment.

Alisha got out; Craig came over and gave her a kiss. "What were you two up to?" he asked her.

"We just made a quick run to the store, that's all. Where were you? I'd tried calling you on your cell phone."

Craig put his arm around her shoulder as they started walking back to the apartment. "Bad reception," he replied.

Chapter 36

"Is that you, Ladona?" Lucky said as he saw her coming from the parking lot.

"Good evening, Lucky," she said back.

Lucky stepped down off his porch and started walking towards her.

"I've had a very good night, Lucky. The last thing I need is for you to come over here harassing me about some foolishness."

Lucky looked Ladona over and started nodding his head. "You look nice. Had you a hot date tonight?"

"As a matter of fact I did."

"You finally work your magic on Craig?"

Ladona rolled her eyes at him. "I don't know why you insist on pushing me on that man."

"Well, see! All you needed was a little fixing up. You've gone and got you a man now. Does this mean you're gonna leave Craig alone?"

"Why do you keep worrying about what I'm doing? What are you doing about Alisha, or have you finally realized you don't have a snowball's chance in hell with that one?"

Lucky started grinning. "Hell has frozen over, my dear, 'cuz this snowball had a chance."

Ladona started walking towards the stairs. "What in the hell are you talking about?"

"Let's just say they don't call me Lucky for nothing."

Ladona looked at him suspiciously. "Yeah, right. You're just wishing aloud."

"She's a wild one," Lucky said, "wanting me to pull her hair and talk dirty to her. Would you believe Miss Sweet and Innocent likes it rough?"

"So what? Why are you telling me this?"

"Well, I was just wondering . . . how does the schoolteacher like it?"

"You'll never find out." Ladona marched halfway up the stairs, then turned back to look at him once again. "Did you really have sex with Alisha?" she asked, walking back down the stairs.

Lucky nodded his head. "We've been sneaking around for the past month. I'm getting a little tired of it, though. I'm looking for some fresh meat. Know what I mean?"

"I know what you mean," she said, feeling good to have Lucky finally look at her as if she was desirable. "You have a girlfriend who does all this wonderful stuff for you, but you still insist on sleeping around with anything that walks. Why is that?"

Lucky shrugged his shoulders and chuckled. "Maybe I'm just starved for attention. Maybe it's the fact that women are like potato chips—you can never have just one. So, are you in a rush to get home, or do you have time to join me on the porch for a drink?"

"What do you have?"

"A little gin to make you sin." Lucky put his hand on her thigh.

"I guess I can have one drink."

She gave Lucky her hand and let him lead her back to his apartment.

Alisha rolled over and looked at the alarm clock, surprised to have still felt Craig in the bed beside her.

"Craig, you overslept the alarm. You're late for work," she told him.

"I'm not going in this morning," he said.

Damn, she thought to herself. She had planned to spend a few hours with Lucky today.

"Why aren't you going in?"

"Because I wanna spend the day with my beautiful and sexy wife. Is that okay with you?"

Alisha got out of the bed and headed for the bathroom. "Fine by me," she mumbled under her breath.

As she stood in the mirror preparing to brush her teeth, Craig walked in. "What is wrong with you?" he asked her.

"Nothing's wrong with me. What's wrong with you?"

"You've been so damn cranky with me lately. It's like you can't stand for me to be around you or something."

"I think you're just imagining things."

"Why is it that when I tried to touch you last night, you nearly bit my head off?"

"I didn't feel like having sex. I swear, sometimes you treat me as if I'm some piece of meat, as if I should just be ready to open my legs anytime you're ready to get between them. Well, it's not like that anymore. It's my body and I'll have sex when I'm ready."

Craig threw up his hands in frustration. "You just took the shit to a whole different level," he said as he walked out of the bathroom.

Alisha started brushing her teeth. As soon as the minty taste hit her tongue, she dashed over to the toilet to spit it out. Craig rushed back into the bathroom when he heard her gagging.

"You okay?" he asked.

"Damn it, I'm fine," she snapped back at him.

Craig walked back out to the bedroom.

Alisha went back to the mirror and continued brushing her teeth, her mind working on how she could slip away from the house to go see Lucky.

"Hurry up and get dressed. I wanna take you out for breakfast this morning. I have a taste for biscuits and gravy," she heard Craig tell her.

The thought of food made Alisha's stomach turn. She quickly got down on her knees, leaning over the toilet again.

Craig walked back into the bathroom, then helped her to her feet. "You should lie down," he said.

Alisha wiped the toothpaste from her mouth and nodded her head. "You're right," she said. "I really do need to lie down for a little while."

"You're not pregnant, are you?" he asked.

Alisha looked at him with a smirk on her face. "What if I am?" she asked.

She saw what looked like a flicker of anger and fear in Craig's eyes. She thought he was going to tell her how much he was not ready to be a father, but instead he just leaned over and gave her a peck on the forehead.

"I'm gonna go fix myself something to eat. Do you want me to get you something? Some water? How about some toast? Maybe you just need to put something in your stomach."

Alisha shook her head. "I'm not hungry," she said. "Don't look so worried. I'll be fine."

As soon as Craig disappeared out of the room, Alisha picked up the phone and dialed Lucky's number.

"Craig is staying home today. I don't think I'll be able

to get away to see you," she said as soon as she heard him answer the phone.

On the other end, Alisha could hear another woman's voice in the background.

"Well, that's cool," Lucky replied.

"Who's that in the background? Is your girl there with you?"

"Actually, that's Ladona. She was just leaving."

"Ladona? What the hell is she doing there?"

Lucky chuckled. "She was nice enough to have a drink with me last night. I didn't want her going home in her condition, so she spent the night."

"She lives just above you!" Alisha hissed into the phone. "You could've let that bitch walk."

"That wouldn't have been polite of me. I would've felt horrible if something had happened to her."

"You didn't have sex with her, did you?"

Lucky started laughing. "Baby, I don't like to kiss and tell."

Alisha heard Craig's footsteps walking toward the room. "Hold on. Craig's coming." She quickly hid the phone under the pillow just before Craig appeared in the doorway.

"I have to run to the store and pick up some milk, honey. Are you sure you don't want me to get you anything?"

Alisha shook her head. "No, no. I'll be fine."

As soon as Craig left, she put the phone back to her ear. "Hello?" she said, but there was silence on the other end of the line. Lucky had hung up already.

Alisha got up, then rushed to the kitchen window just in time to see Ladona walking up the stairs to her apartment, wearing the same clothes she'd had on the night before.

"What are you looking for?" Craig asked.

Alisha turned around, startled, not having noticed him sitting at the kitchen table.

"Looks like Ladona got lucky last night," she sighed, trying to hide her disappointment.

Craig shrugged his shoulders. "Is it that big of a deal that you had to go rushing to the window to see her?"

"She was with the new guy downstairs."

"He certainly does get around." Craig looked at her suspiciously. "He hasn't tried to put the moves on you, has he?"

Alisha shook her head. "Of course not," she said, turning to look back out the window. "He knows how much I love you."

"Guys like that don't make any sense to me. It's like he has something to prove, running around here sleeping with all these women."

Alisha nodded her head in agreement, even though she hadn't heard a word her husband had said. The only thing on her mind was trying to figure out why Lucky would want to be with Ladona when he had her.

Romello came out on the front porch and handed Lucky a beer. He was so relieved to have a day off so he could sit back and enjoy a blunt along with his malt liquor breakfast.

"I saw Ladona creeping outta your place this morning," he said to Lucky as he sat back down.

Lucky started grinning. "Yeah, that's another notch on the headboard."

Romello shook his head in wonder. "Damn, man. I thought I was the man, but you are working your way through the complex and ain't none of these females trying to snatch each other's weaves out over it."

Lucky smiled with pride. "They don't call me Lucky for nothing."

"You plan on tagging every piece here in the complex, bro?"

"Naw. I just got with Ladona 'cuz I could tell she was feeling a little left out. Actually, I'm done messing around. I pretty much got the one I wanted. The other ones were just to keep me entertained."

"Who did you really want?"

Lucky started laughing. "Little Miss Perfect."

Romello nearly choked on his beer as he started to laugh. "You got with Alisha? Bro, you gotta be bullshitting me. How in the hell did you manage that shit?"

"I told you, Lucky is *lucky*."

Romello hit the blunt and started laughing like a madman. "You have got to tell me how it was!"

"I just wanted to find out why Craig is so wrapped up in that pretty little piece of tail, and now I know. The girl is wild. Think porno star."

Romello hit the blunt again, then passed it to Lucky. "Damn, bro," he said in awe. "So you been hitting it on the regular, or was it a onetime thing?"

Lucky passed the blunt, then took a long swallow of his beer. "She pops over as soon as his ass leaves for work."

"Bro, you're messing with all these women, but what about your girl?"

"My baby is my baby. Ain't no other woman's sex better. I'm telling ya, man, I'm just doing this for kicks. Just to prove that I can. It don't mean a thing. At the end of the day, I know where home is. I swear I ain't gonna mess that up."

"You got her whipped too, huh?"

Lucky shrugged his shoulders. "That's right."

"Hey, bro, you ain't still trying to mess with Peaches, are you?"

Lucky inhaled, then let out the smoke slowly. "She's your piece now, right? I wouldn't do no bogus shit like that to you. I know you got feelings for her."

Romello took a drink of his beer, still looking at him with suspicion. "What about my girl Jewel? You ain't never tried to come at her, did you?"

As much as Lucky wanted to tell him the truth, just to see the look of shock on his face, he did not want to lose a good drinking and smoking buddy.

"I wouldn't do no shit like that to you," he replied.

Romello nodded his head. "Well, I just thought I'd ask since you running around here passing out ya dick like it's candy."

"I understand, man. I'd probably ask the same thing about you. You my boy, though. I respect yours more than that. That's why I wouldn't even think about trying to holla at Peaches."

"Thanks, bro."

"How you holding up with the whole Jewel thing, anyway? I can't believe my man came back like that. It's fucked up."

"I'm doing all right, bro," Romello sighed, not wanting to admit that every day he beat himself up over all the things he could have done differently.

A grin spread across Lucky's face when he saw Peaches step out onto her porch.

"Well, look who we just talked up," Lucky said.

Romello looked up and saw her step outside to grab her newspaper, wearing nothing more than a lace bodysuit. While he had always been amazed at some of the sexy things she'd wear to bed, it annoyed him that she would step outside like that. Especially now that she knew how he felt about her.

"That girl is just too much," Lucky mumbled at Romello.

"Don't even think about it, bro. You shouldn't be looking so hard."

Lucky started laughing. "My bad, man."

As Peaches turned to go back inside, she noticed the two men sitting on the porch watching her.

"Hey, Romello. Hey Lucky," she said, greeting them with a wave.

Romello excused himself, then walked over to talk to Peaches.

"What are you doing coming outside like that?" he asked her.

Peaches looked at him with a smirk. "Coming outside like what? This is what I wore to bed."

"Well, don't you think you need to cover up a little? Lucky is out here. He doesn't need to see you like this."

Peaches leaned in closer, amused by his jealousy. "Sweetie, Lucky has seen me in a lot less than this. It's no big deal. Besides, you come stomping over here talking to me like you my man or something."

Romello followed Peaches into her apartment, closing the door behind him so their conversation could not be heard. "All I'm saying is that you shouldn't be stepping outside like this. It ain't right."

"You like it though, don't you?" Peaches taunted him.

"That's not the point, Peaches."

"You're right. The point is that you have a lot of nerve coming over here trying to tell me what I should and should not have on. You walk around here blowing me off every chance you get, but then you wanna act like you my man and keep other niggas from looking at me. You can't have it both ways, Romello."

"Well, you know you kinda like my girl. People around here already know I'm feeling something for you."

"I'm kinda your girl? That is the stupidest shit I have

ever heard. Either I'm your girl or I'm not. There ain't no in between."

"I've told you I need time to get my head straight, Peaches."

"Oh . . . and I'm supposed to sit around until you get it right? I don't think so."

Romello gritted his teeth in frustration. Peaches was as stubborn as a mule, but that was one of the things he found so attractive about her. "Look," he hissed at her, "I'd appreciate it if you didn't come outside looking like that anymore. Don't put yourself on display anymore."

"What's the difference? These men can come down to the club and see me in this and less if they wanted to."

"That's some really fucked-up shit to say to me, Peaches."

Peaches walked over and put her arms around his waist. "Besides, if you want the item taken off display, then you'd better buy it."

Romello gave her a kiss on the lips. "I'm asking you nicely, Peaches."

"Get it before somebody else does," Peaches said coldly.

Romello stormed out of the house, then went back to the porch with Lucky.

Lucky started laughing. "Damn, man! You all right? She got you hot around the collar, huh?"

"I tell ya, bro, that girl drives me crazy," Romello grumbled.

Lucky looked back over at Peaches's apartment and started grinning. "Yeah, man. These damn women will do that to ya."

Chapter 37

Feverishly, Alisha looked around the bedroom, trying to find Craig's ringing cell phone. It seemed more and more that he had become clumsy about dropping things without realizing it. Just the week before, his wallet had slipped out of his pocket somehow. He hadn't even known he was missing it until she called and told him that she had found it under the kitchen table.

This morning, his cell phone had found its way underneath the bed. Alisha bent down to pick it up and saw a number she did not recognize. Not that she would recognize any of the numbers popping up on his phone. He had so many business contacts that she could not keep up. She decided to answer it anyway, curious to hear what voice she would find on the other end of the phone.

"Uh—may I speak to Craig Townsend?" a female's voice asked as soon as she answered.

Immediately, Alisha's curiosity was piqued, even though she knew Craig did come across other females in his business dealings.

"I'm sorry, Craig isn't available right now. May I take a message?" Alisha said in her most professional voice.

"Oh," the woman said, sounding a bit confused. "Is this Mrs. Townsend?"

"Yes," Alisha replied with hesitation. "May I ask who's calling?"

The woman started to chuckle. "Well, Mrs. Townsend, I'm so glad to finally get a chance to speak with you. It seems like every time I speak with your husband, you are always on the go. I'm excited I finally got a chance to reach you there at the house."

Alisha started to tell her that she had actually reached her on a cell phone, but she thought it would be better to listen to what this woman had to say.

"Well, yes," she said trying to sound pleasant. "I'm always on the go."

"Well, I'm sure your husband told you about me. I'm Marjorie Peters with Peters and Peters Travel. I'm the one handling your European trip. I know you must be excited."

European trip, Alisha wanted to scream into the phone. Instead, she bit down on her tongue and forced a smile. "Oh yes. I can't wait."

"Well, Mrs. Townsend, I am so embarrassed about having to call you about this, but your husband came in yesterday to put a payment down. Unfortunately, the card he gave was declined."

"You say his credit card was declined?" she said.

"Yes." Alisha heard a rustle of papers in the background. "It was his Chase Manhattan card. Is there any way you can get in touch with him and let him know? It would be great if he could call me or stop in this evening and give another card. I got you all such a great deal, but I'd hate for you to lose it over something as silly as this."

"Of course not," Alisha said, laughing along with her. "Well, have you tried reaching Craig at work?"

There was the sound of more papers rustling. "Hmm . . . that's the strangest thing. All I have here is his home number. I thought for sure I had gotten his work number too."

Alisha smiled as she gave Marjorie Craig's work number. "Just give him a call. I'm sure he's in the office. And when you talk to him, just tell him his wife said hello."

"Thank you so much, Mrs. Townsend. I know you and your husband are going to love this trip. And I'm so relieved you knew about it. I'm thankful I didn't ruin a surprise."

"Oh no, you didn't ruin a surprise at all," Alisha said before hanging up. *If anything, you've given me the surprise of my life.*

Feeling faint, Alisha sat down on the edge of the bed, not sure if she should scream or cry. Not only did it shock her to find out Craig had been planning a trip behind her back, she couldn't believe Craig had a credit card that she had known nothing about.

She knew there was the credit card they each had from their bank; there were the three department store cards Craig had let her open at her favorite stores; then there was the American Express card he had through his job. Those were the only cards they were supposed to have because Craig had made such a big deal about keeping his credit clean and staying out of debt.

It took every ounce of control to keep from calling him and finding out what was really going on, but the more she thought about it, the more she realized that Craig would be calling her soon enough. She decided the main thing she needed to be doing now was trying to find the credit card statements.

Alisha took another moment to catch her breath, then began tearing through the house like a madwoman. Every drawer, every cabinet—no place was off-limits in trying to find where Craig kept all the bills.

Bills were something she had never concerned herself

with before. She and Craig had a neat and tidy arrangement when it came to the finances: she was in charge of spending; he would pay the bills. As long as she didn't go overboard at the department stores, Craig didn't have any complaints. As much as she loved to shop, Alisha had always made sure to keep her spending within reason. More than spending, she loved her husband. Although he made damn good money, she did not want to send him to the poorhouse.

After nearly an hour of searching, Alisha had almost given up until she remembered the second bedroom. It served as Craig's home office, although he rarely ever did any work in there. It was the one room in the apartment that Alisha avoided at all costs—computers and paperwork just weren't her thing.

Alisha raced from the kitchen to the door of the room. Just as she entered, the phone rang. She knew it was Craig calling. A fire inside her seemed to come alive.

She went and took a seat at his desk and answered the phone. On the other end of the phone, Craig immediately started explaining.

"It was supposed to have been a surprise," he said. "I wanted to surprise you with the tickets next month."

"Oh really?" Alisha said with suspicion that was slowly giving way to excitement.

"I was thinking we could use a little getaway in October. It seems like we've been at each other's throats lately. We could really use a vacation, don't you think?"

"What's with the new credit card, though? When did you get another one?"

Craig laughed it off. "It's for work, honey. Why do you sound so suspicious?"

"Well, why would you use your cell number as your home phone?"

"What's with the twenty questions, baby? I wasn't trying

to do anything sneaky or underhanded. I was just trying to keep it all a surprise. Now you can't honestly think that I would plan a trip behind your back like that, do you?"

That's exactly what I thought, Alisha wanted to tell him.

"Of course not," she told him instead.

Craig promised her he would fill her in on the trip when he got home, but as soon as they hung up with each other, Alisha tore into the desk drawers with a vengeance. Even though his explanation seemed plausible, she wasn't buying it one bit.

Thank God this man keeps meticulous records, she thought to herself as she came upon a file full of credit card statements.

First, there were the store credit cards that were all in her name: Bloomingdale's, Neiman Marcus, and Nordstrom. Next, there were the bank credit cards—a card in his name and a card in hers. Then there was the American Express, his company card that they would use for special occasions.

Alisha's heart sank a little when she found the first credit card bill for Chase Manhattan. She took a seat on the floor and started going through every item listed.

Ladona's heart began to race as she exited the elevator. With each step she took, she thought her knees would buckle under her. This was something she felt she had to do, though. She had finally built up the confidence, and she was not about to back down now. Donned in another new outfit that showed off her shape, and sporting a slick new do, she was ready to do what she had been trying to do all summer.

"I'm here to see Craig Townsend," Ladona announced to the receptionist at the front of the office.

"May I tell him who's here?" the young girl asked.

"Ladona Littleton."

Ladona waited while the receptionist made a phone call to his secretary.

"You can go on back," the receptionist announced as she hung up the phone. "His office is the last one on the right."

Holding her head high, Ladona marched straight to Craig's office. She was met by his secretary, a young black girl who looked no older than twenty.

I wonder if Alisha knows anything about her, Ladona thought to herself.

The young lady stood up from behind her desk. "Craig said to just have a seat. He's on a conference call right now."

I wonder if Alisha knows she's calling him by his first name. Ladona giggled silently.

A few minutes passed like a few hours. Ladona could feel the sweat beading on her forehead, but she promised herself that she was going to go through with this no matter what. Summer was almost over, and even though she had met such a great guy in John, she at least wanted to have one more crack at Craig.

He finally stepped out of his office, looking handsome as ever in his suit. He came over and gave Ladona a hug as if they were the best of friends who had not seen each other in years.

"Melanie, you can go on to lunch if you want to," Craig said to his secretary.

That made Ladona feel a little bit better, knowing there would not be a pair of ears listening outside the door.

Craig let Ladona into his office. She immediately went over to the wall of windows to admire the city view. "This is nice," she commented. "I bet it looks even better when you're up here at night."

Craig closed the door behind him. "So what brings you down here?"

"I was in the neighborhood so I thought I'd stop by. How's your day going?"

Craig shrugged his shoulders uneasily as he thought about the jam that he had just gotten himself out of. He swallowed hard, not looking forward to going home and having to tell Alisha about a trip she was never meant to take. It seemed as though she would be going with him now, though.

"I left my damn cell phone at home today," Craig sighed. "I swear it's caused me more trouble than I could begin to tell you about. I feel lost without it."

Ladona chuckled nervously. "I know what you mean. It's like forgetting your wallet or something like that."

"So what brings you by?"

"Well, I wanted to talk to you about something kinda important."

Craig looked at her with alarm. "Something wrong with Alisha?" he asked. "I just talked to her. She didn't mention anything being wrong."

Ladona shook her head. "Alisha's fine, as far as I know," she assured him. *I bet Lucky's there taking real good care of her.*

"So what's up?"

As Ladona searched for the right way to come out and say what was on her mind, her eyes nervously darted around the office, finally coming to rest on a picture of Alisha nestled among the piles of paperwork on Craig's desk.

Fixating on Alisha's framed photo, she felt a twinge of guilt; and for a brief moment, she thought about apologizing, then excusing herself from Craig's presence. However, she quickly erased that thought from her head.

She figured she had come this far—it was too late to turn back now.

"Is there something wrong?" she heard Craig ask again.

Ladona smiled nervously, breaking away from the trance she seemed to be under. "Nothing is *wrong,*" she began saying after taking a deep breath. She took a step closer to him, deciding that it was now or never.

Trying not to give it another thought, Ladona closed her eyes, then leaned in closer to give him a kiss on the lips. Expecting to make contact, her eyes shot open when she felt his hands grasping her arms trying to hold her back.

Craig stood there looking at her with a look of anger and confusion. Ladona felt as if she wanted to scream. This was the first time she had ever been so close to him—their faces just inches apart; she could feel his breath on her face.

"What in the world are you doing?" he said nervously.

"This is something I've wanted to do for a long time," Ladona replied. She closed her eyes and decided to make another attempt. This time their lips made contact. She felt as if her body would explode. His lips had been everything she had dreamed about.

Craig pulled away from her, wiping his mouth with the sleeve of his shirt. "What is wrong with you?" he gasped. "Alisha's your friend. Alisha's my wife!"

Like a hungry animal that had just had a piece of steak dangled in front of her, Ladona took another step towards him, refusing to let things end right there. In her mind, she was certain she could get more than just a kiss. She was sure she had felt an invitation in the softness of his lips.

"I'm sorry to spring this on you like this, but I didn't know how else to tell you how I felt." Ladona took another step forward; Craig took another step back. "I don't think Alisha's right for you."

He started laughing. "You don't think she's right for me? Why do you think that?"

Ladona paused a moment, trying to figure out the best way to answer that question. In her mind, she had a thousand reasons why Alisha was wrong for him, but she decided to come clean with the best answer she could give.

"Because I'm the better woman," she replied, feeling even more determination. "I can take care of you the way a man needs to be taken care of. Alisha is just some high-maintenance beauty queen who doesn't really appreciate the king you really are."

Maybe it was nervousness or just the absurdity of the entire situation, but Craig let out a cry of laughter. "This is a joke, right?" He shook his head in amazement. "Did Alisha put you up to this?"

Ladona felt insulted. "No," she snapped at him, "this isn't a damn joke, and Alisha didn't put me up to a damn thing. I wanna be with you, and I think you should be with me."

Ladona backed Craig into his desk, then threw her arms around him, giving him a kiss she was sure would light his fire. To her, this was a desperate, last-ditch effort. She put everything she had into it, hoping to get some sort of response.

Just then, the office door opened. "Hey, Craig, I was gonna order something from that roast beef place—oh no! I am so sorry!" Craig's secretary gasped before quickly closing the door again.

A sick look of horror came over Craig's face as he slid away from Ladona again. "I think you should go," he said, looking around the room as if trying to plan an escape.

Ladona shook her head. "I have wanted to tell you this for so long. Now that I'm here, I've got to do it," she insisted. "Craig, I know you're in love with Alisha, but I just don't think she's right for you."

"Look, Ladona, I'm really flattered that you have these feelings toward me, but like you said, I do love my wife. Not only that, but I do feel that she is the right woman for me. In fact, she is the *only* woman for me."

Ladona rolled her eyes at him. She wanted to go after him again, but she knew it was not going to get her anywhere.

"Just what in the world do you see in her anyway?" she snapped at him. "What in the hell is so damn special about her? Other than the fact that she is good-looking, what other reason could you possibly have to be with her?"

Craig stared at her in silence, debating with himself about whether or not he should even answer her question. He finally shook his head. "I don't owe you an explanation about anything," he replied coldly. "You need to leave."

A mischievous grin spread across her face. "Okay, so maybe you don't wanna leave her. I can accept that. I am willing to share you, though."

Craig could not help but laugh again. "You've got to be kidding," he mumbled under his breath.

Ladona shook her head. "Just let me experience you the way Alisha does. Make love to me the way you make love to her. Who else has to know?"

The situation had suddenly lost its humor to Craig, as he went and took a seat behind his desk. "Ladona, I think you need to leave now. Like I said, Ladona, I'm flattered you feel like this, I think you're a nice person, but I love my wife. I'm not gonna cheat on her with you."

"But, Craig," she said, taking a step towards him, ready to get down on her knees and beg if that's what it would take.

Craig reached for the phone on his desk. "Ladona, I'm gonna call security if you don't leave," he said sternly.

Realizing that no amount of begging was going to do any good, Ladona decided to accept defeat and leave with what little dignity she still had left.

"I'm sorry," she said softly. "No need to go calling security on me. I'll leave."

Craig let out a sigh of relief as he watched her head towards the door. "You don't have to worry," he called after her. "I'm not gonna tell Alisha about this."

Ladona shrugged her shoulders. "Thanks," she replied, trying to sound grateful, but it did not matter if he had alerted the newspapers about this.

She held out her hand to open the door, then turned to glance at Craig one last time. "Ya know, I've been in love with you for a long time, Craig. I figured I would at least come here and try. I hoped maybe you felt the same about me."

Craig sat back in his chair. "There isn't another woman who could make me be unfaithful to my wife."

Ladona walked out the office, closing the door behind her. The secretary looked at Ladona and smiled.

"I am so sorry you had to walk in there and see that."

"Don't sweat it. That's not the first time I've walked in on Craig in a situation."

Ladona snickered. "I can imagine. He and his wife are always all over each other, huh?"

The secretary gave her a funny look. "Oh no, it wasn't his *wife.*"

Chapter 38

Alisha pretended she was asleep while Craig got ready for work. As soon as he was gone, she went straight to his computer room to start looking through more credit card statements.

Yesterday had been such an informative day. There were charges for flowers that she had never received, as well as charges for lunches and dinners that she had never eaten. Of course, those charges could easily be explained away, but it was the charge to Bishop Rentals that had her intrigued. Every first of the month, there was an eight-hundred-dollar charge to that company—all on the secret Chase Manhattan charge card.

Is he renting a house? A boat? A storage facility?

Then there were the charges every month to Special One Financing for five hundred and seventy dollars.

No wonder he was always talking about how he didn't have enough money, Alisha said aloud to herself.

Just as she reached in the drawer to find more statements, she heard a knock at the front door. Scared it might be Craig, she gathered all the statements and put them back in the drawer, then went out to the living room to answer the door.

"Good morning, sexy," Lucky said. "I saw your husband leave. Thought I'd come pay you a visit."

"Lucky, I'm not in the mood today," Alisha sighed.

"What's wrong?"

Alisha threw herself on the couch. "My husband is cheating on me," she replied. "I think he was planning a trip to Europe without me, but I found out about it, so now he's trying to say it was a surprise."

"Well, maybe it was a surprise. You're going to Europe. You should be happy."

"And then there is this credit card he's been keeping a secret. I found all these charges on it for a rental company and a finance company. It's like a cheating man's credit card!"

Lucky laughed. "Well, I thought you already knew he was cheating on you."

"Before, it was just a thought. Now I have black-and-white evidence."

Lucky shrugged his shoulders. "Well, so what if he's cheating? Aren't you cheating?"

Alisha rolled her eyes at him. "Yes, but it's not the same thing. I'm not buying you flowers or taking you out to dinner. I don't have mysterious charges on my credit cards! He's buying the woman things. I don't like that."

Lucky tried to give her a kiss, but Alisha moved away. "Look, don't even trip off of what he's doing. Let him keep doing his thing and you just keep doing me!"

Alisha pouted as they both took a seat on the couch. "He's my husband. I can't just let him do his own thing. I need to know what he's doing."

"Well, do you think he's worrying about what you're doing?"

Alisha scoffed at him. "Well, of course not. I'm a woman. I know how to cover my tracks."

Lucky got up and knelt in front of her as she sat on

the couch. "You sound all stressed-out. When you stress, your muscles get all tense, so let me give you a little something to loosen you up."

Lucky tried to spread her legs apart, but Alisha got up and started pacing around the room.

"I don't really know if he's messing around with Ladona or someone at his office, or what. Have you ever heard of Special One Financing?"

Lucky shook his head. "Look, Alisha, what are you obsessing about this for? Your husband is cheating; you are cheating. I'd say you two are pretty even." Lucky walked over to Alisha and started kissing her on her neck. "Why don't you just forget about him right now? Let me take you in the room and help you take your mind off of all this."

"Lucky, please don't do that," Alisha said, trying not to enjoy the way his warm lips felt on her skin.

"I can't stop myself," he said. "You're just so damn sexy when you're angry."

Alisha sighed, her body screaming for her to give in. "Well, we haven't done it in the kitchen yet."

Lucky picked her up and carried her into the kitchen. "Well, we will now."

Peaches glanced over all the statements Alisha had spread out on the table.

She looked up at Alisha and shrugged her shoulders. "There's a lot of shit here, girl, but it doesn't exactly scream *affair,* though. A good liar could come up with a perfectly reasonable explanation for all this stuff."

Alisha picked up one of the bills and glanced through it. "Look at this crap!" she hissed. "Charges at the jewelry store. There are a couple of charges at the hair salon. Whoever the bitch is, she's well accessorized with a badass hairdo."

Peaches couldn't help but laugh at that one. "Well, who's that broad in Unit three-eighteen? Her hair is always looking sharp. I've been meaning to ask her who is hooking her up."

Alisha shook her head. "Craig would never mess around with her. She doesn't look anything like his type. She is way too skinny. The man is terribly picky. You have no idea what I went through just to get him to finally notice me." She sat down at the table and held her head in her hands. "I can't believe this bastard is cheating on me, Peaches! *On me*!"

"What if it's somebody from the office? What if he met someone on one of his business trips? Maybe he's one of those Lifetime movie channel guys, living a completely different life just a block or two away from here. He's got a wife and kids—maybe you pass her in the store every week."

"You aren't helping, Peaches!"

"Okay, so maybe you're right. Maybe he is seeing Ladona. What other female could there be?" Peaches started laughing. "Maybe it's Mrs. Broward."

Alisha looked at her with suspicion. "Or it could be you," she said in a low voice.

Peaches laughed her off. "Girl, you have lost your damn mind. I don't fuck with married men; and if I did, I certainly wouldn't be doing my girl's husband."

"Well, it's not that far-fetched. You're used to having guys pay your bills and keep your hair done."

"I should be offended that you'd say some bullshit like that, but I'll take into consideration you're just stressed."

Alisha continued looking at her suspiciously, but deep down she knew Peaches was not the one. "So what do you think I should do?"

Peaches shrugged her shoulders. "I don't know. Do you think you have enough to confront him?"

Alisha shook her head. "I still feel like I need more . . . like I need actual photos or something."

"Hire somebody to follow his ass around."

Alisha shook her head. "Too much damn money for something I could just do myself. Besides, that seems a little desperate."

"You're sitting here going through the man's things. Don't you think that's a little desperate?"

Alisha chuckled. "They're only credit card bills, and technically, they are mine too. I accumulated most of them."

"Alisha, you've got a good-ass man, girl. The man treats you like a queen. And whether he's cheating on you or not, he still brings his ass home every night and makes you feel like you're the only one, right?"

"But you're the one who told me I shouldn't trust a man. You said something about how men will screw you over if you don't keep a close eye on them."

"Yeah, but I have since softened my heart. Besides, you have a good-ass man. You should give him a little credit. I don't think he's like the rest of these jerks out here."

"So I should just accept it? Since he treats me so well I should turn the other way and forget that he's a cheating bastard?" Alisha shook her head. "Uh-uh. He is married to me. He should not be screwing some other bitch during the day, then coming home to me at night. I'm supposed to be the only one he makes happy. I'm the only one who should be getting diamonds and trips to the salon. My bills are the only ones that should be getting paid."

Peaches nodded her head in agreement. "I hear ya, girl," she sighed. "Well, have you thought about confronting Ladona about it? Scare that bitch into telling you the truth. Show her your mean side."

"I don't really have a mean side."

"If you find out the bitch is sleeping with your husband, that mean side will definitely come out."

"She'd probably just deny it anyway."

"Her hair sure was looking nice the other night with that fresh perm from the beauty salon."

"Do you really think Craig would mess around with her, though?" Alisha asked in disbelief.

Peaches shrugged her shoulder. "Well, Ladona sure did clean up rather nicely, don't you think?"

"She was with that white guy, though. She's got a man."

"And Craig has a wife. What's your point?"

Chapter 39

"Are you about ready to head out to your car?" CJ, the bouncer, asked Peaches as he poked his head into the dressing room.

She looked around and realized she was the last one in there, hiding out ever since the end of her last stage performance. Unlike other nights, she just did not feel like mingling in the crowd or trying to hook up a private dance with any of the big-money ballers who had filled the tables.

Her heart just was not in this anymore. Gone was the fascination with money and the power she had over guys that she loved so much. None of it seemed worth it anymore. She felt like there was more she needed to be doing than just being some dancing piece of meat on the stage every night; however, she just didn't know what.

"I'm the last one here?" Peaches said, chuckling.

"A couple of the girls are still out near the bar," the bouncer replied. "If you aren't ready yet, I can come back and check on you in a few."

Peaches waved for him to come into the dressing room. "No, no. Don't leave. I'd rather you sit here with me for a while. I'm not quite ready to go."

The bouncer came in and took a chair sitting against

the wall. "So what's up with you tonight? I didn't see you out there too much after your dance. As a matter of fact, I've noticed you missing a lot of nights lately. You aren't thinking about trying to move to another club, are you?"

Peaches shook her head. "I wouldn't go anyplace else. This is where I started dancing, and this is the place I'll retire from."

"Hey, I'd heard some of the other girls talking about that shit that went down with William. I know that shit's got to be messing with your head."

Peaches shrugged her shoulders as she took a sip of the rum and Coke she had been nursing most of the night. "It's on my mind every now and then," she lied, knowing that there was not a moment she didn't think about William shooting Jewel.

"Look, Peaches, what you do ain't none of my business, but have you ever given some serious thought to getting out of this mess? A pretty face and a bad-ass body don't mean you have to be stripping."

"The thought's crossed my mind a couple of times," Peaches lied. In all honesty, getting out was on her mind more and more these days.

"This is all I know, though," she replied, waving her hand around the room. "I've been doing this since I was seventeen. What else could I do that would pay me this kind of money? Could you see me in some office answering phones while some old-ass bastard is trying to cop a feel on my ass? Some stupid little office job isn't gonna buy me the Marc Jacobs or the Gucci or the Prada I want."

Peaches paused to take another sip of her drink before going on. "Just the other day I dropped over three hundred on these Manolo Blahniks I had been dying to get. How could I do that working behind the counter asking people what size Slurpee they want with their hot dog?"

CJ shook his head. "I have no idea what a *Momo Baba* even is, but three hundred dollars is probably too much to be paying for it anyway. Yeah, you probably bring in just as much money as a lawyer bills in a month. Is it worth it, though? So what if you can buy pretty much whatever you want? Can you honestly say you actually have what you *really* want, though? Are you happy?"

Peaches knew she did not have what she really wanted, and lately she hadn't had anything to be happy about . . . except Romello.

"I know asking a woman this is like flirting with death, but how old are you?" CJ asked.

Peaches smiled. "I'm twenty-eight," she lied. CJ gave her a look telling her that he did not believe her. "Okay, okay. I'm twenty-three."

"Aww, girl, you still a baby!"

"A baby? And just how old are you?"

CJ smiled big. "You wouldn't believe me if I told you," he replied. "Let's just say I got socks as old as you."

"Well, you look mighty good for whatever age you are."

"You'd give an old man like me a second glance?" CJ asked. "Anyway, baby girl, you're still young. Maybe you should take your butt to school. Go get yourself an education. Lord knows you can't be 'round here shaking that pretty ass in front of these niggas' faces for the rest of your life. I know damn well you don't wanna end up like Goldie, do you?"

Peaches started laughing at his reference to the strip club's resident grandmother. She was a woman in her late thirties with a few strands of gray and a body full of stretch marks. Goldie had been in the stripping game long before Peaches even knew what a G-string was. Goldie was a permanent fixture around this place, the perfect example of someone who had been stuck.

"That definitely wouldn't be me," Peaches said, chuckling.

"Do you even have a plan to get outta this shit? Please tell me you at least have some of your paper stacked. Don't be like a lot of these chicken heads who can barely pay their rent, but drive around in cars that cost more than a house."

Peaches nodded her head. "I've been smart about my shit," she assured him.

Even though she loved her shopping, she had still managed to put a little bit away for a rainy day.

"And do you ever worry about love? Peaches, you are a beautiful girl, and I know you have no problem getting a man. Hell, if I thought an old man like me had a chance, I would have asked you out a long time ago. Don't you want a serious relationship?"

Peaches thought about Romello. "I've thought about it," she replied.

"I'm gonna just be blunt with you 'cuz you seem like one of those no-bullshit kinda people. Do you really think a man is gonna wanna be serious about a stripper? Would you wanna be serious with one of those niggas shaking his ass every night for the ladies?"

Peaches thought back to the male stripper that she had dated a few years ago. She went into the relationship thinking that things would be okay since they were both in the same business. She quickly learned that jealousy was an ugly thing.

"So what the hell should I do, CJ? I need the money. No, I *love* the money."

CJ leaned over and rested his elbows on his knees. "But do you love Peaches?"

"Hey, CJ, me and the other girls are ready to head out to the parking lot," one of the other girls said as she walked into the dressing room.

CJ got up from the chair, never taking his eyes from Peaches. "You think about what I said, beautiful," he told her. "I've gotta run and do something right quick, then I'll be ready to walk you girls out." He walked out of the room.

The other girl went over to her locker to get her things.

"I see CJ was giving one of his famous 'do-something-else-with-your-life' pep talks," she said to Peaches.

Peaches nodded her head. "The man's got some knowledge."

The girl shook her head and started laughing. "Don't let that dirty old man fool you, girl. He uses that shit on everybody, trying to get into ya damn pants. I swear he's run that game on just about everyone here."

Peaches smiled and nodded her head as if she agreed with the girl, but CJ had spit too much truth for it to have all been a pickup.

"Do you ever think about getting out of all this?" Peaches asked.

The girl looked at her as if she had lost her mind. "Get out of what, dancing? Hell naw. Niggas around here make too much damn money and are giving it up too damn easy to make me wanna quit. You thinking 'bout walking away?"

"We aren't gonna be beautiful forever, ya know. Just look at Goldie."

"Girl, what is you talking about? Goldie is my idol. I wanna be out there shaking my booty when I'm her age, driving the niggas crazy, taking all they money. The only thing I ain't gonna do is have kids. I don't want no nasty stretch marks fucking up this body."

Peaches could not believe how silly the girl sounded, but she felt like she was listening to herself. "So you've never thought about leaving?"

"Sure I have. I'll leave the day I find some dumb nigga with a fat-ass bank account and six months to live." The girl paused to think, then started laughing. "I wanna be a black Paris Hilton. If I leave this sonofabitch, I need a man who can take care of all my wants and needs. I have grown used to a certain standard of living, ya know. I've been po' before, and I'll be damned if I go back to being po' again."

"What about love?"

The girl started laughing hysterically. "What about it?

Peaches, ain't no piece of dick worth giving up all this unless he's got deep pockets."

"Hey, I'm just curious . . . what kind of car do you drive?"

"I just bought that badass Infiniti Q45 truck out there. Girl, that shit is fully loaded. You wouldn't believe how much I paid for it!"

Peaches watched as the girl walked out of the dressing room.

As soon as she saw Romello come to the door, Peaches's face lit up like a Christmas tree. "I hope I didn't wake you up."

Romello stepped out onto the porch and grinned. "Actually, I don't go to sleep until I hear you go into your apartment," he said.

Peaches smiled, feeling better that Romello was at least thinking about her sometimes.

"Well, I really didn't want anything. I saw your light on and I thought I'd stop by to tell you good night."

"Is that all? You look like you got something else on your mind."

"I do, but I don't wanna keep you awake."

"If something's bothering you, Peaches, I don't mind."

Peaches shook her head. "Maybe I shouldn't have come by. You get yourself some sleep." She gave him a kiss on the cheek.

"Was work okay?" Romello asked.

Peaches shrugged her shoulders. "It was just like any other night," she replied.

"I know I probably don't have any right telling you this, but maybe you should think about finding another job. Do you really wanna strip for the rest of your life?"

Peaches smiled. "Everybody wants to lecture me tonight," she said, chuckling. "Me being a stripper is a problem for you, isn't it?"

Romello shook his head. "I'm sorry. It's not my place to say anything about what you choose to do with your life."

"But if you said that, that means you must have a problem with it."

Romello chuckled. "Well, let's be real. What man would want his girl being a stripper? I mean, if he cares about her."

"Well, is that man capable of taking care of his girl so she wouldn't have to be a stripper?"

Romello looked at her and shook his head. "I've thought long and hard about this. Even though I'm working a legit job now, making decent money, I don't think I'd ever be able to take care of you. Maybe if I hit the lottery, but you are used to things that I could not do for you. You need one of them brothas who hang out at the club just sliding money to you left and right."

"Maybe money really isn't everything, Romello."

Romello looked at her in exaggerated amazement. "What? I can't believe that just came out of your mouth. You can't be the Peaches I know."

Peaches pushed his arm. "Don't be so damn sarcastic. I'm being serious with you. I'm starting to wonder if there are more important things in this life than money."

"But it is all about the money for you. That's why you strip. That's why you be having those guys spend the night. You make more money in one night than I do in two weeks, maybe more."

Peaches reached out and touched his arm. "Romello, are you ever gonna be able to forgive me for Jewel?"

Romello lowered his head and said in a soft, apologetic voice, "Peaches, I can't even forgive myself."

Without another word spoken, he went back into his apartment and shut the door.

Chapter 40

Ladona looked up and was surprised to see Alisha standing at the side of the car. "Oh hey, girl," she said to her as she continued unloading the few bags of groceries from her trunk.

Alisha stared down at her with cold, accusing eyes. "Ladona, you and I need to have a serious talk," she said in a tone that was icier than her stare.

Ladona nodded her head. "Well, I've been meaning to come and talk to you about something, but I have just been so busy this past week. School is gonna be starting soon. I swear the summer just goes by too fast for me."

Ladona saw that Alisha didn't seem the least bit interested in making small talk with her.

Alisha folded her arms across her chest and let out a hard sigh. "Look, I'm just gonna come right out and ask you this. Are you sleeping with my husband? Better yet, have you ever slept with him?"

"Of course not," Ladona replied. Even though she was telling the truth, she still felt guilty, thinking about all the nights that she spent wishing she'd had the chance to sleep with him.

"Now see, I was hoping you'd be woman enough to

just admit what you were doing. Why do you have to stand here and lie to my face?"

"What?" Ladona gasped.

"I know all about your little trip to Salt Lake, the trip you claim was a Vegas getaway with John."

"What are you talking about? I did go to Vegas. In fact, I brought back souvenirs."

"And what about all those morning trips downtown? What about all those nights you were out when Craig had to work late?"

Ladona shrugged her shoulders. "They're just coincidences."

"You are a lying, backstabbing bitch!"

Ladona turned and looked at Alisha. "Excuse me?"

"You heard what I said. You have been running around here fucking around with my husband. You've been caught, so just be a woman and own up to it."

"I don't have shit to own up to. I've never slept with your husband," Ladona said again.

"So were you trying to sleep with him? Was he trying to sleep with you?"

Ladona drew in a deep breath. This time Alisha had asked a question that was not so easy to lie about.

"Alisha, maybe we should talk about this some other time," she said.

Alisha shook her head. "Why? So you can run to Craig and make sure your stories match?" She took a step closer to her. "I'm here right now. I wanna talk about it right now."

"Is it gonna make you feel better to know? It seems to me you shouldn't be trying to jump on me about cheating when you've been in and out of someone else's bed yourself."

"What are you talking about?" Alisha asked, trying to sound innocent.

Ladona laughed at her. "Don't think I don't know

about you and Lucky. He sure is proud of the fact that he got in your pants, as if you're some kind of grand prize."

Alisha tried to hide the fact that she was hurt that Lucky would be bragging out them sleeping together. She wondered how many other people knew.

"Did he tell you about me that night you had sex with him?"

Ladona looked shocked that Alisha knew. "So what if I slept with him?" she said, regaining her composure. "At least I'm not the one who's married. So before you go off calling somebody a lying, backstabbing bitch, you need to take a long hard look in the mirror."

"But you are the backstabbing bitch who's been fucking with my husband."

Alisha had never been a violent person. She thought it was too barbaric to put down a mousetrap. However, today she had reached a point where she could not control her emotions. Before she could stop to think about her actions, she grabbed Ladona by the hair and started dragging her around the parking lot.

"This'll teach you not to mess with another woman's husband!" Alisha screamed.

Ladona started kicking and scratching. "I didn't sleep with your husband!"

Out of nowhere, Lucky came running over to break the two ladies up. He held Alisha back by the waist, trying to get her to calm down.

"What the hell is wrong with you two?" he shouted at both of them.

"The bitch is crazy," Ladona said as she started picking up the few groceries that had spilled onto the ground.

"This bitch has been sleeping with my husband!" Alisha roared, as she squirmed to get out of Lucky's grip.

"I haven't slept with your husband, Alisha." Ladona turned to Lucky. "I'm not the one he's been cheating with."

Alisha stopped squirming. "What do you mean, *you're* not the one?" she asked her.

"You heard what I said. I'm not the one you're husband's cheating with." Ladona continued glaring at Lucky. "Why don't you calm your girlfriend down? You're a lot of the reason all this mess is getting started in the first place."

Lucky smirked. "Me? What do I have to do with any of this?"

After gathering her groceries, Ladona slammed the trunk closed, then started walking to her apartment.

"You wait a minute, bitch! Get back here! Who in the hell is Craig cheating with? What do you know? You're supposed to be my friend! Why won't you tell me?"

"Alisha, calm down. You're causing a scene," Lucky said calmly.

"Just let me go."

"You have to promise me you won't go running after the girl. You're a grown-ass woman. You can't be out here acting like this."

"I won't run after her," Alisha said, heaving, as she tried catching her breath.

As soon as Lucky let her go, she started pounding his chest with her fists. "Why in the hell would you go and tell her that we had sex?"

Lucky grabbed her by her wrists. "Who in the hell cares what that girl thinks?"

"She could go back and tell Craig!"

"Well, maybe Craig needs to know. I mean, if he's not gonna take care of home, then he needs a wake-up call to let him know that somebody else is."

"You are such a bastard! You have no right going around telling her my business."

Lucky pulled her closer. "I'm the bastard you can't get enough of, though."

"Who else have you told?"

Lucky smirked. "Romello knows, but it's not like he's gonna go back and tell Craig. He and I are cool."

"Why would you go around telling people about this, like it's some big deal?"

"Why wouldn't I tell people? How many men around here have the pleasure of saying they got to be with someone as fine as you?"

Just as Alisha opened her mouth to fuss at Lucky, she saw Craig's truck pull into the parking lot. She quickly backed away from Lucky, hoping Craig hadn't seen her in his arms. From the way he swung the large truck into the parking space, she knew he had seen it. As he got out of the truck and marched over to them, she could only imagine the reaming she was about to receive.

"Uh-oh," Lucky said teasingly, "it looks like the hubby isn't too happy."

Lucky turned and started to walk back towards his apartment, but stopped when he heard Craig call out his name.

"What's going on here?" Craig demanded.

"Hey, honey," Alisha said, trying to act as if nothing was going on.

Craig brushed passed her and walked up on Lucky. "I saw you with your hands on my wife."

Lucky smirked as he nodded his head in Alisha's direction. "She's your wife. Shouldn't you be questioning her about what's going on?"

"I don't want you near her."

Alisha walked over and put her hand on Craig's shoulder. "Honey, it's not what you think."

Lucky nodded his head, "Yeah, Craig, it's not what you think," he said, with a taunting look.

Alisha shot him a nasty look. "Baby, let's go into the house and talk about this. Lucky wasn't doing anything wrong. He was just trying to calm me down."

Craig glanced at his wife in disbelief, then turned back to Lucky, who still had that sarcastic smirk on his face.

"I don't care what you were doing. I don't want you around my wife anymore. Is that clear?"

Lucky held up his hands as if offering a truce. "No problem, man," he said before turning to go back to his apartment.

Craig looked down at Alisha. "I don't like him," he grumbled under his breath.

Alisha slid her arm around his. "What are you doing home so early?"

Peaches carelessly threw her things into the duffel bag. "I'm quitting," she said again.

CJ stood in the doorway of the dressing room shaking his head at her. "Look, beautiful, when I was saying all that stuff to you the other night, I was trying to put some shit on your brain. I didn't mean for you to pack up your shit and leave like this."

CJ walked in the room and took a seat in one of the chairs along the wall. "And just what are you gonna do? The other night you had no idea what you would do if you left here. So in a matter of days you've come up with this wonderful, foolproof plan?"

Peaches paused to look at him. "I have money saved up. That should take care of my bills for a few months." She went back to throwing stuff in her bag. "As far as a plan, I really don't have one yet. Maybe I'll do like you said and register for some courses at the college."

CJ shook his head again. "Who is he?" he questioned.

Peaches looked up in alarm. "Who is who?"

"Who is the man? I know there's a man behind this life-altering decision you're about to make. There's always a man."

Peaches smiled. "Why does there have to be a man behind my decision?"

"Peaches, I've been here a long-ass time, and I've seen a lot of girls come and go. Most of the time these girls leave 'cuz there's some nigga who has their noses wide open. So once again I ask who he is."

"CJ, a lot of the things you said to me the other night made a lot of sense. One thing that really stuck in my head is that no man who truly cares about me is gonna want me being a stripper." She paused to look at him. "And for your information, his name is Romello."

CJ shook his head and started laughing. "Damn, girl. As hard as you are, I never thought you would be one to fall in love with somebody."

"To tell you the truth, neither did I."

"So are you sure he's the one? I mean, is he worth walking away from all this? It's a lot of money to walk away from over some man."

"It's now or never, CJ."

"Is he worth it, though?"

"I sure hope so."

"The brotha's got a job, right? 'Cuz if he ain't got no job then he's only after your money, your body or both."

"He's got a job."

"I can't believe you're leaving, beautiful."

Peaches zipped up her bag, then let out a nervous sigh. "To tell you the truth, I can't believe it either. I've gotta do it, though. I don't wanna be stuck here."

CJ stood up and gave her a hug. "Girl, I hate to see you going. I know everybody's gonna trip when they find out you're gone."

"Life goes on, though. They will be someone else filling my seat by the end of the week."

"Yeah, but there ain't gonna be no other ass as pretty

as yours shaking around that stage, though. I really do hope everything works out for you."

"I hope so too."

"Of course you'll always have a place here if you wanna come back."

Peaches shook her head. "I won't be back. It's time for a change and getting my life together."

"If you need me . . ."

"I know exactly where to find you."

The End of the Game

Chapter 41

Despite the knots in her stomach, Peaches was sure she was making the right decision. She had not given much thought to what she was doing, but she was sure everything was going to work out just fine. She was a person who always seemed to come out on top no matter what happened.

I'll get into school, find a decent paying job. Everything will be okay, she told herself.

As Peaches walked from her car to her apartment, she saw Romello come outside carrying a box in his arms.

"You doing some spring cleaning?" she asked with a chuckle.

Romello looked surprised to see her standing there. "What are you doing home this early? Aren't you supposed to be working tonight?" he asked.

"I decided to cut out early. What's going on with you, though? You finally clearing out some of Jewel's things?"

Romello set the box down and let out a long sigh. "I thought I'd be able to get all of this done before you got home in the morning," he said, unable to look her in the face.

"What do you mean?"

"Peaches, I'm moving out," Romello said softly.

"Moving out? You were trying to creep out of here without telling me?"

"Peaches . . ." Romello exhaled.

"Wait a minute, Romello, what the fuck is going on here? Why are you moving?"

"I can't do this anymore!" Romello snapped at her. "I can't keep living here. I can't keep being around you."

Peaches felt like someone had just knocked the wind out of her. "You can't be around me? So you were just gonna pack up and leave without saying a word to me?"

Peaches wasn't sure whether to believe if he was telling her the truth or playing a cruel practical joke. She started running towards his apartment; Romello took off after her. When she stepped into the living room, she found all the furniture gone.

"Where is everything?" she asked, turning to look at Romello in the doorway. "You really are leaving."

"Jewel's mother came and got most of the stuff last night while you were at work."

"So you were just gonna leave. You weren't even gonna say good-bye."

Romello lowered his head in shame. "Peaches, I don't wanna be here anymore. It's too hard for me."

"What's too hard? You make it seem like I've been making your life miserable or something."

"It's the guilt. It's the memories."

Peaches pushed his shoulder. "Man the fuck up, Romello!"

"Look, I can't stay in this place anymore. I'm sorry."

"But you were gonna just leave without saying anything to me. What was all that talk about you caring about me and wanting us to be together?"

"I do care about you," he said in almost a whisper.

Peaches pushed his shoulder again. "You care so

much that you'd pack up and leave in the middle of the night, huh?"

"I didn't wanna have a scene like this."

"You selfish sonofabitch!" she shouted in his face. "You don't even have the guts to face me like a real man. You don't care about me."

Romello finally looked up at her. "I do care about you," he shouted back at her. "I just don't think I can be with you. Every time I'm around you I just feel so damn guilty about Jewel."

"But this is what you wanted! *I'm* what you wanted!"

"I wanted to be out of a relationship with her. I didn't want her dead!" Romello walked out onto the porch. "And I'm not sure what I want anymore. I'm not sure about anything."

Peaches came up behind him. "And to think I quit my job for your ass."

Romello turned around and looked at her in surprise. "You quit your job for me? Why would you do that?"

"You wouldn't want your girl being a stripper, would you?"

Romello started blinking fast to fight back the tears that had started filling his eyes. "You didn't have to do that for me."

"I did it for us."

"There is no us."

Peaches started punching his back. "You sonofabitch!" she screamed.

"Stop it!" Romello turned around and grabbed her wrists.

Peaches stopped struggling with him, then walked back inside the apartment to calm herself down. Romello followed her inside.

"All that stuff about you loving me, I believed it," she mumbled under her breath. "It was all just a lie, though."

"I didn't lie," Romello said.

Peaches shook her head. "Oh, no, it was a damn lie, otherwise we wouldn't be standing here having this conversation."

Romello walked over and took Peaches into his arms. "Peaches, I told you I've got to clear my head."

Peaches pushed him away from her. As badly as she wanted to feel his arms around her, she did not want anything to make her emotional. She refused to let him see her cry.

"So where are you gonna stay?" Peaches asked.

"My boy Gino said I could crash with him for a while 'til I got myself another place."

Peaches nodded her head. "So that's it, then. Poof! You're outta here, never to be heard from again?"

Romello put his arms around Peaches and buried his face in her shoulder, hiding the tears that he could not hold back anymore.

"If you didn't want to stay in the apartment, you could just stay with me," Peaches said, trying not to sound too anxious.

Romello squeezed her tighter, afraid that if he let go she would somehow blow away.

"I can't stay with you," he said softly.

Peaches calmly stepped away from him. "Well, let me let you get back to your moving," she said.

Before Romello could open his mouth to say another word, Peaches walked back outside, grabbed her bag off the ground, then went back to her apartment. For a few moments, she stood at the door, hoping and waiting to hear Romello's footsteps on the front porch. Instead, she heard a car door open. When she went to the window, she saw him loading his things into the backseat.

Alone in the darkness of her own kitchen, Peaches finally let her emotions come out. One tear was followed by three, then five, until a whole stream of them came flowing down her face.

She rested her head on her arm as she sobbed softly into the glass table, hating herself for having been so stupid to believe Romello cared about her. Her sobs became louder and louder until she could no longer hold in the anger. She let out a scream of frustration as she pounded her fist on the table.

"Peaches," she heard a voice say.

Peaches looked up and saw Romello standing at the end of the table. She quickly wiped her tears away, not wanting him to see her cry. She had always thought it was the worst thing to let a man see that you had any type of emotion toward him.

"Your door was unlocked," was all Romello said before walking over and taking her by the hand.

Peaches stood up and let him take her into his arms. With his cheek, Romello wiped away the tears that were left on her face, and then ever so gently, he kissed her lips. Peaches could not hold back the tears anymore.

"What did you come here for?" Peaches asked.

"I just can't walk away from you like that," Romello said softly in her ear.

Peaches wrapped her arms around him tightly. "I don't want you to leave, Romello," she said. "I want to try and make things work."

In the moonlight of the window, Romello looked into her eyes. "You have no idea how bad I want things to work between us," he said.

"Don't leave. Stay here with me."

The two of them embraced in a long, passionate kiss.

* * *

Romello followed close behind as Peaches led him into her bedroom. He stood at the doorway as she walked over to the nightstand to cut on a dimly lit lamp.

"Why are you standing over there?" she asked him. "You scared?"

Romello shook his head. "I'm not scared, just a little nervous."

"Why would you be nervous?"

Romello put his hand to his chest to feel the strength of his heart pounding against his rib cage. "I feel like I did the night I had sex for the first time," he said, chuckling. "Ten years old . . . she was my babysitter, ya know."

"In a way this will be like our first time. No interruptions. No worrying about anyone finding out about us." Peaches dropped her shirt to the floor. "You can't leave, Romello. You and I need to be together. We need each other."

"What makes you say that?" Romello asked.

"You need a woman who can deal with your shit. I need a man who can keep me in line. I'm the plus to your minus . . . the yin to your yang." She slid her arms out of her bra and let it fall to the floor.

Romello nodded his head in agreement. He wanted to tell her he agreed with her, but he was too fixated on watching her wriggle out of her miniskirt.

"So you can't leave," Peaches said, pausing to give him a good look at her in her purple-laced thong. "Tell me you don't want to leave."

"I don't want to leave," Romello said as he watched the thong fall to her ankles.

Peaches walked over to him and pressed her naked body against his. At that moment, Romello did not want to leave. He wanted to stay right there forever, touching her and feeling himself inside her.

"I love you," he whispered in Peaches's ear.

Peaches walked over to the bed to lie down. "Come show me," she whispered back.

Peaches opened her eyes to a flood of sunlight coming through the bedroom window. With a smile on her face, she felt as if she were waking up to a dream.

It had finally happened. She had finally been with Romello the way she thought she was meant to. What they had done in the bathroom was nothing compared to what she had experienced last night. If she had not been in love before, she had certainly felt like she was in love now.

"Romello, you still sleeping?" she asked, rolling over to find the spot next to her was empty. "Romello?" she called out again, with no answer in return.

Peaches got up and looked in the bathroom, then looked in the kitchen. She finally came back to the bedroom and realized Romello's clothes were gone. Trying not to panic, she threw on her robe and rushed outside to his apartment. As she approached the front door, she heard voices inside.

She took a step towards the door; someone from maintenance came walking outside.

"Where's Romello?" she asked.

"He turned in his keys this morning," the man replied before going on about his business.

Chapter 42

Alisha stared hard at the little plus sign in the window as if she could will it to turn into a negative sign. Being pregnant was supposed to be something she could be happy about and celebrate. There could not be much celebration since she did not know which man she was pregnant by.

She threw the test stick across the bathroom, slamming it into the wall.

"This can't be happening," she sobbed into her hands, starting to entertain the idea of getting an abortion.

Just then, there was a knock at the bathroom door. "Alisha, you okay in there?" she heard Craig ask.

"I'm fine, honey," she called out to him. "I'll be out in a second."

"No rush," Craig said. "If you aren't feeling well, just take your time. If you need me to get anything, just let me know."

"Sure," Alisha said before going back to crying in her hands. She so badly wanted to open the door and wave the stick in Craig's face, then pretend as if everything was all right.

In her mind, she figured everything would be all right

until the moment of delivery. She pictured a baby coming out looking just like Lucky. She could not imagine the words Craig would have for her then.

She picked up the stick from the floor, then hid everything under the sink in the cabinet. After splashing some water on her face, she ventured back out into the bedroom, where Craig was already nestled under the covers waiting for her.

"You sure you okay?" he asked.

Alisha nodded her head as she got under the covers next to him. "I'm fine, honey. Just a little upset stomach."

"Or a little pregnancy," Craig mumbled.

Alisha looked at him in alarm. "What?"

"Don't even try to act like you don't know what I'm talking about," Craig sighed. "Baby, I know your cycle like the back of my hand. You didn't have a period, you've been sick and irritable, and much to my satisfaction, your breasts feel a lot fuller than usual."

"You're pissed, huh?" she asked, with part of her hoping that he would go into a fit of anger and insist that she have an abortion as soon as possible.

To her surprise, Craig responded with calm. "Not really. Maybe now is a good time to start a family." He rolled over and gave her a peck on the lips.

"Are you serious?" Alisha gasped, wishing she could be more excited.

Craig chuckled. "You sound surprised. Of course I'm serious. If we start a family, maybe that will get that silly idea out of your head that I'm messing around with another woman."

Alisha smiled as she reached over to cut off the light. *Dear God, if you get me out of this, I swear I will never sleep with Lucky again . . . without a rubber, that is.*

Alisha closed her eyes and drifted off to sleep, not

knowing that Craig was in the dark, saying his own little prayer to God.

Thank you for the distraction, Lord. May she never find out the truth.

Alisha awakened to find Craig standing in the mirror getting dressed. She glanced at the alarm clock.

"What are you doing up this early on a Saturday morning?" she asked him. "Come on back to bed."

Through the mirror, Craig smiled at her. "I just have some errands to run. I promise I won't be gone too long. Go on back to sleep."

"Well, bring me back something for breakfast."

Craig walked over to her side of the bed and gave her a kiss on the cheek. "Like what?" he asked.

"I have a taste for waffles."

"Well, I'll hurry back so I can serve my beautiful lady breakfast in bed." Craig touched her stomach. "I've gotta take care of both my babies."

Alisha forced a smile. "Hurry back," she said.

Craig walked out of the room as Alisha closed her eyes and drifted back to sleep. A few moments later, she thought she heard voices coming from the living room. She quietly got out of bed and crept into the hallway. She could hear Craig involved in a hushed conversation on the phone.

"She says she's pregnant. I don't know what the hell I'm going to do. You know I didn't want any kids. This is a fucked-up situation to be trying to bring a kid into . . . yes, I know you've been saying you want to have one, but what am I supposed to do?" Craig paused, listening intently to what was being said on the other end of the line.

"I do love you, but you have to understand she's my wife. I love her too . . . well, I think this pregnancy will keep her occupied. She won't be so hot to find out about us if she's busy getting ready for a new baby. . . . I'll pay off one of the credit cards so she can shop 'til she drops. That should keep her happy." Alisha watched as Craig looked around the room as if to make sure no one was around. "I love you too," he said to the person on the other end before quietly hanging the phone in the cradle.

Alisha was paralyzed with a pain in her chest. Even as she heard Craig's footsteps coming towards the room, she still could not bring herself to make a move.

"Alisha!" he said, coming around the corner, surprised to see her standing there. "I thought you were asleep, baby. You need me to get you anything?"

She felt a single tear run down her cheek as she shook her head. "I didn't realize you were still here," she managed to squeeze out through her tightening throat.

Craig looked at her with worry, wondering if she had caught any of his conversation. "You're crying," he said. "What's wrong?"

The moment he took her into his arms, Alisha felt a stream of tears come down. "Are you still going out?" she asked.

"Yeah," he replied, "unless you want me to stay here with you."

"I'll be okay," Alisha said, sniffling.

"Why are you crying?"

Alisha wanted to tell him why, but it angered her that she could not open her mouth to say it. For weeks, she had thought about how she would rant and rave if she ever found hard evidence that Craig was cheating on her. Now that she had a chance to hear it from his own mouth, she didn't know what to say to him. All the anger she felt had given way to sadness. Instead of fussing, all she wanted to do was cry.

"Craig, I really do love you," she said.

Craig kissed her on her forehead. "I know that, baby," he said. "I love you too."

In her mind, she kept hearing Lucky say, "But you're cheating too." That did not make the hurt any less painful, though. So what if she was cheating? Craig was not supposed to be cheating on her. She was supposed to be the only woman he would ever want for the rest of his life.

Even after Craig had left the house, Alisha stood in that same spot, still too shocked to move. She slid down to the floor and wrapped her arms around her legs, not wanting to believe Craig wanted her pregnant just to keep her from finding out about his indiscretions.

I'm gonna find out who she is even if it kills me, she vowed.

Chapter 43

"I can't believe he just left like that," Alisha said as she put her arm around Peaches's shoulder to comfort her.

Peaches sighed. "Men are just no fucking good," she said. "I swear I will never let another man get close to me for as long as I live."

Alisha nodded her head. "All they do is lie to you and use you up. They're no good."

"And the nerve of Craig. I can't believe you actually heard him say all that."

"It's killing me, not knowing who this woman is, Peaches."

The two of them watched as John came out of Ladona's apartment. Over the last week, he had become just another one of the familiar faces around the complex. Everyone knew the schoolteacher was dating a white man. That was enough to convince Alisha that Ladona was not sleeping with her husband.

"So if it ain't Ladona, then who in the world could it be?" Alisha said aloud.

"Maybe you should go check out his secretary. How does she look?"

Alisha shrugged her shoulders. "I don't know, but I

doubt he'd be with his secretary. Craig is too anal to mix business with pleasure."

"You should really think about having his ass followed, Alisha. Or do you still think that's too desperate?"

"I'm getting desperate!"

Lucky walked over to the two of them as they sat out on Peaches's front porch.

"What's up with your boy Romello? How is he gonna just up and leave like that? Next time you talk to him, you tell him I said he could still come through and smoke a blunt with a brotha."

Peaches shrugged her shoulders. "Don't feel bad. He up and left without saying a thing to me too."

"Damn . . . sorry about that," Lucky said, sounding not the least bit sincere. He turned his attention to Alisha. "I understand why Peaches is down in the dumps, but what's got you looking so sad?"

"Nothing," Alisha replied.

Peaches nudged her arm. "You need to tell him, girl."

"Tell me what?" Lucky asked.

Alisha shot her an evil look for having put her on the spot like that. Even though she knew she needed to tell Lucky that she was pregnant, she did not want to say anything to him in hopes this would all go away.

"Nothing," Alisha replied. "We can talk about it later." She got up and started walking up the stairs to her apartment.

Lucky turned back to Peaches. "Well, since you and Romello ain't an item anymore, does this mean you're back on the market?"

"You're fucking my girl!" Peaches snapped at him.

Lucky started laughing. "I was just asking," he said as he turned and walked back to his apartment.

Alisha stared across the table and watched as Craig ate his dinner. All evening he had been wearing a smile on his face that Alisha wanted to rip away. Her own dinner she did not have an appetite for. All she wanted was to know the truth. She wanted to find out who the other woman in his life was.

"You need to eat something, baby," Craig said. "The baby needs nourishment."

"Who is she?" Alisha finally blurted out.

"Who is who?"

"The woman I heard you on the phone with the other morning. I heard you tell her that you loved her."

Craig tried to laugh it off and say he had been talking to his mother, but Alisha knew better.

"I heard the conversation, Craig. That definitely wasn't your mother. Why do you have to lie? Who was she?"

Craig tried desperately to think of another lie to get himself out of this one, but there was nothing he could say to turn this around in his favor.

"Alisha," Craig sighed.

She shook her head. "Don't even think about giving me bullshit, Craig. All I wanna know is who she is and how long it's been going on."

Craig's calm expression suddenly turned to anger. "If I tell you, what are you gonna do about it?" he snapped at her. "I treat you like a damn queen, Alisha. I give you anything and everything you could ever want; and I've managed to do this and still cheat on you." Craig snickered. "So what difference will it make if you know who it is? You are not going to leave me. You need me."

"I need you?" Alisha scoffed.

Craig snickered. "That's right. You need me. You need to be taken care of, honey. You wouldn't make it out there without me, and you damn sure won't be able to find anyone better than me."

"What I need is a man who loves me."

"And you don't think I love you?" Craig asked. "You want for nothing, Alisha. I don't deprive you of affection. I don't deprive you of money. I don't deprive you of time. I spoil you rotten with love. You always have been and always will be my number-one lady."

"So I should be grateful for what I have and just let you continue on with your little affair?"

"In a marriage, you sometimes have to take the good with the bad, honey."

Alisha shook her head in disbelief. "You aren't my husband. I have no idea who you are, but you damn sure aren't my husband."

Craig shrugged his shoulders. "I'm still the same man you married. I haven't changed a bit."

"The man I married never would have cheated on me."

"Who's to say that man wasn't cheating on you when you got married?"

Alisha jumped up from the table. "Craig, you must be out of your mind if you think I'd sit around here and just let you cheat in my face like it's no big deal." Alisha got up from her seat and started walking towards the front door.

"Isn't marriage supposed to be about compromise? After all, I'm willing to let you walk around with another man's baby growing in your damn belly."

Alisha stopped dead in her tracks, unable to believe what she had just heard. She slowly turned back around to look at her husband, who stared back at her with a smug look of satisfaction on his face.

"What are you talking about? Another man's baby? Craig, I don't . . ." She was not sure what else she could say.

"Just don't say anything else, Alisha. You'd be insulting my intelligence. I know all about you sneaking around with Lucky. I've known about it for a couple of weeks."

Alisha walked back over to her husband, trying to hide

the shock of her dirty little secret being discovered. In the brief moment of silence, she studied Craig's face, wanting to find out if there was more to the simple smile spread across his lips. She wondered if he really knew anything or if he was simply taking a shot in the dark.

"Well, if you really believed I was seeing another guy, why did you wait until now to say something about it?" she responded in a slow, deliberate tone.

Craig shrugged his shoulders. "As long as Lucky kept you busy, you weren't nagging me about things."

"Nagging you?" Alisha gasped.

Craig looked at her and started laughing. "Yes, my beautiful princess. You are a bit of a nag. Besides, as long as you were busy doing your thing with Lucky, I figured you wouldn't be too concerned about what I was doing."

Alisha slapped Craig in the back of the head, and then walked out the front door.

It felt good to have the cool evening air in her face. Now that she was away from Craig, all she could do was cry.

What in the hell just happened in there? she asked herself.

She stood there a few moments longer, trying to get herself together before going down to Lucky's and letting him know about everything that had just happened. Alisha prayed that he would not be busy. She needed a shoulder she could cry on.

Lucky came to the door. His face lit up with a smile when he saw it was Alisha.

"Everything okay?" he asked her as he ushered her inside the apartment.

"Lucky, he knows. Craig knows all about us. I don't know who told him. I bet it was Ladona." Alisha went to take a seat on the couch.

"Well, I told him," Lucky replied matter-of-factly.

Alisha looked at him in shock as she slapped him across the arm. "Why would you do something like that?

Have you lost your mind?" Alisha broke down into tears again. "How could you tell my husband about us?"

"Look, Alisha, I told you I was gonna do it."

"Yeah, but I thought you were just joking, Lucky! I didn't actually think you'd go and do something so stupid!"

Lucky shrugged his shoulder. "He was cheating. You were cheating. I was cheating. It's all one big game. Besides, I thought he should know about us. I mean, he needed a damn wake-up call to let him know that he needed to do more to take care of home, otherwise someone else would come in and take care of it for him."

Alisha glared at him. "You think this is some kind of game, don't you? It's not a game, though. This is my damn life—my damn marriage you're screwing with!"

"So is he pissed?" Lucky asked with a look of amusement.

"This isn't funny, Lucky. What if your girlfriend found out about me? How would you like it if I called her up and told her about us? Better yet, why don't I call and tell her I might be pregnant with your baby?"

"You're pregnant?"

Alisha nodded her head. "Yes."

A smile spread across Lucky's face. "So what did Craig have to say?"

Alisha threw her hands up in frustration. "Lucky, why in the hell are you so damn concerned about what Craig says? You think this is a damn game, don't you? I keep telling you it's not a game, though. This is serious shit, Lucky!"

Lucky put his arm around her to comfort her. "I'm sorry. I didn't mean to cause all this drama," he said, although Alisha didn't believe a word he said. "I tell you what. Why don't we go for a drive? I think the fresh air will help you calm down a little."

"How can you be so calm about this?"

"Have you ever seen me lose my cool over anything?" Lucky asked. "You just sit here and relax a few minutes.

I'm gonna run and change, then we can take a drive around, maybe get something to eat."

Alisha nodded her head. "That'd be great. I really need to get away."

Lucky got up and went to his room. Alisha got up and started pacing around the room. "So how did Craig react when you told him about us?" she called out to Lucky.

He called out from his room. "There was a scuffle, a few words exchanged, but that's it."

Alisha let out a sigh of relief at the news that Craig at least had some kind of reaction to Lucky. She was afraid Lucky was going to tell her that the two of them sat around laughing and telling jokes.

Alisha walked over to the kitchen table. Even in a time of crisis, she could not help but be nosy, going through a stack of opened letters that had been thrown around on the table.

I wonder if there's something in here from her, Alisha thought to herself as she began looking through the papers. She paused to laugh at herself, thinking of how Craig often teased her about being too nosy for her own good. *I'm not nosy, I'm just inquisitive,* she thought before continuing to go through the pile. All of a sudden, there was one piece of paper with a letterhead that caught her attention.

As she picked it out of the pile, her heart began to race. Suddenly feeling her inquisitive nature was justified, but sick from what her eyes beheld, she read:

Dear Mr. Craig Townsend,

Thank you for your recent car payment of $573.00 for your 2007 Mercedes-Benz SLK. This payment was made on your Chase Manhattan Visa card ending in 2335.

Special One Financing

Alisha looked up from the paper and was surprised to find Lucky standing there in front of her.

"Okay, sexy," he said, "you all ready to go?"

Alisha nodded her head, not wanting to believe what she had just read. She held the letter up to Lucky.

"What is this?" she asked. "What is Craig's mail doing here?"

Lucky looked at the letter, then started smiling. "I told you my baby pays for my car, didn't I?"